SUSANNE O'LE... ...
1946. After gra... ...
married an Iri... ...
world. She is a trained fitness instructor, and has
recently published two health and fitness books, *Look
Great, Feel Great for Life* (Gill & Macmillan, 1999) and
The Life in Your Years (Gill & Macmillan, 2000).

Diplomatic Incidents

Susanne O'Leary

beeline

First published in 2001 by Blackstaff Press Limited

This edition first published in 2002 by Beeline
an imprint of Blackstaff Press Limited
Wildflower Way, Apollo Road
Belfast BT12 6TA, Northern Ireland

© Susanne O'Leary, 2001
All rights reserved

Susanne O'Leary has asserted her right under the
Copyright, Designs and Patents Act 1988
to be identified as the author of this work.

Typeset by Techniset Typesetters, Newton-le-Willows, Merseyside

Printed and bound in Great Britain by Omnia Books Ltd, Glasgow

A CIP catalogue record for this book
is available from the British Library

ISBN 0-85640-719-4

www.blackstaffpress.com

To Olivia

CHAPTER I

The drawing room at the Dutch embassy in Paris was packed with people, and was very hot.

Anna dabbed her forehead with a napkin and looked at the tray of tiny sandwiches that a waitress was offering her. They looked very tempting. But she knew that even if she ate the whole trayful, she would still be hungry. That was the trouble with cocktail party food. She looked around for somebody to talk to, but saw no one she knew.

The huge room was full of people engaged in animated conversation. Anna could distinguish at least four languages. The air smelled of expensive perfume, cigarette smoke and food. The women were dressed in the latest designer chic and wore exquisite jewellery. The men wore superbly tailored suits. Everybody seemed to know each other, judging by the kissing on both cheeks that served as greeting, but she saw no one that she wanted to kiss or even say hello to. She was beginning to feel seriously fed up.

She took another glass of champagne from the tray of a passing waiter. Where was Conor? Why couldn't he rescue her? He had been ignoring her more and more since they came to Paris five months ago. His job as number two at the Irish embassy was taking up most of his time. Paris was turning out be less exciting than she had anticipated when they moved here.

Anna had always dreamed of living in Paris. As a schoolgirl in Stockholm, she had fantasised about marrying a gorgeous Frenchman with title and money. In her imagination, she had seen herself living in a big house surrounded by several beautiful, well-dressed, perfectly behaved French children. She would have an army of servants and her handsome French husband would spoil her with expensive presents and make love to her every night. Anna would always be dressed in designer clothes. And be thin . . .

A few years later, she had met Conor and forgotten about the handsome Frenchman. Conor had looked at her across a crowded room and she had been in love with him before they had spoken one word to each other.

She had never thought she would fall for a tall, red-headed Irishman, but his brown eyes and broad smile were irresistible. When he held her in his strong arms and told her she was beautiful, she had never felt happier. That his career came before anything else and he had no idea that men and women were supposed to be equal were things she discovered later. But then it was too late. She was lost.

She caught a glimpse of herself in one of the huge mirrors that covered the wall. Her white silk blouse was wrinkled and the black skirt looked very tight.

Her dark auburn hair, piled on top of her head, was escaping in tendrils around her face. Not what you'd call chic, she said to herself. If I had married a handsome Frenchman, he would have headed for the hills by now.

She walked through the french window, which was open to the mild evening air, and out to the garden. It was not yet dark. There were a few people walking around, admiring the beds of tulips. She sat down on a bench under a big oak to rest her sore feet and aching back. She wanted to leave the party, but Conor would still be talking to 'important contacts' as he called them. This was often how he acquired bits of information about the positions of other countries on foreign policy questions. Anna couldn't care less.

When she had met Conor, she had had no idea what diplomats did apart from entertaining and going to lots of parties. She had thought that as his wife, she would help him in his job. She soon found out how wrong she had been.

One of Conor's colleagues had told her that the wife of a diplomat was not an important person. The only thing she had to do was to accompany her husband to dinners and receptions, stay reasonably sober and not look too bored. She didn't have to be intelligent, witty, particularly well-read or even elegantly dressed. It did not matter if she only spoke Norwegian, dressed like the Spice Girls, or ate peas with her knife. She could serve hamburgers and spaghetti on paper plates without causing anything more than a little ridicule. She had no influence on her husband's career. She could be the best hostess in their foreign service, or the worst. It did not matter.

A diplomat's career depended on only two things: his ability as a diplomat and how good he was at something called 'arse-licking' (an expression Anna had not come across when she studied English at school). This meant sucking up to politicians. In fact, arse-licking was the more important skill.

Anna had been both surprised and relieved at this discovery. She thought it would take the tension out of entertaining. But Conor didn't agree. 'Even if the Department doesn't care about the way we entertain, I do,' he said during a heated argument. 'A terrible dinner reflects badly on me and on Ireland, even if it has nothing to do with my career.'

Although he was critical about her ability as a hostess, he didn't notice her clothes. She had always had her own style of dressing, preferring to look sexy rather than elegant. Now she could wear what she liked without worrying that the length of her skirts or the depth of her neckline would influence her husband's promotion prospects. But she never managed to find out what diplomats actually did when they were in the office.

Somebody sat down beside her on the bench and Anna was jolted out of her reverie. She looked up. It was Monique du Jardin, wife of a French diplomat at the moment on a home posting at the French foreign office, and Anna's long-time friend.

'So this is where you're hiding,' Monique said in her excellent but accented English. 'You just missed a great conversation about opera.'

'Opera?' Anna asked.

'That's right,' Monique replied, 'or that's what those pseudo-intellectuals thought we were talking about. I was talking about ice cream.'

'What have you been up to now?' Anna demanded, confused. Monique's sense of humour was bizarre at times.

'I got drawn into this group of women who were trying to be sophisticated. One woman asked what I thought of *Le Nozze di Figaro*, and I said I loved it. Especially the crunchy bit at the end.'

'They might still have thought you were talking about opera,' Anna suggested.

'They would if I had stopped there.' Monique giggled. 'But I added that the combination of vanilla and nuts was especially delicious. You can imagine the rest. They looked at me as if I had two heads. But I think they suspected I was having them on, so I left.'

Anna smirked. Monique loved to pretend she was the dizzy blonde she looked like. 'You didn't talk about Proust and Kafka this time?' she asked.

'No,' Monique replied. 'What a shame. I love to talk about their mysterious quality, their fascinating personalities and their ... their ...'

'Melancholy and depth,' Anna filled in.

'That's right,' Monique laughed. 'And I wouldn't have mentioned that they're my cats.' She sighed happily, took a small mirror and a lipstick out of her evening bag and proceeded to touch up the deep red of her full lips.

'Who's that man?' Anna asked suddenly, as she looked into the drawing room. 'Now that's what I call good-looking.'

'Who? Where?' Monique closed her handbag and scanned the garden, her eyes squinting. 'I'm not wearing my contact lenses. I can't see a thing. Describe him to me.'

'He's standing just inside the door. And he's absolutely divine. Dark, tall and dressed to perfection.'

'Not a diplomat then,' Monique decided.

'Probably not,' Anna mumbled. 'He looks like a young Cary Grant. Maybe he's an actor.'

'Let's see if we can get to know him,' Monique suggested, getting up and walking towards the door.

'He's gone. I can't see him any more. Maybe it was just a mirage.'

'Wishful thinking,' Monique sighed and sat down again. 'Men like that are very rare these days.'

'That's true,' Anna replied. 'Talking about men, things are going to be a bit more interesting *chez nous* in the next few days.'

'Really?'

'Conor told me today that we are going to have an Irish journalist to stay with us. He's arriving tomorrow. He will be in Paris to cover the visit of the Taoiseach.'

'The T-shirt?'

'The Taoiseach. It is Irish for prime minister. He is coming to see the French president. Something to do with the European Union.'

Anna had only a sketchy knowledge of politics and what was going on in the world. She skimmed through the newspapers in the mornings, quickly going through the main headlines without reading the articles. 'Political crisis in Germany', she would read, only to skip to the television programmes, the cartoons and the weather. She would know that there was a crisis but not what it was about. If someone asked her about the political situation in Ireland at a dinner party, she would quickly change the subject. On the other hand, she knew all about the private lives of film stars, members of all royal families and other celebrities. She read *Hello!* magazine from cover to cover every week and *Howerya!*, its Irish equivalent, not missing a single scandal or tragedy in the world of the jet set. She felt that this type of know-how was much more interesting for her table companions at dinner than the latest developments in world politics.

'We have journalists staying with us all the time when we are abroad,' Monique replied. 'At our embassies, the ambassador looks after the politicians. We get the journalists.'

'It's the same for us, but we haven't had any of them actually staying with us. This is the first time.'

'French journalists are terrible house guests,' Monique stated.

'Why is that?'

'Because they are such macho pigs. When they stay with us, they behave as if our home is a hotel and treat me like some kind of tart. They either pinch my bottom, or try to order room service. I don't know which I hate more.'

'The Irish aren't like that,' Anna said. 'And this is a very nice man. I have spoken to him on the phone several times. He has this sexy, gravelly voice. I bet he is really good-looking. I can't wait to meet him. It will be a contact with Ireland and I can catch up on all the news.'

'It might be fun, if he's nice. You certainly have lots of room.'

The O'Connors' large, comfortable apartment was situated in an old house in Neuilly, a very chic part of Paris. It was on the top floor with a big terrace, where they could have breakfast on warm spring and summer mornings. It overlooked the Bois de Boulogne and the rooftops of the city beyond. The apartment had high ceilings, parquet floors and period fireplaces in every room. There were three reception rooms, a huge kitchen and four bedrooms, all with bathrooms *en suite*. It was beautifully furnished by the landlord, who lived in the south of France.

'When Mícheal O'Huiginn arrives, I'll invite you and Jean-Pierre for dinner. You'll really like him.'

'He sounds like the kind of man I'd want to meet,' Monique replied. 'But how are you going to cope with two Irishmen in the house? Conor is enough trouble on his own.'

Anna was annoyed at the criticism. 'Conor is not difficult.'

'But he is, darling, don't deny it. I never knew a man to take up so much space.'

'I don't know what you mean. He's not fat.'

'It has nothing to do with size, it's his personality,' Monique explained. 'And he has a very strange attitude to women. It's the rugby. It makes men think they can rule the world. He makes me nervous. I don't know how you cope with him.'

'We're very happy,' Anna protested.

'ok, *chérie*,' Monique soothed. But she didn't look convinced.

It had become dark, and the breeze was beginning to feel chilly. Anna and Monique walked inside to join the party again. As Anna followed Monique through the door, she bumped into someone standing just inside.

'Oops! Sorry!' she exclaimed. She was embarrassed to see that she had knocked into the man's glass and made him spill champagne all over his suit. She looked up and saw that he was the very good-looking man she had spotted earlier. He was even better-looking close up. But his dark eyes were angry. Anna felt suddenly annoyed. His precious suit got a little bit wet, she thought, so what? She studied him in more detail. He had dark wavy hair, dark brown eyes and he was very tall. He was dressed in a superbly cut suit. On the little finger of his left hand he wore a gold signet ring bearing some kind of crest, and she could glimpse a paper-thin Piaget watch under the cuff of his white shirt.

The man dabbed at his suit with a paper napkin. He knew exactly who she was, and their bumping into each other was less than accidental, but he would have preferred not to have sacrificed his suit for the purpose. He studied her as he tried to blot the champagne from the fine cloth. She was not the kind of woman he would normally have flirted with, his tastes running more towards leggy blondes who were easy to please. This woman was the exact opposite, with her ample hips and interesting cleavage. She had a wanton, careless look, which he found very sexy. He tried to gauge her mood and assess how to play his cards. Her blue eyes were rebellious, and they now studied him intently.

'Is this your first time serving in an embassy?' he said in perfect English with just a hint of an accent. There was laughter in his dark eyes.

'I'm not a waitress,' she exclaimed.

'Then who are you?' he asked. 'I really want to know.'

'Why? So you can have me arrested?'

'No, so I can avoid you. I don't have that many suits.'

'Ha, ha,' Anna drawled.

The man turned his attention to their hostess as she came towards them with a plate of *maatjes*, a Dutch speciality consisting of raw herring that you were supposed to take by the tail and eat whole. And they say the Scandinavians have strange food, Anna thought, declining with a little shake of her head. The man looked at the plate with a face like a trapped animal. He bravely took one, tipped his head back, opened his mouth and the *maatje* disappeared. 'Most delicious,' he lied with a forced smile. He had turned a little pale. Anna had to admire his impeccable manners, and his bravery.

Monique had turned back to see what was keeping Anna. 'What are you doing?' she asked. 'Oh,' she stammered, looking up at the man. Then she smiled. '*Bonsoir*. I don't think we've met,' she purred. 'I'm Monique du Jardin.' She held up her hand in a way that indicated she wanted him to kiss it, and he duly obeyed. He turned to Anna.

'And who is your charming friend?' he asked, taking Anna's hand and looking into her eyes.

'This is Anna O'Connor, the wife of the counsellor at the Irish embassy,' Monique replied, annoyed at being ignored. 'And who are you?'

'My name is Juan Valverde,' he murmured over Anna's hand.

Anna looked into his eyes and blushed slightly. Juan Valverde. She had heard of him. He was the number two at the Spanish embassy and one of the most popular men in Paris. Heads turned and cutlery dropped when he entered restaurants, as women admired his athletic frame and handsome face. He drove a Mercedes sports car, rode like a god, and always, always said the right thing. All the ladies of the diplomatic corps loved to have him at their dinner parties, as he was single, good company, mad about women, and able to talk to anybody about anything. He also spoke six languages fluently, making him extremely useful. The fact that he was not very good at foreign policy or other diplomatic skills was beside the point.

This party suddenly seems a little more bearable, Anna thought.

'You don't look like a typical Irishwoman,' he remarked.

'I'm not.'

'Not typical?'

'Not Irish.' She smiled.

'Oh. So what are you? A typical German? Or maybe a typical Dutch woman?'

'I'm Swedish. But not a typical one.'

'Pity. The typical Swedish girl is any man's dream.'

'I'm sorry to disappoint you.'

'Anna isn't one hundred per cent Swedish,' Monique interrupted, 'she's part Russian.'

'Oh,' Juan replied. 'Which part?'

'Moscow,' Anna said without thinking.

'I meant which part of you is Russian,' he asked with a little smile. 'Is it your eyes, your mouth or your lovely figure?'

'Oh, I don't know,' she stammered.

'Was your grandmother a Russian aristocrat who had to flee during the revolution?'

'No,' Anna answered. 'She was an actress. And not a very good one. She met my grandfather after she had been kicked out of the theatre company. He was on a business trip to Moscow. He fell for her when she tried to steal his wallet in his hotel. It all happened in the late nineteen thirties. Nothing to do with the revolution.'

'How exciting. Are you like her?'

'You mean will I steal your wallet?'

'That's not what I meant.' He smiled broadly. Anna suddenly felt a little dizzy.

'I am *so* pleased to meet you,' Monique cooed. 'I have heard so much about you.'

'Really?' Juan murmured, still looking into Anna's eyes. 'How interesting. How long have you been in Paris, Mrs O'Connor?'

'Only five months,' Anna replied. 'We came here from Ireland.'

'And we've been here two years,' Monique

volunteered, 'we came back from ...' But nobody was listening.

'Is your husband here tonight?' Juan asked Anna. 'I would like to have a word with him.'

Anna told Juan where he could find Conor. Juan bowed over her hand and the hand of Monique in turn, and walked away. The two women looked at his elegant back.

'So that's Juan Valverde,' Monique said. 'Not bad.'

'Bad? A nun would have trouble sticking to her vows when he's around.' Anna sighed.

'Dishy man. But terribly rude.'

'I thought he was lovely.'

'You would. He was all over you. How strange.'

'Maybe you weren't his type,' Anna teased. 'You're too skinny. God, I'm starving. Are you coming to get something to eat?'

'OK,' Monique murmured, still looking at the retreating figure of Juan Valverde.

They went into the big, richly decorated dining room. It was furnished with Dutch antiques. Venetian chandeliers hung from the high ceiling, and the french windows overlooking the garden were framed with heavy yellow silk curtains held back with tasselled ropes. The walls were covered with paintings, and giant urns had been filled with peonies and roses. It was the typical opulence of a small, wealthy country.

The big table in the middle of the room bore plates of prawns, smoked salmon and caviar. There were also chicken pieces and spring rolls. Chatting happily, the women nibbled on the delicacies and sipped champagne.

'This beats the raw fish and turpentine they are serving in the other room,' said Monique. 'Thank goodness the Dutch are civilised enough to give you an alternative.' She licked some caviar off her fingers.

Anna was trying not to eat too much. She had put on a lot of weight lately. I'll just have a little snack, she said to herself, stuffing three of the tiny sandwiches into her mouth at once. They were followed by two spring rolls, a scampi in garlic mayonnaise and some bite-size pieces of chicken in batter.

'That's better,' Anna muttered. She suddenly stopped eating as she noticed a tall, blonde woman at the other side of the room. She was eating a piece of herring with obvious relish. The woman looked up and stared at Anna with hard eyes.

'Oh, no, I don't believe it,' Anna hissed. 'What's *she* doing in Paris?'

'You mean Susanna?' Monique replied. 'She has been in Paris a long time now. We all work out with her in St-Cloud. Her classes are tough, but very good.'

Susanna Fuchs was not only the wife of a Dutch diplomat, but also a champion of women's hockey and a keep-fit teacher. Anna had made her acquaintance four years earlier when she and Conor had been on a posting to the Netherlands. They had not been friends. In fact, Anna couldn't stand her.

'Herring is such healthy food,' they could hear Susanna say. 'Full of vitamins and Omega-Three oils for strong bones.'

'Everything she does is healthy and good for you. I bet she hasn't had a piece of cake or a chocolate since she was five,' Anna muttered.

'I know. She's a pain in the neck. But she's a great teacher. She would soon get you into shape.'

'You want me to look like that?'

'No, darling, nobody could. She doesn't look like a woman. And she can't dress. Look at that awful suit. Like something from a nineteen eighties soap opera. And she should at least try to look shorter,' Monique declared.

'Why is she wearing such enormous shoulder pads?'

'She isn't. They're her shoulders.'

'Very sexy.'

'Not very, no,' Monique agreed. 'But no one can work you out like she can. It's thanks to her I'm still wearing a size ten.'

Anna was putting another piece of chicken into her mouth and promising herself to go on a diet the next day when she spotted Conor's red head in the crowd. He was talking to a group of diplomats, and he was looking alarmingly unsteady. He must have overdone the *genever*. The Dutch schnapps had a kick like several mules.

When they first met, he had told her he was a 'pioneer'. She had been very impressed. The word conjured up images of a rugged man in big walking boots going across rough countryside, scaling mountains and wading through wild rivers. The truth was brought home to her at a party in Stockholm.

Conor had turned to a waiter. 'Could I have a glass of milk? – I'm a pioneer,' he had explained in response to her puzzled look.

'I know, but what has that got to do with it?'

'It means that I'm a member of the Pioneer Total Abstinence Association.'

He had gone on to explain that children in Ireland were made to take 'the pledge' at their confirmation. You didn't have to, but many did, mainly to please their mothers. It meant that for the rest of your life you promised not to drink alcohol. That was what the term 'pioneer' meant in Ireland. Many broke their pledge later on. In fact, the worst drinkers in Ireland were those who had broken the pledge.

'But,' Anna stammered, 'you said *total* abstinence. What else did you promise to give up?'

'Just alcohol. Nothing else,' Conor assured her.

'But not drinking will cause serious problems for your diplomatic career,' Anna exclaimed. 'And drinking wine is not the same as being blind drunk on home-made brandy.'

Conor had looked thoughtfully at Anna. She was right. The old tradition in Ireland was really meant to protect you from the terrible effects of strong spirits. A glass of wine was not the same thing. He decided that night to break his pledge. To hell with his mother and the aunties!

'It's a bit like losing your virginity,' he had explained. 'Once you have had a drink, there is no going back.' Anna had been delighted. One in the eye for his mother, she had thought.

Now she muttered something to Monique, and walked quickly over to Conor, who was helping himself to yet another glass of *genever*. Anna had a feeling this could end in disaster.

'Conor,' Anna hissed, 'how much have you drunk?'

'Lots!' He beamed. 'And it's luuvvly!'

'That's enough,' Anna said, putting his glass back on the tray. 'Time to go home.' She took him by the arm and tried to lead him toward the door. Jean-Pierre, Monique's husband, who happened to be standing nearby, came over and took Conor's other arm. 'Let's go and say goodbye to the ambassador,' he said to Conor.

'OK,' Conor meekly agreed.

Together, Anna and Jean-Pierre walked Conor through the big room. The door seemed miles away. On the way, they passed a couple they knew, who tried to stop them for a chat.

'A bit tired,' Conor muttered and tripped over his own feet. 'Time for a little lie-down.' They straightened him up and continued to steer him towards the door.

Their hostess was standing in the hall saying goodbye to some departing guests. Susanna Fuchs was beside her, putting on her coat.

'Hello, Anna,' she said. 'Fancy meeting you in Paris.'

'Hi,' Anna replied lamely, struggling to keep Conor upright. 'Nice to see you again.'

'You should come to my keep-fit class soon,' Susanna announced, glancing at Anna's waist. 'In Paris you have to choose between *haute cuisine* or *haute couture*. In your case, the *cuisine* seems to be winning.'

'Awful cow,' Conor muttered to Jean-Pierre. 'You can't smoke, drink, eat or even fucking sit down when she's around. Bloody rude name too.' He giggled and Susanna glared at him.

'Typical,' she sneered. 'The Irish can't hold their drink.'

Anna made a superhuman effort not to lose her temper, but failed. 'That's what happens when they serve you paint stripper,' she snapped.

Anna and Jean-Pierre managed to get Conor into the car, where he put his head back against the head-rest and fell asleep, snoring loudly. Anna drove quickly home through the heavy traffic.

By the time they reached the apartment, Conor had sobered up somewhat. He flopped down on the sofa in the living room to watch the evening news. Anna went into the bedroom to change out of her party clothes. She put on a pair of comfortable trousers and a cotton blouse. At last she could relax with her family.

'How was the party?' Assumpta, their diminutive au pair girl from County Kerry was in the kitchen cleaning up after the children. She had bright blue eyes and wild black curly hair.

'Another magic evening.'

'Really?'

'Oh, absolutely. The place was full of people I didn't know, two people thought I was a waitress and tried to order a drink, my best friend told me I was fat and I spilled champagne all over a very dishy man. Then I met someone I had hoped never, ever to see again and Conor got sloshed on Dutch paint stripper and had to be practically carried out.'

'Sounds lovely,' Assumpta smiled. 'I have finished

here,' she continued. 'I'll be off now.'

'All right,' Anna replied. 'Have a good time.'

'Don't worry if I'm a bit late.'

'I won't. See you in the morning.'

The children were in the living room, trying to catch their father's attention. They both had his red hair and brown eyes. They were asking about the party and who was there. They lost interest when they realised that it had not been their sort of party.

'You never do anything at your parties,' Lena, who was ten, complained. 'We have much more fun at ours.'

'Yes,' nine-year-old Declan added. 'At Billy's party last week there was a fight and a big Coca-Cola bottle exploded. Then Billy said a bad word and his mummy slapped him. Sam was sick all over the sofa. *That* was cool!'

'Grown-ups don't behave like that at parties,' Anna replied.

'Much more fun if they did,' Conor muttered.

'I heard a Dutch woman's husband call her a very bad name when they were here for dinner last week,' protested Declan. 'He said *ya hoour* to her.'

'They were speaking Dutch,' Anna explained. '*Ja hoor* means Yes indeed in Dutch. Anyway, what were you doing out of bed at that time? You know you are not allowed to go into the dining room when we have guests.'

'I just wanted to see what you were doing. But it was really boring so I went back to bed.'

'Isn't it time you were asleep?' Conor said without taking his eyes from the screen.

Anna went to get the children into bed. They would play up if she wasn't there to check on them. They went to an international school, where they were being turned into juvenile delinquents by the incompetent staff. Conor had threatened to send them to boarding school in Ireland if they continued to misbehave. Anna didn't want to send them away, but Conor said that an Irish school would be better than 'that hen factory'.

When the children were finally in bed, Anna joined Conor on the sofa in front of the television.

'Mmmm, you smell nice,' he muttered, putting his arm around her. 'How about some quality time with your husband?' He kissed her neck and started to unbutton her blouse. Anna was pleasantly surprised. She put her arms around Conor's neck and kissed him. They were nearly ready to retire to the bedroom when the doorbell rang.

'Ignore it, maybe they will go away,' Conor said, slipping his hand inside Anna's bra. The doorbell rang again, this time followed by the sound of fists banging on the door.

'Damn,' Conor growled and went into the hall. He was followed by Anna, hastily buttoning her blouse, and Lena and Declan who had been awakened by the noise.

Conor opened the door.

CHAPTER 2

A tall, bearded, rather fat man dressed in a dirty beige Aran pullover, baggy corduroys and sandals was standing on the landing. He carried two huge battered suitcases and a laptop computer.

'Godzilla downstairs didn't want to let me in,' he said. (The concierge was a suspicious woman whose mission in life was to stop anybody who did not meet her high standard of respectability entering the building.) 'I am Mícheal O'Huiginn,' he continued. 'I think you are expecting me.' He dropped the suitcases on the floor.

'But we thought you were coming tomorrow,' Anna stammered, her eyes wide both with surprise at his early arrival, and shock at his appearance. She couldn't believe her eyes. The name Mícheal was to her the name of someone good-looking and romantic. This man looked more like a Trevor or a Hugh. His voice on the telephone had been deceptively deep and sexy. Where was the Richard Gere look-alike she had hoped for?

'But you're not good-looking!' Declan exclaimed.

'Mammy said you would be handsome! And you're not. You're really –'

'Go back to bed at once,' Conor snapped, before Declan could finish his sentence. 'Please come in,' he said to the man. 'I'm sorry about the concierge. She takes her duties a bit too seriously at times.'

It was midnight before their visitor had had a bite to eat in the kitchen and settled into the guest room. He had spent the entire evening either winking at Anna behind Conor's back, or leering in a suggestive way.

He could not be described as even remotely attractive. He didn't even look very clean. Anna thought he probably slept in his clothes. The pullover seemed to have fused to his beard, and the trousers looked as if they had never been pressed or even hung up.

Anna showed Mícheal to his room as Conor had already gone to bed. The guest bedroom had a bathroom *en suite*, and she pointedly showed Mícheal this.

'This is for you alone,' she said. 'You don't have to share.'

'You diplomats certainly live in style' was the only reply.

Anna went into the bedroom hoping to pick up where she and Conor had left off before the doorbell rang. She was met by the sound of gentle snoring.

Juan and Anna were dancing. He twirled her around the ball-room making the white tulle dress float around her legs. He looked deep into her eyes and said: 'Anna, you are the most beautiful woman I have ever met. I have a yacht in the Caribbean. Please come with me. We'll sail around the

world. You will never have to go to one single cocktail party or
talk to boring old men at dinner. I will take you away from all
that. From now on, your life will be full of fun and steak with
Béarnaise sauce. I will feed you chocolates and we will only
drink champagne. Please, say yes.'

Someone was screaming. Anna woke with a start.
She squinted at the clock on the table beside her bed. It
was two o'clock in the morning. Conor turned in the
bed and buried his head in the pillow with a grunt.

She quickly put on her dressing gown and ran
out into the hall.

There was another scream. Assumpta was in the
hall staring wildly at Mícheal O'Huiginn, who was
standing in the doorway of the kitchen dressed in a
pair of rather grey, baggy underpants and matching
vest with holes. 'Just getting a snack,' he said, showing
them a sandwich.

'Who . . . who is that?'

'It's all right, Assumpta, it's our guest, Mícheal
O'Huiginn. You were gone out when he arrived.'

'Have you never seen an Irishman before, girl?'
Mícheal growled.

'Not with underwear like that.' Assumpta had
recovered her confidence.

Mícheal suddenly realised that he was less than
decent. He hastily went into his room and closed the
door with a bang.

'Not exactly to die for,' Assumpta laughed.

One morning a week later, Anna wandered up the
Champs-Elysées looking into shop windows. The
spring sunshine was warm, and there was a gentle

breeze. She was wearing a navy linen suit she had bought at last year's sales. She had a few hours to herself before meeting Monique for lunch at a small bistro nearby. 'I must talk to you,' Monique had insisted. That could mean anything from the opening of a new boutique to the outbreak of World War Three.

The shop window displays were showing the latest spring and summer fashion. The skirts were short and pencil-slim this year, requiring a wearer to have the body of a twelve-year-old. Anna sighed. She would have to lose a lot of weight fast if she were to fit into this year's clothes. During their years in Ireland, her weight had crept up as she turned to food for comfort during evenings alone while Conor pursued his career. Nobody seemed to notice how she dressed, and so she had stopped bothering to make an effort. But Paris was the city of style. French women were so well turned out, and Anna wanted to be like them.

Somebody bumped into her so roughly that the bags of shopping she was carrying fell on to the pavement. At first startled, then angry, Anna looked at her things spread across the pavement, and turned around to glare at the person who had been so clumsy.

'If you weren't so busy window-shopping, you would not bump into people, my darling Anna.' Juan Valverde was standing there looking impossibly handsome. Anna wanted to scream. Why did this kind of thing happen every time they met?

Juan knelt down to recover the scattered shopping. T-shirts for the children, three pairs of embarrassingly large knickers, a pair of stockings (she didn't like tights), a bag of liquorice all-sorts and a string of fake pearls. All purchased at Prisunic, the low-price department store at the end of the Champs-Elysées.

Anna knelt down beside Juan in an attempt to put away the items before he could see them.

'A thrifty shopper, I see.' He picked up the underwear.

'They're for my mother.' She snatched them away from him and quickly stuffed them back into the bag.

'She must be one hell of a woman.' He gave her the rest of the items. 'Stockings? Are they for your mother as well?' he said with a cheeky look.

'Never mind!' Her face felt even hotter. She just wanted to get away from him.

He helped her to her feet. His smile spread all over his face, showing his white, even teeth, until he was grinning like a mischievous boy. 'How about a cup of coffee to help you recover?' he offered.

A cup of coffee seemed suddenly very attractive to Anna. She was tired and longed to sit down for a while. 'That would be nice,' she said.

They sat down at a table outside one of the many cafés. She sighed contentedly, taking off her jacket to reveal a pink silk sleeveless T-shirt. The gentle wind felt delicious on her bare arms and there was a smell of flowers, coffee and French cigarettes. She closed her eyes to the sun.

'*Deux verres de champagne, s'il vous plaît,*' she heard Juan order.

'No, no, just coffee for me.'

'But it is such a lovely day. It calls for something more than coffee.'

'Please, I don't want champagne.'

He reluctantly changed the order and sighed. 'How can such a lovely woman be so unromantic?'

'What are you doing here at this time of the day? It isn't even lunch time.'

'I am pretending to be at a briefing at the Quai d'Orsay. Nobody will notice my absence.'

'Won't you have to write a report about it?'

'I will make something up. The outcome is rather predictable.'

'You mean you're going to lie?'

'A successful diplomat, my darling Anna, needs to have many talents but honesty and zeal are not among them.'

'But Conor works very hard. He's an excellent diplomat.'

'Yes he is. Despite his hard work and honesty.' Juan leaned closer, his elbow on the table, his chin in his hand, looking Anna deep in the eyes. 'You see, my darling Anna,' he drawled, 'and this is the first lesson in diplomacy that I'm going to give you, a good diplomat, a really excellent diplomat, is never where he is supposed to be and never does what he is expected to do. Going to briefings and official dinners, taking notes and reporting a country's official policy is easy. You can find out all you want by reading the newspapers. A child of five could do it. The trick is to catch people off their guard. You have no idea the amount of interesting information one can receive by being in the wrong place at the wrong time with the right people.' He gave her a little wink and straightened up. 'And that's much more fun.'

'Oh,' Anna said. She had the feeling that he had not been talking about diplomacy.

'Now, let's forget about duty and enjoy this beautiful day. How about a slice of cake, or a croissant?'

Anna shook her head.

'Don't tell me you're on a diet! You have a beautiful, feminine figure, don't spoil it.'

'It isn't fashionable to be feminine. This year women are supposed to be thin.'

'Fashion! Women's clothes are not designed by real men. To me, a beautiful woman does not look like a boy. You are a real woman, Anna, don't change.' He ran his hand up her arm, barely touching her. It made her shiver slightly. The arrival of the coffee broke the spell. Anna started to chatter to cover her nervousness.

'I'm meeting Monique for lunch later. She has something important to tell me.'

'It's probably something to do with boats.'

'I beg your pardon?'

'Tell me, Anna, do you like the sea?'

'Yes, I do. Why?'

'Never mind.' Juan now quickly changed the subject. 'Have you been to see the Picasso museum?' he asked. Anna happily talked about the museums in Paris and the most recent exhibitions. Then Juan asked how she and Conor had met. She told him how Conor had been on a posting to Sweden and how they had met at a party, fallen instantly in love and been married very soon after that. Juan laughed at her story of how her mother had thought marrying a diplomat was a great career move.

'How come she thought it had something to do with your career?'

'Well, I suppose she didn't think there was any future in being a receptionist. And she was delighted when I gave up the notion of being a dancer,' Anna explained.

'You wanted to be a dancer?' Juan enquired incredulously, glancing at her figure.

'Hard to tell now,' she laughed, 'but I worked hard to join the Stockholm Opera ballet.'

'Why did you give it up?'

'I was no bloody good. And ballet is absolute murder. If you ever tried on a pair of point shoes you'd know.'

'If I had, I wouldn't admit it,' he joked. 'But I know what you mean.'

'Ballet is not for wimps. That's for sure,' Anna declared.

'So,' Juan continued, 'how did your husband's family react when he brought home a Swedish girl? They must have been a little startled.'

'Startled?' Anna said. 'They were grief-stricken. His mother cried for a week and said it would be the end of her. If my mother wasn't already dead, this would kill her, she sobbed. They thought I was something from outer space. The girl from the planet Sex.' She laughed. 'They didn't calm down until we had children.'

Conor's aunts had tried to explain to Anna how an Irish mother feels about her son. 'It was nothing personal,' one of them had said. 'If the Queen herself came over from England to marry Conor, she would not have been good enough for his mother.'

'Yes,' added another aunt, 'and if the Virgin Mary had come down from heaven to marry him, she would not have measured up either.'

'Irish mothers seem to be rather terrifying.' Juan smiled.

'They'd scare you to death.'

'You don't look as if you scare easily.'

'That depends.'

'I hope you're not afraid of me,' Juan joked.

'Should I be?'

'Of course not.' He smirked.

'Good. Then we can be friends.'

'Friends!' he snorted. 'Men and women can't be friends. I will certainly never be yours.' He looked suddenly angry.

'Of course they can. I have lots of men friends.'

'Then they are either gay or just wimps. A real man could never be your friend, Anna. There is always sexual tension between a man and a woman. It is only natural. Don't tell me that you are not aware of that.'

Anna felt suddenly angry. What a self-centred, macho pig.

'Who do you think you are, God's gift to women?' She grabbed her jacket and got up from her chair. 'And you can keep your sexual tension.' She stomped up the street. She had only gone a short distance when she remembered her shopping still on the chair beside Juan. Red-faced, she turned around, marched back and took the bags. Juan rose, laughing and shaking his head. He grabbed her hand and kissed it.

'I love feisty women.' He laughed.

'Oh, get lost.' Anna charged up the Champs-Elysées.

Juan paid the bill and turned to leave the café. He was still smiling when he spotted Susanna seated a few tables away. She was looking at Anna's retreating figure.

In the small bistro, Monique was waiting for Anna at a table near the window.

'Hello, Monique darling. What's up?'

'Let's order some lunch before I tell you. I need food.'

'Is it that bad?' Anna knew that only a disaster would make Monique break her never-ending diet.

'It's terrible.'

Anna ordered a *salade niçoise* and Monique chose a plate of *cassoulet*, a heavy pork stew with haricot beans, a favourite of French truck drivers. Something was obviously seriously wrong. Anna always turned to food in a crisis – being depressed would even lead her into serious bingeing – but she had never known Monique to resort to this form of therapy.

While they were waiting for their lunch, they talked about Conor's minor disaster at the Dutch embassy the week before.

'I don't blame Conor for getting drunk,' Monique consoled her. 'That *genever* is lethal stuff. Jean-Pierre once got so drunk on it that he fell down a flight of stairs and landed on top of the wife of the mayor of Paris.' She laughed, and then was suddenly serious.

'What's the matter?' Anna asked. 'What's happened?'

Monique didn't reply, but started to cry. Tears

were streaming down her face and she made no effort to wipe them away. Her expertly applied make-up was dissolving and her mascara made black rings around her eyes.

'Monique! Has someone died?'

'No, but someone will.'

'Who?'

'Me,' Monique exclaimed. 'This is the end of my life,' she sobbed, burying her face in her hands. All the customers in the small restaurant were now staring at Monique. This was exciting. A beautiful woman having a nervous breakdown at lunch time. The French were used to dramas in restaurants. But it was usually a couple having a row. This was more interesting.

'Monique,' Anna snapped. 'Pull yourself together and tell me what's wrong. Everybody is looking.'

'OK.' Monique sighed, and took a deep breath. 'I'll tell you. We are moving again. To somewhere horrible.'

'Where?' Anna demanded.

'Australia,' Monique exclaimed and her eyes filled with tears again. 'We have to leave in September.' She looked expectantly at Anna as the tears rolled down her cheeks.

Anna stared back. 'So?' she asked. 'What's so terrible about that? It's far away and I'll miss you but . . .'

'Hello?' Monique exclaimed. 'Did you hear me? I said Australia. You know, kangaroos, koalas, spiders and snakes.'

'I heard. But . . .'

She was interrupted by the arrival of the food. Monique gulped down two huge forkfuls of the pork and haricot bean stew as if she had been starving for weeks. Then she started to cry again.

'Oh, Anna,' she moaned. 'You know what I mean. It's a terrible place. They dress in shorts, T-shirts and sandals. And they wear hats with corks hanging from the brim. They drink beer straight from the can and eat only barbecued steaks.'

'Yes,' Anna filled in. 'They burp and swear. And that's only the women. Unlike France, where the people go around in berets with strings of onions around their necks.' She looked at Monique and shook her head. 'You're such a twit.'

'OK.' Monique sniffed. 'Maybe I'm exaggerating a little. But I do know that Australian men are rough. And they treat women badly. If anyone calls me Sheila I will scream.'

'It's a beautiful country,' Anna declared. 'There are flora and fauna there that you will not find anywhere else.'

'Flora? Fauna? You mean in the, the ... bush?' Monique was looking frightened. 'I will *not* go camping. Can you honestly see me in the Australian bush? I will die first.'

The thought of Monique cooking over a camp fire and sleeping in a tent in the Australian bush made Anna laugh. But then she felt suddenly sad. Monique was her best friend. She had helped her cope with the first few difficult months in Paris.

They had known each other for a long time, ever since Anna spent a year in Monique's boarding school as an exchange student when they were both sixteen. With Monique, she had spent her free time sitting in cafés, drinking strong black coffee, ogling men and smoking Gauloises, feeling grown up and very French.

They had kept in touch ever since through letters and phone calls. There had been a tearful reunion when Anna arrived in Paris five months ago. And now Anna would have no one to call when she was fed up, no shoulder to cry on when things went wrong, and nobody to ask to stand in for a dinner guest who had dropped out at the last minute. Who would fill her in on the latest gossip, tell her where to get a bargain, listen to tales of woe about her marriage, and cheer her up with silly jokes?

Monique, having eaten with alarming haste, now finished the huge helping of stew and burped discreetly. 'I'm going to have dessert. How about you?'

'OK. Profiteroles or chocolate mousse?' Anna asked, consulting the menu.

'What do you mean *or*?' Monique asked as she tried to attract the attention of a passing waiter.

'Monique, you'll make yourself sick. Stop eating, darling, and calm down. Australia may turn out to be a wonderful adventure. After all, it is only for a few years.'

'It is easy for you to say that, being on a posting to Paris. You don't have to pack up and go to the other side of the world. You don't have to live in a place where there is no ... no ... fashion!' she spluttered. 'And what about my darlings? I have to leave them behind.'

'The girls? You can't leave them behind!' Anna exclaimed. 'They're only five and three.'

'Not them,' Monique snapped. 'The cats. Proust and Kafka. They will never forgive me. Oh, God. This is the pits.'

'For God's sake, Monique, stop moaning,' Anna commanded. 'It's not the end of the world. Your mother will take the bloody cats. You'll be fine. You'll be the toast of Canberra and the most stylish woman in Australia.'

'The toast of Canberra,' Monique replied in a flat voice. 'Big deal.' She blew her nose and sighed deeply. 'I should have known I wouldn't get much sympathy from you. You always look on the bright side. It's very irritating.'

'What do you want me to do?' Anna demanded. 'Cry? I don't see that it's such a tragedy. And you'll probably find a handsome tennis instructor to flirt with.'

'But I don't play tennis.'

'Who said anything about tennis? Before you know it, you'll be back in Paris with a great tan, telling us all about the gorgeous Australian men, and we'll all be jealous.'

'Maybe,' Monique replied without much conviction. She sighed and dried her eyes. 'There is another thing I wanted to tell you.'

'Yes?'

'We are going on a cruise in the Mediterranean in July.'

'You and Jean-Pierre?'

'Yes, and so are you.'

'What? How do you mean?' Anna asked, bewildered.

'The Greek millionaire Pavlos Patmos is inviting some French officials and other European diplomats on his yacht. He thinks Greece will improve their relations with the EU this way. Juan Valverde is going too. You and Conor will be invited.'

So this was what Juan had hinted at. 'Why? We are not exactly important. I don't see how the Greek economy would benefit from our presence.'

'Can't you guess? It is Juan Valverde who has organised your invitation. I think he is a little *amoureux* with you, Anna.'

Anna blushed. What was the man up to? A cruise in the Mediterranean! 'It sounds wonderful, but Conor would refuse to go if he knew why we are invited.'

'Don't tell him. Only Jean-Pierre, you and I know the truth. Juan would not tell, he is too clever.' She sighed. 'I rather fancy him myself. But for some reason, he seems to be more interested in you.'

'Oh, Monique. Stop.'

'Oh Anna,' she mimicked. 'Don't be coy. Admit you find him attractive.' She closed her eyes. 'I bet he's great in bed,' she murmured. 'A little fling with him would cheer you up. It would bring colour to your cheeks and you would lose some weight. It is the best lift a woman can get.' Monique opened her eyes and looked at Anna. 'So he's not your type. You don't have to marry him or introduce him to your parents. Think of it as therapy.' Monique, in her French way, made adultery seem like a holiday, from which you came back invigorated and stimulated. She had had one or two affairs during her ten-year marriage, but that didn't seem to have affected her relationship with her husband. Monique had a strange attitude to love and marriage, Anna thought.

'Every girl needs a boyfriend to flirt with,' Monique stated.

'Not if you're married.'

'*Especially* if you're married.'

'No, I wouldn't want a boyfriend,' Anna protested. That would be too much trouble. But it would be nice to have an admirer.

It was true. She would love to have a good-looking man on the side who would cheer her up and tell her she was beautiful when life became dull. But that was really all she wanted. She didn't need to make problems for herself. Conor would kill her if she cheated on him. The sex would have to be spectacular to risk being murdered. (With Juan it probably would be.) In any case, the reason Anna would never consider having an affair was more to do with her stretch marks and cellulite than with any moral scruples.

'Oh, don't be so prissy. Come on the cruise,' Monique pleaded. 'It will be fun. And Juan will not cause trouble if you're careful.'

Anna thought how marvellous the cruise would be. She could handle Juan. There would probably be many women on the trip who were much more glamorous than she. Thinking of glamour, and of Juan's interest in her, made her think of clothes. She would need a new wardrobe for the cruise. And a new body.

Anna was interested in clothes, but was not

prepared to spend as much money, time and effort as Monique. Anna's clothes shopping was a hit-and-miss affair, and her wardrobe was full of the results of impulse buying. To Monique, buying clothes was not just a pleasant shopping trip, it was a crusade, the search for the Holy Grail of the perfect outfit at a rock-bottom price. It took Anna as long to choose which of her outfits to wear for a party as it did Monique, but for a very different reason. Monique would spend a long time thinking about what sort of party it was going to be, who would be there, and which dress had been seen the least often. Anna's choice was based simply on whatever she could find that had all its buttons and was reasonably clean.

She was just not organised enough to look after her clothes. Unlike Monique, who after a party would check her dress for stains, wrinkles or loose buttons, and who would repair any damage before hanging the dress in the wardrobe, Anna would simply dump her outfit on a chair, promising herself to check it the next morning. It would usually end up shoved back in the wardrobe without a second glance. She would have to improve. Surely it would be worth it to look as polished as Monique.

'What about clothes?' Anna asked. 'I have nothing to wear. I can't afford Armani.'

'Who can? I buy most of my clothes in the sales.'

'Oh, yeah, as if you could buy Armani, Chanel and St Laurent at sale prices.'

'But you can,' Monique protested. 'I will tell you my secret. Twice a year, the most important designers send what is left of the past season's collection to a warehouse outside Paris. There is a list of women who are then invited to buy from that selection. Don't ask me how, but I managed to put my name on that list. You can find the most fantastic bargains this way.'

'Really?' Anna asked.

'Absolutely. I'll bring you next time. But I warn you, it is hard work. You will have to fight for what you want, and I really mean fight. The place is usually packed with French society ladies. They are very fierce. A friend of mine lost a tooth at a summer sale. I almost broke a rib last year because a woman shoved her elbow in my side to get to the last Dior jacket. I managed to grab it at the last moment. I was covered in bruises.'

'What sort of damage did you inflict on her?'

'Oh, she was all right. Just a black eye and a split lip. Anyway,' she continued coolly, 'that is not all. If you have to try things on, you must strip in front of *le tout Paris,* because there are no changing rooms. This means that your body is scrutinised by every bitch in town. They will see each flaw on your body. But,' she added with a malicious smile, 'we can also scrutinise theirs. You will see more scar tissue than in a hospital. Every woman over forty has had corrective surgery.'

'Nip and tuck, you mean?'

'More like major re-upholstery.' At thirty-three, Monique could still be smug about her looks. 'I must go,' she continued, 'I have a full afternoon before I collect the children from school. I have an appointment at Carita's for a full facial, a cellulite treatment,

eyebrow dye and a manicure. God knows I need it.'
She sighed, trying to wipe some of the mascara from
under her eyes. 'You should try Carita. They really
take care of any problem you have with your body.'
She sounded like somebody who was having the car
serviced. Like most French women, Monique spent a
lot of time and money on her body.

Anna did not put her beauty routines at the top of
her list of priorities. She had slipped into the habit of
not bothering with the many time-consuming
grooming jobs that needed regular attention. She only
occasionally plucked her eyebrows, shaved her legs or
applied body lotion. She wore her hair long more for
convenience than because it suited her.

'Why don't you let them look after you, Anna?'
Monique suggested. 'They are really good at reducing
cellulite.'

'How do you know I have any?'

'Don't be silly, all women do. The cosmetics
industry wouldn't survive if we didn't. Let's go to
Susanna's workout tomorrow. We have to train for
the summer sale. And darling, it wouldn't do you
any harm to lose some weight. I have to rush now. *A
demain, chérie.*' She got up, kissed Anna, and left the
restaurant with the air of someone rushing to a vital
appointment.

Anna walked into the apartment to the sounds of
scuffling in the living room and a crash of broken
china. She quickly went into the room, where she
found Lena and Declan wrestling on the floor. A
broken vase lay on the carpet. The children were

shouting and pulling at each other. The television was on full blast and Mícheal O'Huiginn was lounging on the sofa with a glass of Guinness.

'What's going on?' Anna exclaimed angrily. 'Stop fighting.'

'Yes,' Mícheal said. 'I can't hear the television. I'm trying to watch a programme about French contemporary literature. The children are on their own. Dementia's gone out.'

'Who?'

'That garden gnome you call a nanny.'

'Her name is Assumpta. Surely you have heard that name before? Ireland is full of Assumptas.'

'Of course I have,' Mícheal quickly replied, looking oddly uncomfortable. 'I sent her out for more Guinness. Get the children out of here. Appalling behaviour.'

Anna looked at him with distaste.

'I agree,' she replied, 'but it's not *their* behaviour that's appalling. They usually watch their favourite programme at this time. And you have no right to send Assumpta out to do your shopping. Declan and Lena, go to your rooms. I'm sure you have some homework.' The children left the room, looking sullen.

'Children should be seen and not heard,' Mícheal grunted. 'And you were out of Guinness.'

Anna looked pointedly at the litter of cans on the coffee table. 'Whose fault is that? My children don't drink a lot of Guinness. And you have a very negative attitude to children for an Irishman.'

'Well . . .' Mícheal muttered, 'I . . . I was an only child.'

'You must be the only one in Ireland,' Anna said, studying his red face. Why was he suddenly so embarrassed?

Mícheal was turning out to be the worst house guest. He had only been with them for a week and was already getting on her nerves. He left a mess of newspapers everywhere, he never as much as brought a coffee cup back into the kitchen and he was constantly looking for food in the fridge. His table manners were appalling. It was as if he thought that being an 'intellectual' excused him from behaving in a civilised way, or even from keeping clean. He obviously hated children and treated them with barely disguised dislike. He was appallingly rude to Anna and Assumpta.

'He was probably stood up by some woman in college,' Assumpta had said. 'And now he is taking it out on us.'

'Probably,' Anna agreed. 'I can't imagine that any woman would ever have wanted to go out with the creep.'

'What happened to hospitality? It seems to be unknown in this house,' Mícheal now grunted.

'And good manners in yours,' Anna retorted.

'I'm going out for dinner. Don't wait up,' he announced as he got up from the sofa and shuffled to the door.

'Please, don't worry about tidying up.' The irony was dripping out of Anna's voice.

Mícheal closed the door without answering.

Later that evening, Anna had a hot bath in order to

relax and rest. She loved her bathroom. It was the first time in her life that she had one of her very own. She mentally blessed the French for putting in lots of bathrooms in these big apartments. This one was huge and pink. The floor was covered in a thick, white carpet. Not practical, but lovely. There was a big window overlooking the rooftops of Paris.

Anna could admire the view as she was lying in the pink marble bath with warm scented water up to her chin. The sky was becoming dark. There is an hour in Paris between twilight and night which is magical. The French call it *l'heure bleue*. The sky turned royal blue, but it was not quite dark. The lights started to come on in all the apartments. Anna watched Paris turning into *la ville lumière*, the city of lights. It was beautiful, and she never tired of watching it.

She got out of the bath and wrapped herself in one of the huge, fluffy white towels she had bought especially for her bathroom.

The children ran into the bedroom as she was sitting at the antique dressing table brushing her hair. She had changed into a loose, comfortable dress. At last an evening at home.

'Mammy,' Lena called, 'Assumpta says that your wan is on the phone.'

Your one? Who could that be? Anna wondered as she went out into the dark oak-panelled hall to take the call.

'Anna, my love.' She recognised Juan's deep voice. It gave her a jolt. 'I am so sorry about what happened this morning,' he continued. 'I was being silly. Will you forgive me?'

'Of course,' she stammered.

'I will try to be your friend.' Anna could hear him choking on the word. 'We are going to have a wonderful time in the Mediterranean. A whole week together.'

'We're not going to be alone. I believe twenty people are coming on the trip, and one of them is my husband. If he agrees to go, that is. I can't help wondering why we are being invited. Why didn't you tell me about it?'

'I thought you wouldn't want to come if you knew I had something to do with your invitation.'

'You were right. In any case, it all depends on Conor. It's going to be hard to convince him to go.'

'Very few people would refuse such an invitation.'

'You don't know Conor.'

'That's true. I don't really know your husband at all. Is he the kind of man who has strong principles?'

'That's right.'

'I thought the Irish were more flexible.' Was there a touch of regret in his voice? 'I don't understand them,' he continued. 'They are so unpredictable.'

'That's what makes them so interesting.'

'Anna, don't be mean,' Juan pleaded. 'I want to see you again soon. I promise to keep my distance.'

'I'm very busy at the moment, Juan. My family take up most of my time these days.'

'Are you playing hard to get?'

'I *am* hard to get.'

'I like a challenge.'

'You're being too optimistic.'

'Who said, the difficult things we do straightaway,

the impossible takes a little longer?'

'Camilla Parker-Bowles? It sounds very boring to me. I have to go now, I'm very busy, actually.'

'I hope we will meet very soon again. Goodbye for now, *querida*.' It sounded like a caress. Anna smiled as she put down the receiver and went back into the bedroom.

The children were jumping on the bed on top of the suit she had taken off when she came home.

'Stop it! Look, it's all crumpled. Assumpta,' she called, 'try to control these children!'

'All right, all right.' Assumpta was looking hassled. 'I was doing the ironing and checking on their homework at the same time when your wan rang,' she explained. 'A person can only do so many things at once.'

'Your wan! Very funny. See if you can do something with this suit, Assumpta. It's one of my favourites.'

When Conor came home, all was peaceful again. The suit had been rescued, the children had finished their homework and had dinner, and they were seated watching television in their pyjamas. Conor sank into the sofa beside them, loosening his tie.

'Hard day?' Anna looked at his tired face.

'Yeah.'

'Is it the Taoiseach's visit?'

'Yes. And bloody tourists,' he grunted.

'What was it this time? Lost passports?'

Irish tourists got into trouble in Paris with irritating regularity. If they didn't have their pockets picked in the Métro, they managed to forget the names of their hotels, lose their passports, or their luggage, or their cars, husbands, wives and children. Some people got drunk and fell into the Seine, others were involved in fights in the many Irish pubs around Paris and were arrested, or had to be admitted to hospital. There was no end to the amount of problems the personnel at the Irish embassy had to sort out. Anna knew the Irish were well-behaved compared to other nationals judging by the complaints from friends of other embassies. British diplomats had to deal with soccer hooligans, the Dutch with drug addicts, and the Greek and Turkish embassies with illegal immigrants. Taking care of your countrymen's mishaps abroad was part of a diplomat's duties.

'We had one woman who had her handbag stolen, a couple who couldn't remember where they had parked their car, and a little boy whose parents had left him in the crèche of a department store and forgotten to pick him up.'

'God Lord,' Anna exclaimed. 'What did you do?'

'We got them all sorted out in the end.'

'Even the lost child?'

'Yup. The parents arrived at the embassy only half an hour after he did. They thought he had been kid-napped. They didn't realise they couldn't leave him there for eight hours.'

'Some people shouldn't be allowed to leave the country,' Anna declared. 'Bedtime, kids,' she added, producing a chorus of grunts and groans from the children. Lena went off to her room, but Declan refused to budge.

'It's my favourite programme,' he shouted.

'Since when is *Cooking with Delia* dubbed into French your favourite programme?' Anna asked. 'If you are not in bed in five minutes, you won't be watching *any* programme for at least a week.'

'OK then.' Declan grunted and got up from the sofa. 'You're such a bitch.'

'Charming manners they are picking up at school,' Conor remarked. 'You'd better go to bed at once, or you'll feel the back of my hand, young man. And I don't want to hear you call your mother names again. Is that understood?'

'That's child abuse!' Declan shouted. 'It's against the law. Our teacher said . . .'

'Your teacher isn't here now, is she?' Conor purred menacingly. 'So I can do what I like to you in my own home.' He bent down and looked Declan in the eyes. 'What would be the smartest option for you right now, do you think?'

'OK, you win,' Declan muttered. 'I'll go.'

'A very intelligent choice,' Conor agreed. 'I'm proud of you.' Declan sloped off to bed.

'At last an evening to ourselves,' Anna sighed.

'Sorry, darling, I forgot to tell you that I have to go out to dinner tonight,' Conor said. 'The ambassador wants to go through the programme for the Taoiseach's visit. I only have time to shave and change. Where is Mícheal? He should be there too.'

'Probably on a pub crawl with his grotty friends,' Anna muttered.

'I know he is a bit hard to take. Try to put up with him for a few days longer. He will soon be gone.'

'The sooner the better.'

When Conor had left and the children were in bed, Anna went out to the kitchen to get something to eat. Assumpta had gone up to her small bedsit on the top floor of the building and Mícheal was still out. Anna had decided to go on a diet to lose weight for the cruise, but she would have a last pig-out. It would be her farewell-to-food night.

There was a lot of food in the fridge. Anna took out paté, smoked salmon, salami, Camembert and some crab salad with mayonnaise. She found a stick of French bread in the bread basket, also half a bottle of her favourite wine. She put all the food on one big plate and placed it, the bread and a glass of wine, on a tray. There was a good film on television, so she would have her improvised feast in the living room.

An hour later, she was watching the film, eating chocolate ice cream straight out of the carton, and sobbing quietly. The heroine had just said goodbye to her lover who was leaving to go to the front during World War One. The fact that she also had a husband and three small children was beside the point. She was nobly going back to them and would never see her handsome lover again. It was a very French film.

Anna heard the front door open. She wiped her tears away. Maybe Conor was back? She looked up to see Mícheal standing unsteadily in the doorway of the living room. He was wearing a grubby beige rain-coat over the dirty Aran pullover and baggy pants he had arrived in. His only concession to the warm weather had been to take off his socks and wear his sandals on bare feet that didn't look too clean.

'Had a little feast I see. I like a woman who can eat.

You have a bit of flesh on your bones. I find that very sexy.' He came closer and squinted at the television screen. 'What's that shite you are watching? Romance? A load of crap, if you ask me.'

'I wasn't going to.'

'Where's your husband? He shouldn't leave a beauty like you alone.'

'My husband is at a working dinner at the embassy,' Anna said, getting up from the sofa. 'They are discussing the Taoiseach's visit. Shouldn't you be there too? Aren't you supposed to be a journalist?'

Mícheal didn't seem to have heard. He tried to put his arm around her. 'How about a little cuddle?'

'Don't be ridiculous!' She quickly moved away.

'Oh come on, me darlin', just one little kiss.' Mícheal was lurching towards her, his lips pursed. 'I'm feeling affectionate. And I can tell you're getting fond of me.'

'Leave me alone.'

'Don't fight it. I know you have feelings for me.' He put out his arms as he moved closer. 'Come here, sweetheart.'

Anna put out her foot, and he crashed to the floor. There was a deathly silence. She looked down at him, suddenly frightened that she might have killed him.

Mícheal was lying in a heap on the floor. He stirred and grunted something.

'What was that?' she asked.

'Is that yes or no?'

CHAPTER 3

Anna's heart was pounding. Her face was burning and she was soaked with sweat. She could hardly breathe, the blood was thumping in her ears, her muscles ached, and she could scarcely see for the sweat stinging her eyes. And this was only the warm-up.

'And one and two, lift your legs higher, pull in your stomach...' Susanna's voice boomed above the ear-splitting music. Anna was trying to keep up with the rest of the keep-fit class in the American club, where Susanna pushed the ladies of the diplomatic corps to the limit of their endurance three times a week.

Anna knew that she would be in agony the next day. She could see her thighs and stomach wobble up and down in the full-length mirrors that lined the room. I shouldn't have worn a leotard, she thought. She had finished the bottle of wine to calm her down after the scene with Mícheal and as a result she felt unwell.

'How long is this class?' panted Teresa beside Anna.

'She's the teacher from hell,' she continued. 'No mercy, no consideration . . .'

'. . . and no hips,' Anna gasped.

Susanna's perfect body was moving effortlessly in time with the music. She was not even sweating. Anna felt a flash of hatred. Maybe she could sneak out while they were lying down doing the leg-lifts. If she crawled out on all fours, Susanna might not notice. Anna hated those leg-lifts. They made her feel as if her legs weighed two hundred pounds.

Good, they were going to lie on the floor.

'Time for some stomach crunches.' Susanna's voice was irritatingly cheery. The crunches were as painful as they sounded. Anna felt a burning sensation in muscles she didn't know she had.

'Fifty-four, fifty-five, and lift higher! Anna, don't slacken off.' Anna had only been able to do three crunches and lay panting on her mat, hoping Susanna wouldn't see her. But Susanna didn't miss a thing. There would be no chance to sneak off. Maybe she should have tried yoga instead? But then the weight would not come off so quickly. Anna had hardly eaten anything for breakfast, which made her feel even less energetic.

Oooh, the leg-lifts. Her leg would fall off. Anna mentally cursed Jane Fonda and all the aerobic instructors in the world. She wished she had never seen a leotard. Women were not supposed to work their muscles like this. Her body was not that bad, was it? She caught sight of herself in one of the mirrors. Yes, it was. There were rolls of fat around her waist, her stomach bulged and her thighs were lumpy. She was a mess.

The music had slowed. They were doing the stretching. The class was finally over. Anna's breathing slowly returned to normal. She felt like a piece of limp spaghetti. The mirror showed her red face, her hair plastered to her head and the leotard soaked with sweat. She staggered out behind Teresa to the bar. Monique was already there having a glass of orange juice.

'Two glasses of water,' Teresa said to the barman.

'And call an ambulance,' Anna added. She dried her face with the towel she had draped around her neck.

'You wouldn't feel so bad if you exercised regularly.' Susanna was standing further down the bar. Her hair was neat and there was only one small drop of sweat on her smooth forehead, which she dabbed away with a towel that matched the colour scheme of her leotard. There was not an ounce of fat on her lean body. 'How nice to see that you have taken my advice,' she said. 'A body like yours needs a lot of hard work.'

'I just want to get fit,' Anna replied. 'I don't care how I look.'

'That's obvious,' Susanna replied. 'And you don't seem to care how you behave either. Especially with men who are not your husband. Your little tête-à-tête was very public. I would be a bit more discreet if I were you.' Susanna swished out of the bar.

Monique looked at Anna's face which was now redder than during the aerobics class. 'What was that all about?' she asked.

'I had coffee with Juan on the Champs-Elysées

yesterday morning. We just happened to bump into each other. She must have seen us.'

'You have to be careful with Susanna. She can be really vicious,' Monique remarked. 'You had better not let her find out about your little fling with Juan.'

'But I am not having a fling with Juan or anyone else,' Anna snapped.

'What is the big deal?' Teresa asked. 'If Juan was flirting with *me*, I would be more than pleased. It would be a relief from the boring life I have at the moment. I am so programmed to looking after small children I have to stop myself cutting up the meat for the person sitting beside me at a dinner party. I would love an evening with a gorgeous man like that.'

'Wouldn't we all.' Monique sighed. 'I could do with some cheering up.'

'What's the matter?' Teresa asked.

'They are moving to Australia,' Anna replied.

'Oh no,' Teresa exclaimed. 'That's terrible.'

Monique agreed. 'The worst thing is that Jean-Pierre is delighted. He can't wait to go.'

'I don't believe you,' Teresa said.

'It's the only place on earth where men are still allowed to be men and women shut up, he said. Last night he kept calling me Sheila and slapping my bottom. He said he was practising.'

'He'll love Australia,' Anna laughed.

'That's what I'm worried about,' Monique said. 'He'll be hell to live with when we're there.'

'I'd better go and have a shower and change,' Anna said as she gathered up her things. 'I've got to do some shopping on the way home. Our house guest eats like a horse.'

'Oh, yes,' Monique said. 'The attractive journalist. What's he like?'

'Incredible,' Anna replied.

Anna decided to do her grocery shopping on her way home from the Métro station. This meant going into at least four different shops. In France, the supermarket was where you stocked up on staple goods like bottled water, milk and yoghurt; the rest of the shopping was done in 'real' shops. Fruit and vegetables, bread, cheese, and meat were all bought in different shops. And you had to be nice to the shopkeepers, or they would not give you the best. The customers examined everything as if they were carrying out a scientific experiment. Anna had been amazed at first at the squeezing, prodding and sniffing that went on before French housewives were satisfied that they were buying good-quality food fit to be eaten that very day. But she had soon acquired the habit of touching and feeling everything, which had earned her great respect from the shopkeepers. Food was almost as important as making love to the French.

Anna loved food shopping in Paris. The smell of the food made her ravenous, and the handling of it had a sensuous quality. It was certainly an improvement on a weekly dash through an Irish or Swedish supermarket, where you would end up always with the same tasteless fruit and veg, boring bread and mousetrap cheese wrapped in plastic. Shopping in Paris was sexy. In Ireland or Sweden it was just shopping.

She walked home with her many little parcels. There was a dinner at the Danish embassy that evening, which she was looking forward to, but it meant that there would be little chance of a chat with Conor. She would be glad when the Taoiseach's visit was over. Everybody at the embassy was very tense about it. Even Sarah Maloney, the First Secretary in charge of European affairs. She was normally cool-headed and unflappable. But she had taken to phoning Conor about every little problem that arose in connection with the visit.

Sarah was an ambitious career woman, organised and efficient. Anna hated her. But she often felt that Sarah would make a much better wife to Conor than she herself did. Sarah would never put the wrong date on invitation cards and have fourteen people arrive a week early for dinner only to find Conor out and Anna, dressed in an old tracksuit, eating a large pizza in front of the television. Sarah would not forget people's names, mislay official documents, or spill sauce on her best dress. Sarah would be the *perfect* wife.

Conor was writing the Taoiseach's speech for the lunch with the French president, and Sarah was helping with the research. They spent a lot of time together and Anna was beginning to wonder if Sarah did not have a crush on Conor. Was it really necessary to phone Conor every evening, to call to their apartment at the weekend for 'forgotten' pieces of paper, and to discuss work over long lunches? Once, at a cocktail party, Anna had even found Sarah talking earnestly to Conor, hanging on to his tie. Sarah had lately taken to walking her cat past their building in the evenings (whoever heard of exercising a cat?), probably hoping to bump into Conor. When the visit was over, Anna would make sure that there were no more 'consultations'.

When Anna stepped out of the lift with her shopping, Esmeralda, their Brazilian cleaning lady, was just leaving the apartment. There was an angry look on her normally cheerful face.

'*Madame*, I could not do it,' she said. 'I have never seen anything so horrible in all my life.'

'What on earth are you talking about? Is it Declan's room? I told him to clean out the budgie's cage. Wait till I catch him!'

'It is not the birdie. It is the room of the man with hair on the face. I cannot clean it. It is clothes everywhere. I do not know where I start.'

'It's all right, Esmeralda. I will have a look. You don't have to do anything. Just go on home.'

'*Merci, madame*.' Esmeralda left, looking relieved.

Anna went into the apartment, put the groceries in the kitchen and marched down the corridor to the guest room. She flung open the door, not caring if Mícheal was there or not.

She could not believe her eyes. This could not be the room of an adult. Declan sometimes got his room in an awful state, but this was worse. The bed looked as if it had not been made for weeks, the floor was strewn with clothes, there were books, magazines and newspapers everywhere, remains of a meal could be seen on a sticky plate on the desk, along with dirty socks, half-finished glasses of Guinness and empty coffee cups with cigarette butts inside. The room reeked of stale cigarette smoke and sweat. The man had only been with them a week. How was this possible?

'Has there been an accident?' Assumpta was standing behind Anna staring into the room.

'No, but there will be one if this place isn't cleaned up at once. Where is that pseudo-intellectual? I'll give him hospitality.' Anna was so angry she could hardly speak.

'I think he is at a briefing for the visit. He said something about it this morning,' Assumpta answered.

'He should clean up his own briefs before he worries about any other ones,' Anna said, looking at a pair of large underpants hanging from the doorknob of the wardrobe. She started to laugh. It really was too ridiculous. 'I think I will call this room *Nightmare on Elm Street*. Remember that movie?'

'Or how about *Tornado*.' Assumpta giggled.

'I will have to clean up this mess. If I complain to Conor, he'll only be annoyed.' Anna remembered that she needed Conor to be in a good mood so he would agree to go on the cruise.

'I'll help you,' Assumpta offered. 'I don't have to be at my class until two o'clock today.' Assumpta studied French at a special course for foreign students at the Sorbonne.

'OK. We will need the hoover, some rags, plenty of disinfectant and room freshener.'

'Don't forget rubber gloves,' Assumpta added. 'I'm not touching any of his stuff without them.'

'We haven't seen the bathroom yet, it might be even worse,' Anna groaned. But the bathroom was surprisingly neat.

'That's because he doesn't use it,' Assumpta suggested.

Two hours' hard work later, the room was clean and tidy. They had stacked the newspapers and magazines on the small table by the window, removed plates, cups and glasses and put them in the kitchen sink to soak, and thrown away any food that was still stuck to some of the plates. There had even been a half-eaten pizza under the bed. The dirty clothes and sheets were put in the washing machine to wash on the hottest cycle. Finally, Anna had thoroughly hoovered and dusted the room, changed the sheets and opened the window to the warm spring air.

Anna and Assumpta were having coffee at the kitchen table, exhausted but satisfied with their work, when the front door slammed. Mícheal was back.

'I'll be off to my class now,' Assumpta announced nervously. She got up from the table and went out through the door that led to the back staircase. This way she did not have to confront Mícheal.

'Coward,' Anna said to her departing back. She was not sure how she was going to handle the situation. She wanted to give Mícheal a piece of her mind, but she knew that would make Conor angry. He had to take care of journalists when they were in town, taking them to lunch and organising meetings. Conor had told her to make Mícheal feel welcome, and she knew he was worried about any criticism of the embassy that could appear in the press. It would damage the name of the department and, heaven forbid, his career. 'Keep the press sweet' was his motto.

Mícheal's loud, angry voice interrupted her thoughts. 'Who the hell has been in my room!' she heard him shout. 'I can't find anything. And what's that smell?'

Anna found him standing in the middle of his room looking angrily at the neat piles of magazines and newspapers. His laptop computer was on the middle of the desk with the papers that had been found on the floor neatly stacked beside it.

'I just tidied up,' she said. 'The room was a disgusting mess. And the smell is furniture polish, clean sheets and fresh air.'

'I liked it the way it was. I knew exactly where to find everything. It will take all day to get it back to normal.'

Anna didn't know what to say. She decided that the best policy would be to humour him.

'I'm sorry if I upset your papers. But the room has to be cleaned and aired occasionally. I also took care of your laundry. It will be ready tomorrow.'

'Did you look at any of my work?'

'No, I just straightened up the pieces of paper and put them in a pile.'

'What about the desk? Did you snoop around in the drawers?'

'Of course not,' Anna protested.

'You didn't look at my passport, or read my letters?' Mícheal pushed his face forward and stared at her. He looked really worried now.

'Why would I?' Anna asked, mystified. 'Is there something wrong with your passport? Is it out of date?'

'Never mind,' he replied. 'I would be grateful if you left my room alone in future. I can't stand interfering women. You don't understand how important my work is. I'm not only writing a political report, I'm also writing a novel. It's based on my childhood in the west of Ireland.'

'That'll be a best-seller,' Anna remarked sarcastically. 'Look,' she continued, 'let's compromise. I will not go into your room if you promise to give me your dirty clothes, only eat and drink in the kitchen or dining room, and open the window from time to time. That will not be so hard, will it?' She tried not to show her impatience.

'If that's what it takes to have some privacy, OK. But I will keep the door locked in future. I don't want anybody to look at my work.'

'Don't worry, nobody will.' Who would want to? Anna thought.

'They better not. Leave me alone now, woman.' He grasped her roughly by the arm and pushed her out, closing the door with a bang. She could hear him mutter to himself. She shook her head in bewilderment and prepared to leave the apartment to pick up the children from school. If that is being an intellectual, I prefer to be ignorant, she thought, as the lift brought her downstairs.

That evening Anna spent some time staring into her wardrobe, trying to find something to wear for the dinner at the Danish embassy. The children were in bed and she was trying to get ready in time. Why did dressing to go out always take so long? It normally involved standing there for half an hour looking at her clothes as if she had never seen them before. Why did the tops not match any of the skirts? She usually changed outfits at least ten times before she found something halfway wearable. It's time I smartened up in the clothes department, she thought, promising herself that she would sort out her wardrobe the very next day.

After a lot of rummaging around, Anna found a black straight skirt and a pale pink silk embroidered jacket that she had bought in last year's sale and forgotten she had. It was black tie tonight, and this outfit was perfectly dressy for the occasion. She picked out a pair of diamond and pearl earrings and a pendant with one large single pearl. Her hair was held up with a pair of tortoiseshell combs and twisted into a french knot at the nape of her neck. She was pleased with her outfit even if the skirt was a little tight around the waist. It will remind me not to eat, she thought.

Where was Conor? If he didn't come home soon, they would be late. The phone rang as she was fastening her earrings.

'I'm running a bit late here,' Conor said. 'You will have to go on to the Danes on your own. I'll meet you there. I have asked someone to give you a lift.'

That's typical, Anna thought, work comes first. She hated arriving at a party on her own.

'But don't you have to change into your dinner jacket?'

'I brought it with me to the office just in case. And I can shave here.'

'ok,' Anna replied, annoyed, 'but who's bringing me?'

'It's Juan Valverde. I asked him because I knew he had been invited. You don't mind? I thought you liked him.'

Liked him? Anna thought, that's the understatement of the year.

'I had lunch with him today,' Conor continued. 'He's very interested in Irish politics. He wanted to know all about the various politicians. When I told him that I was from County Cork and my father is on the county council, he was fascinated.'

'He was?' Anna asked, mystified. Juan had not expressed any particular interest in her husband's country when they had met, and he had even confessed complete ignorance of the Irish when they had been speaking on the telephone.

'Yes, yes, he loves that part of Ireland. His family has connections with Ireland and his grandmother had Irish blood. I think he said that she had an ancestor from Kinsale. Of course, Cork is also the Taoiseach's constituency. Juan said he would love to meet the Taoiseach when he comes, but that will be a little difficult to organise.'

'Juan wants to meet the Taoiseach?' Anna asked, bewildered.

'He says he's a great fan of Seamus Nolan. But I haven't time to discuss this now. Just tell me it's all right for you to go to the party with Juan.'

'Yes, yes, that'll be fine,' Anna replied. 'See you at the party.' She hung up with a startled look on her face. Bloody hell. She went into the living room and poured herself a drink from the bottle on the side-board. The whiskey hit her empty stomach and made her feel immediately calmer but at the same time somewhat elated.

'Tanking up before the party? Don't you get enough drink at the embassies these days?' Mícheal was lounging on the sofa with a glass of Guinness.

The doorbell rang.

'Mind your own business,' Anna said as she took her small evening bag and went to open the door.

'That's a nice way to greet a visitor.' Juan was lean-ing against the doorpost looking more over-the-top than ever. His dinner jacket fitted him to perfection, emphasising his athletic frame. The pristine white shirt made his light tan look darker. He was the only man Anna knew who in black tie didn't look like a head waiter. His dark eyes sparkled as he looked at her.

'Jesus, Mary and Joseph,' Assumpta whispered to herself from the kitchen door. She was staring at Juan with wide eyes.

'What a pleasure to meet such a beautiful young lady,' said Juan and went over to kiss Assumpta's rather grubby hand. She looked as if she was going to faint.

'Eeeh ... eeer' was all she managed to stammer before Juan swept Anna out of the apartment and into the lift.

'It's very naughty of you to tease a young girl like that.' Anna laughed as the ancient lift brought them slowly down. In her high heels, she was nearly as tall as he and could look him straight in the eyes. They were standing very close together in the confined space. He looked back at her with a smile.

'I was just having a little fun. How lovely to see you. You look . . .' Before he could continue, the lift reached the next floor and came to a halt. An old lady opened the iron grille doors and stepped inside. Anna and Juan were now squeezed even closer together. The lift creaked lower and lower. The old lady sniffed and cleared her throat. Juan was looking at Anna with amused eyes. Being so close to him made her feel dizzy. She could smell his aftershave and feel the warmth of his body. She was nearly sorry when the lift finally stopped at the ground floor. She could have stayed in the lift with Juan all night.

He was driving his white Mercedes sports car – what else? – the most beautiful car in the world. The roof was down and Anna could feel the warm wind in her hair as they drove through the city. The car radio was playing a romantic French song. Juan had to concentrate on the very heavy traffic and could not talk much, but when they stopped at a traffic light, he put his hand on her thigh.

'I wish I wasn't taking you to a boring embassy dinner,' he said. 'I would rather take you dancing.' She took his hand and put it back on the steering wheel.

'Please keep your hands to yourself,' she murmured. Juan just shook his head and grinned. A car horn hooted, followed by loud swearing.

'*Merde!*' Juan swore back, and put his foot down hard on the accelerator. The car took off so fast that Anna was thrown back roughly against the seat.

'Sorry, my darling, the traffic is impossible at this time of the evening.' Juan turned to her with an apologetic smile. 'Has your husband decided to bring you on the cruise yet?' he asked when the traffic had calmed a little. 'I will be very disappointed if you don't come.'

'Oh, you will soon find someone else to flirt with.'

'But do you want me to?'

'I really don't care if you do,' she replied. Juan glanced at her without answering, lifting one eyebrow.

'So, I hear that you're a great admirer of Seamus Nolan,' Anna continued, to change the subject.

'Who?'

'Seamus Nolan, the Irish prime minister. You're supposed to be one of his fans.' Probably the only one, she thought to herself.

'Oh. Yes, that's right, I have a great respect for him. He is an interesting man with great charisma.'

'Hmm.'

'You don't seem to like him. I thought women loved him. He has had several wives.'

'Most of them other people's.'

'Really? He is a womaniser?'

'That's right. He screws around.'

'That's not very romantic,' Juan remarked with a little laugh.

'With him, it wouldn't be. Is that why you admire him?'

'No, no. He's a very shrewd politician and a great statesman. I would love to meet him. There is something I want to discuss with him. Maybe you could help, Anna?'

'How could I help? I'm only the wife of the counsellor. I will probably only get to shake hands with him. That's all. I don't get to discuss matters of state, or anything else with politicians.'

'But you might be able to get me an invitation to the party at the embassy. Could you talk to Conor about it? It would mean a lot to me,' Juan pleaded with a soft little smile.

'I'll mention it to him. But that's all I can do.'

'Thank you, darling.'

Anna secretly thought the whole thing was decidedly fishy, but she loved it when Juan called her darling.

They had arrived at their destination. Juan opened the door of the car and helped Anna out with a hand under her elbow. Susanna and her husband were arriving at the same time. Susanna looked at Juan and Anna with a knowing smile.

'When the cat is away . . .' Susanna muttered.

'The cat is on his way,' Juan purred, 'and I am escorting this lovely kitten to meet him.' His voice was teasing, but his eyes were hard as he looked at Susanna, who tossed her head and entered the building ahead of them.

The Danish embassy was situated in an old private mansion which had once belonged to one of Napoleon's ministers. The interior had been carefully restored to its former magnificence. The Danes had furnished the building with exquisite period pieces. The carpet and curtains were of the best Danish design, and soft lamplight gave a cosy and inviting feel to the rooms.

'Anna, welcome,' said their hostess. 'You look wonderful. Have you been on holiday?'

No, just a thirty-minute drive with the sexiest man in Europe, she thought to herself. 'It must be the lovely spring weather,' she said aloud. As she glanced out into the hall, she could see Conor signing the guest book. The pen fell on the floor, and he bent to pick it up. Anna went to greet Monique and Jean-Pierre, who were already holding glasses of champagne.

'Anna, you are sitting beside me,' a voice said. She turned around to discover Olaf Trondheim, the Norwegian ambassador, a tall thin man with thinning grey hair and glasses, grinning at her. He had obviously already had several glasses of champagne. His left arm was in a sling.

'What happened to your arm?'

'I slipped and fell out of a window of the embassy when I was taking in the flag after our national day.'

'What bad luck.' Anna knew that at dinners he had the habit of groping ladies under the table. This injury would curtail his little games.

'Where are we sitting?' Together they consulted the seating plan. Anna's name was on the left of Olaf's. She would be sitting on the same side as his broken arm. What a relief. On her other side, she could see the name of the newly arrived Canadian ambassador, Patrick Daly. Diplomats were seated according to how long they had been in a post, the longest-serving being the most senior.

'Anna,' a voice exclaimed in Swedish. 'How marvellous to see you. What are you doing in Paris?'

Anna looked up from the seating plan and found herself facing a tall, blonde woman.

'I'm sorry? Have we met before?' she stammered.

'We certainly have' came the reply. 'Don't you recognise me, Anna?'

Anna stared at the pretty face with the big, green eyes, the small upturned nose and the wide, full mouth. She was so familiar, but . . .

'Or should I call you Anna-Karin?'

It startled Anna to hear her full name, a name she hadn't used since she left school. She looked again at the stranger. Of course! How stupid of her. It was Betsy Lindström, her childhood friend. But Betsy looked so different from the girl who had sat beside Anna in fourth grade. In those days, Betsy had been fat and her hair had been a mousy light brown. She had worn glasses. Big fat Betsy, who had always covered for Anna when she was in trouble. They had lost touch when they left school.

The woman before Anna did not look at all like the fattest girl in the class. She was as tall and slim as a supermodel and dressed in the latest avant-garde chic; an ankle-length light blue silk sarong skirt tied up with a bit of string at the waist and a baggy lilac angora pullover that looked as if it had accidentally been washed on the wrong cycle in the washing machine. She wore black sandals with thick soles, and her shaggy light blonde hair looked as if someone had attacked it in the dark with blunt scissors. Anna knew that this look was both expensive and hard to pull off, making most women look like a bag of spuds. Betsy looked stunning. Now Anna was the one who was embarrassed about her weight.

'Talk about a transformation!'

'You have changed too,' Betsy said as she looked at Anna.

'Yes, but not for the better. But that is what having babies does to your body.'

'You've had a baby?' Betsy asked, looking delighted. 'Congratulations! How old is he?'

'Nine,' Anna replied, turning red.

'Nine weeks?'

'No, years. He was a big baby. I just couldn't get my figure back. Not that I have been trying very hard,' she had to admit. 'But what are you doing in Paris?' Anna was babbling. She wanted to ask Betsy a thousand questions. She saw Conor beckoning her on the other side of the large drawing room. He was looking worried. Anna knew she should join him to find out what the problem was, but she wanted to talk to Betsy.

'I'm here because of a job I'm doing. I'm an interior designer,' Betsy replied.

'What?' Anna stammered, remembering that Betsy had had very strange taste. 'Design?'

'That's right. And what about you?' Betsy asked. 'Did you manage to join a ballet company?'

'No,' Anna replied, realising that she couldn't possibly look less like a dancer if she tried. 'I got married twelve years ago. My husband is a diplomat. We have been here only five months.'

'You gave up your career for a man? He must be something special.' Betsy looked astonished at this revelation.

'You're not married?' Anna enquired. What career? she asked herself.

'You bet I'm not. I'm no man's slave. But let's get together soon. Maybe we could meet for lunch and catch up. Give me a call tomorrow, and we'll organise it.' She gave Anna a card with a number on it and looked up.

'Who's that man with the red face?' she asked. 'He looks as if he desperately wants to talk to you.' Conor was approaching, walking stiffly across the carpet.

'Hello, darling,' Anna said, 'glad you could make it in time.' She turned to introduce Betsy, but she was gone.

'I have a bit of a problem,' Conor muttered. 'I don't know what to do.'

CHAPTER 4

Anna could not imagine what sort of problem Conor could be having. He looked as if he was in pain. Had he been mugged on the way from the embassy? She could see no sign of injury. Was he feeling unwell? Apart from looking worried, he seemed in perfect health. He gripped her arm hard and brought her over to a corner of the room where they would not be overheard.

'I have a huge tear in the seat of my trousers,' he hissed in her ear. 'What am I going to do?'

'What?' Anna could not take it all in at once. 'Are you sure? How did it happen?'

'Of course I'm bloody sure. I could feel it go when I bent over to sign the guest book.' His face was pale. 'I could say I am feeling ill, and go home, but I have to speak to Juan.'

'Why? What about? Can't it wait?'

'Stop asking so many bloody questions! Try to help,' Conor hissed back.

'I don't see how I can help. In any case, the tear isn't noticeable. The jacket covers your bum completely,'

Anna reassured him, after a quick glance. 'Who are you sitting beside?' Anna thought that if Conor had a nice neighbour at the table, he would calm down.

'Susanna bloody Fuchs, that's who. And fecking Penelope ffrench on the other side.' Conor looked like a prisoner who was about to be toasted slowly over a very hot fire.

'Oh shit.' Anna started to giggle. Susanna Fuchs was bad enough, but Penelope ffrench! Conor is in no state to cope with her tonight, Anna thought, but he deserves it.

'Why the bloody hell did you not buy a new dinner suit when I told you?' she muttered. 'You knew the trousers of this one were getting worn.' This was typical of Conor. He had been so proud that he still fitted (only just) into the dinner jacket and trousers of his student years. He was attached to some of his clothes, and refused to replace them until they fell apart. Well, this might teach him a lesson.

'Trust you to start giving out now. Try to think of a solution instead of bitching.' Conor now looked angry instead of worried. Anna knew that everything would somehow turn out to be her fault as usual.

'You'll just have to manage,' she whispered, trying not to laugh. 'Try to keep the jacket from riding up. You'll soon be sitting down.'

Conor sighed. 'It's just like you to find it funny. Can't you take anything seriously? This is a real crisis. It's all I need, on top of everything else.'

'Everything else?'

'Mmm, yes. The Taoiseach called me in the office. That's why I was late.'

'Seamus Nolan called you and not the ambassador?'

'That's right. He wanted to add something to the programme. Something private. I don't know what to do about it.'

'Private? You mean like sightseeing?'

'Yeah, we could call it that,' Conor smirked. 'He wants to see the sights. I don't really know how to organise it, so I thought I could ask Juan to help.'

'That's a great idea. Juan knows all about Paris,' Anna replied. 'I'm sure he would be delighted to take Seamus Nolan on a little outing after the official part of the programme is over.' And that way Juan will meet Nolan, just as he wants, she thought, pleased with herself.

'Come on now, you two lovebirds. We are going in to dinner.' The Danish ambassador came between them and took them both by the arm, propelling them forward into the dining room.

'Just don't make any sudden moves,' Anna had time to whisper to Conor as he walked stiffly to his seat and sat down, forgetting to pull out the chair for Susanna first. She looked at him disapprovingly.

'The Irish are socially terribly gauche,' she announced loudly to nobody in particular. The Canadian ambassador, who was passing on the way to his seat, looked at her, surprised.

By this time Anna was beginning to find the situation terribly funny. A big smile spread across her face.

'It is lovely to see you so happy.' Olaf looked at her fondly as he pulled out her chair. Anna looked around the lovely room.

The big table in the dining room was covered with

a cloth of fine damask linen with the Danish royal crest woven into the fabric. The china was the famous Flora Danica service, delicately painted flowers on a white background with gold-leaf edging on each plate. It seemed nearly sacrilege to put food on such beautiful china. Pink and white roses mixed with blue freesias decorated the centre of the table. The room was lit exclusively by candles set in vast silver candelabras, which gave it a romantic and old-fashioned feel.

'The Danes are very sophisticated people,' said Patrick Daly while Anna helped herself to the first course, delicately cooked sole in a white wine sauce, from a big silver platter.

'Are they?' She didn't want to give too much praise to another Scandinavian country. She was very proud to be Swedish. In any case, there was a rough side to the Danes too, just look at the size of their sausages, not to mention the fat ladies who smoked cigars. Swedish sausages were much daintier, and no Swedish woman would be caught smoking cigars, or a pipe for that matter.

Anna looked around the table to see if she could spot Monique. The size of the portions to which she felt she could help herself would depend on whether or not Monique could see what she had on her plate. Monique was sitting at the top of the table, beside the host. Good, that would keep her too busy to worry about Anna's calorie intake.

Anna looked casually across the table. Directly opposite sat Juan, with Betsy at his side. They were talking animatedly. Oh, no, Anna thought, Betsy will

tell him all the embarrassing details about my childhood. There were a few things that Anna would not
want anybody to know. But the table was so wide
that it was impossible to hear their conversation.

Anna turned to her neighbour. Patrick Daly was a
tall man in his late forties with greying thick dark hair
and brown eyes. He was attractive but there was an
arrogant look in his eyes. He had ignored Anna, and
was talking across the table to a French EU official
about the economic situation in Germany. Now he
turned briefly to Anna. 'Sorry, we're talking shop. I
know it's not something a woman would understand,
but I couldn't pass up a chance to get some information.'

'Of course,' Anna muttered, 'it's too much for us
brain-dead. Just ignore the women.'

'I didn't quite catch that,' Patrick Daly said. But the
Frenchman across the table had heard, and gave Anna
a little smirk. Then he resumed his exchange with
Daly.

Anna soon lost the thread of their conversation. She
was trying to suppress a yawn, and turned to her other
neighbour, but he was occupied with trying to chat
up a lady from South America on his other side. Anna
sighed and studied her nails. Maybe she should have
put on some nail polish? She looked down the table
to check on Conor. He was listening to something
Susanna was saying with a wooden expression on his
face. Anna knew he was both suffering from boredom
and worrying about his exposed posterior.

'I hear that the Irish prime minister is coming to
Paris soon,' Patrick suddenly remarked, and Anna

was jerked out of her apathy. 'Is his party conservative or more left-wing? Maybe you can tell me about the different political parties in Ireland.'

Anna looked down at her plate. The room felt suddenly hot. This plate knows more about Irish politics than I do, she thought. The crumbs on the tablecloth looked enormous, and she saw every detail of the pattern on the silver cutlery with terrible clarity. What was she going to say? She looked at Olaf for help, but he was still talking to the vivacious South American woman. Across the table, Juan was busy admiring Betsy's cleavage.

Oh, if she had only read the *Irish Times* more carefully, instead of using it to line the budgie's cage. If she had only listened to Conor when he tried to explain the intricacies of Irish politics. All she knew about the Taoiseach, Seamus Nolan, was that he was a womaniser and a ruthless politician. She knew that many people were terrified of him. But she had no idea of his actual politics. She knew he was with a minority party, but why, in that case, had he been made Taoiseach? Well, she had to bluff her way out of this. Daly probably knew even less about Irish politics than she did. He wouldn't know if she was telling the truth or talking rubbish.

Anna lifted her exquisite crystal glass of white wine and took a desperate swig. 'Well,' she said, 'it's like this.' She cleared her throat and launched in. 'You see,' she started, as if she was telling a story to a small child, 'the main parties are Fianna Fáil and Fine Gael. There is no great difference between them, except that Fianna Fáil attract mostly businessmen and Fine Gael have mostly lawyers and farmers among their supporters.'

'Who is in power at the moment?' Daly asked.

'Fianna Fáil.'

'If Fianna Fáil are in power, how come your prime minister is the head of the Liberal Socialists?' Patrick asked.

'Eh, well,' Anna stammered, 'there's a coalition. The Liberal Socialists are a minority party. Fianna Fáil made him Taoiseach so they could keep an eye on what he was up to.'

'Oh?' was all Patrick Daly managed to say before Anna was off again.

'In any case,' she continued, feeling more confident, 'it's easy to recognise a Fianna Fáil politician. They wear pin-stripe suits and loud ties. The members of Fine Gael have a more homespun, nerdy look. Sandals and knitted ties.'

'And what about *their* policies?'

'Well, they ...' Anna stammered, trying desperately to remember anything at all about Fine Gael. 'They oppose everything Fianna Fáil stands for.'

'Everything?' Daly asked. He was beginning to look amused.

'Absolutely everything,' Anna exclaimed. 'If Fianna Fáil propose something, Fine Gael are against it. That's their main political ideal.' She drained her glass. This was more fun than she had thought. And she was really good at it.

'Well,' Daly drawled, 'this is very interesting. How about the other parties? Labour, and – what is the other one called?'

'The PDs.'

'And that stands for . . .?'

'The Progressive Democrats!' Anna exclaimed triumphantly. She felt as if she had just passed a test at school. 'They are right in the middle,' she babbled, 'just so they can fill the gap in case one of the main parties need someone to enter into a coalition with and they don't want to ask Labour. They only have a few seats, which are mainly occupied by women.' She stopped for breath.

'And how do you recognise them? How do they dress?'

'They don't,' Anna replied, 'I mean, they aren't interested in clothes. They prefer to iron out their policies.'

'Really?' Patrick Daly said and suddenly had a fit of coughing into his napkin. 'That leaves the Labour Party,' he continued when he had recovered his breath. 'Tell me about them.'

'OK. Well, Labour,' she started. 'This may surprise you . . .'

'Go on,' Daly said. 'I'm ready.' His voice was shaking a little. Was he not well? Anna wondered.

'Yes. The Labour politicians are the most right-wing of them all.'

'They are?' Patrick Daly exclaimed. 'Why?'

'They dress beautifully, have lots of money and are very well-educated. The best-dressed man in the Irish Parliament is the leader of the Labour Party.'

'What do the workers think of that?' Daly asked.

'They love it,' Anna replied. 'It cheers them up.'

'I see.'

'So that's it,' she declared, before Daly could ask her anything else about the Labour Party. 'That's the political scene in Ireland. I hope my explanation will be of some use to you. I mean,' she suggested helpfully, 'maybe you could write a report about it?'

But Patrick Daly was coughing into his napkin again. 'I could write a book about what you just told me,' he remarked, when he finally drew breath.

Anna smiled, feeling proud of herself. There isn't that much to political analysis, she thought. Thank God he hadn't asked her about the situation in Northern Ireland. Then she would have had to pretend to faint. That was one subject about which she wouldn't dare pretend knowing anything at all.

They had finished the main course of roast duck with sautéd potatoes and Madeira sauce. Anna had been so engrossed in the conversation that she had forgotten to eat. The waiter removed her nearly untouched plate. The dessert, nougat ice cream on a strawberry *coulis*, was being served. The Danish ambassador rose. He was introducing the first speaker. Why was ice cream always served at dinners with long speeches? It was guaranteed to turn into mush before you were allowed to eat it.

During the many speeches, Anna tried not to fall asleep. She looked longingly at her plate of ice cream which was slowly becoming sauce. Around the table, most of the guests were looking increasingly bored: the third speaker was droning on about Denmark's relations with the rest of the world. On the other side, Juan's eyes were closing, and Betsy looked as if she had lost the will to live. Anna felt a terrible urge to stand up and scream.

Suddenly something touched her leg under the table. Had Olaf managed to feel her knee despite his handicap? No, he was holding hands with a clearly delighted Mrs South America. His other arm was safely in its sling on Anna's side. Juan was asleep and, in any case, too far away to reach. It had to be Patrick Daly. What a creep! She glanced sideways. He seemed to be listening to the speech and Anna could see only one of his hands. Well, the nerve of the man!

'Please!' she hissed in his direction. 'Stop.'

'What?' he hissed back. 'I . . .'

'Take your hand off my knee,' she whispered angrily.

'What the . . . I'm not.' He held up both his hands.

She felt something touch her again and a soft beating on her leg. She peeped under the table and looked straight into the smiling, panting face of a golden labrador. He was wagging his tail. He gave her face a lick. She pulled back with a little squeal. The speaker paused in surprise and, as Anna got up, she found the entire company turning to stare at her. Some of the guests looked as if they had just woken up from a coma.

'Sorry,' she stammered, 'the . . . eh . . . the dog . . .' The dog had obviously fallen in love with her, and continued to lick her hands and arms. He was wagging his tail furiously .

Their host rose from his seat and grabbed the dog

by his collar. 'He is very friendly,' he said proudly.

'Isn't he just,' Anna replied with a stiff smile. She was trying to regain her composure and brush the dog hairs off her skirt. The ambassador pulled the unwilling dog out of the door. The speaker made an attempt to catch the attention of the guests and continue his speech, but there was now a low murmur in the room. He sat down and glared at Anna. Patrick Daly was also looking at her, lifting one eyebrow.

'I'm so sorry,' she stammered. 'I thought . . .'

'Forget it,' he drawled and looked at Anna as if she was a worm he had just found in his salad. 'I'll certainly try to.' He rose from his chair and wandered out of the dining room.

'Coffee in the drawing room,' the wife of the ambassador chanted. Anna was relieved to file out of the room with the other guests.

'That was quite a performance, my dear,' Juan murmured behind her. He had adopted a serious expression, but his eyes were smiling. 'I didn't know you were such an animal lover.'

Anna didn't reply, but gave him an angry look.

'I must thank you for breaking up the dinner,' he continued. 'I was so bored I nearly fell off my chair.'

'If you took your job more seriously, you would be paying attention and take notes during important speeches,' she muttered.

'I do, darling. But the foreign affairs of Denmark are nothing to write home about.'

'You seemed to have enjoyed yourself with Betsy,' Anna remarked.

'We had fun. But she is not really my type. A bit of

a nut-cracker, if you must know.'

'You mean ball-breaker.'

'Do I? Sounds painful.'

'Let's introduce her to Patrick Daly,' Anna suggested.

'The Canadian ambassador? Why?'

'Never mind,' Anna mumbled and went in to the drawing room to find Conor. He was standing with his back pressed to the wall drinking brandy out of a big glass, with a morose expression on his face.

'Are you all right?'

'Only barely, ha, ha. The tear got bigger as I sat down. I was sitting by the open window and could feel a draught on my behind all through the dinner.

'How did you cope with the two ladies?'

'It was a nightmare. Susanna was trying to be seductive, touching my knee and leaning against me the whole time, while she gave me a lecture on healthy living. She said I should do at least fifty sit-ups a day to make my stomach muscles firm.'

'How does she know they aren't?'

'She put her hand on my stomach.' Conor shuddered. 'Penelope wasn't much better, All she could talk about was the rich and famous people she has met, and how she and Jasper have been invited to the château of a French count for the weekend.' He looked even more morose than before. 'I want to go home,' he pleaded, 'I can't stand much more of this. You'll have to walk behind me. My trousers must be in shreds by now.'

Conor looked so miserable that Anna felt really sorry for him. 'We'll go as soon as you have spoken to Juan,' she reassured him.

Conor sidled over to Juan, keeping his back to the wall. They were soon engrossed in conversation and Conor began to look more cheerful. Anna was hoping that Juan would be able to help Conor. It would mean a lot to Conor's career if the Taoiseach had a favourable impression of him. Conor would never try to suck up to a politician, but doing someone a favour was not the same thing, Anna thought.

Some of the guests had taken their leave and were drifting towards the front door. Conor had finished his conversation and he and Anna joined them in the hall after saying goodbye to their hosts. Juan blew Anna a kiss from the far corner of the drawing room, but she was too concerned about Conor and his predicament to notice.

Anna walked closely behind Conor through the hall and out of the front door, holding on to his waist. They did a kind of strange two-step down the steps in front of the embassy, waving farewell to their friends. Conor carefully eased himself into the driver's seat. He sighed with relief.

'Let's hope we aren't stopped by the police on the way home. I would probably be arrested for indecent exposure.' He smiled for the first time that evening.

When they finally arrived home, they found Mícheal still on the sofa with his feet on the coffee table. He was surrounded by empty beer cans and packets of crisps. There were potato crisp crumbs in his beard and on his pullover. Anna sighed. Conor went quickly into the bedroom to take off the torn trousers.

Mícheal looked up as he was disappearing through the door. 'I've heard of having your arse out of your trousers, but I didn't know diplomats suffered from it.'

'We have had a difficult evening,' Anna replied stiffly. 'Would you mind tidying up before you go to bed?'

'What a prissy family,' he grunted, as he heaved himself up in a shower of crisp crumbs. Anna closed the bedroom door with a bang.

Conor held the trousers up in front of his face, looking at her through the tear. 'Now do you see why I panicked?'

Anna looked at the trousers, the huge rip, and Conor's face, and started to laugh. Conor joined in, tossed his trousers on the floor and grabbed her by the waist. Together they collapsed on the bed, still laughing. Conor kissed her as he started to unbutton her jacket. They undressed each other, flinging clothes and underwear on the floor.

'You looked really cute tonight,' Conor said, undoing the clasp of Anna's bra.

'I thought you were too miserable to notice,' Anna muttered into his neck. 'What *are* you doing?'

'I thought we could try something new. I saw this in one of your women's magazines. If I put my leg like this, you can put your knee ...'

'That was yoga, you fool.' Anna giggled. 'I can't ... No ... It's not a rugby match. Please stop,' she panted. 'It's not possible. Conor please don't ...

Conor please . . . Conor . . . Oh. Yes. Oh God.'

'See?' Conor smiled. 'I knew you'd love it.'

Anna woke up with the sun on her face. Had she forgotten to close the shutters last night? Yes, of course. She remembered how the evening had ended, and smiled. They had not had that much fun for a long time. She turned to Conor's side of the bed, but it was empty. The clock on the bedside table said eight o'clock. Anna jumped out of bed. God, she was stiff! Aerobics and Conor's 'yoga' were too much for an unfit body to cope with.

When she limped into the kitchen, she found the children and Assumpta having breakfast.

'Daddy has already gone to the office,' Lena announced. 'Sarah rang *very* early to say that she needed Daddy to be there at once. She woke me up,' Lena complained with a long-suffering expression on her face.

'Did she?' Anna muttered between clenched teeth. The Taoiseach was arriving the next day. Anna wouldn't see much of Conor during the next few days.

'This arrived for you early this morning,' Assumpta said, waving a big bunch of flowers wrapped in cellophane.

'What? Oh, thanks.' Anna took the flowers. 'I didn't know that the florists delivered so early.'

'It was brought by a chauffeur. There is a card, but I don't recognise the handwriting.' Assumpta craned her neck, trying to read the card that Anna had just taken from the envelope.

'Never mind,' Anna muttered, and turned around so that Assumpta could not see the message.

Darling Anna, you looked lovely last night. I tried to find flowers that match your beautiful blue eyes. Thank you for finding a way for me to meet you-know-who! I would still love to come to the party as well. Do your best, please darling. Looking forward to the next time we meet, all my love, J.

Blushing, she quickly tore up the card. 'It's from a friend of Conor,' she explained as she took the wrapping off the exquisite bouquet of cornflowers and red roses.

'What pretty flowers, Mammy,' Lena exclaimed. 'How nice of Daddy's friend.'

'Yes,' Assumpta giggled. 'Conor will be so surprised.'

'Oh, shut up, Assumpta, and take the children to school.' Anna was sometimes irritated by Assumpta's nosiness.

Assumpta and the children had just left and Anna was putting the flowers in a vase, when the doorbell rang. It was the concierge, Madame Bernard, with the morning's mail.

'You have a postcard from your mother and two letters that look like invitations,' she said as she handed Anna the post.

Madame Bernard took her job very seriously. She thought that her main duty was to stop visitors from entering the building and, after that, to scrutinise everybody's mail: she unashamedly read postcards and unsealed letters. She took the fact that some of Anna's letters were in a language she could not understand as a personal insult. Anna would have preferred to collect the post from the box downstairs herself, but delivering it like this was a Parisian tradition that went back centuries.

Anna looked at Madame Bernard, taking in the bulging eyes, the bleached long hair worn in a girlish style held up with two bows at the temples, the frilly dress and the high-heeled slippers. She was at least sixty years old.

'Thank you, *madame*,' Anna said and started closing the door.

'That strange man, how long is he staying? I do not like him in my building. He is not normal, you know.' Madame Bernard's eyes bulged more than before. 'He throws papers in the entrance downstairs and he comes in *very* late. And he sings in the lift.'

'He will be leaving soon,' Anna replied. At least they agreed on something.

'Good.' Madame Bernard clattered into the lift.

The concierge had been right. Apart from the postcard, there were indeed two invitations. One was for the ball at the Opéra Garnier to celebrate the end of the *haute couture* season and the other one was for a weekend in the country at a château in Normandy. *The Comte and Comtesse de Bailleul would like the honour of the company of Mr and Mrs Conor O'Connor and their children for a weekend in the country,* the invitation said in French. It was for the weekend after next. How wonderful. And how strange.

The Comte and Comtesse de Bailleul were a lovely

old couple who often invited diplomats to their sixteenth-century château in Normandy, near the little seaside town of Honfleur. Anna and Conor had never been invited to one of their famous weekends because Conor, being the counsellor at the embassy of a small country, was not considered important enough to be a guest at such a place. Anna had heard that these weekends were always good fun. She was sure that Conor would want to go. He loved the country.

Anna took a closer look at the invitation to the ball at the Opéra. It was three weeks away. There would be a performance of the Opéra Ballet and dinner and dancing in the foyer afterwards. Another invitation to a top-notch event. Was it a mistake? Not that Anna would refuse to go, but why were she and Conor suddenly welcome at every glamorous bunfight in town? These were parties she had only read about in magazines. Now she was invited to join the upper crust. She knew that Juan had fixed their invitation to the cruise, but surely he would not be able to rewrite the Parisian social calendar? Anna had read about the ball the previous year and now she would go herself! (Conor would certainly need a new tuxedo.)

It would be fun to watch the in crowd of the world of fashion. The dresses were always spectacular, the food would be exquisite and the surroundings beautiful. It was the event of the year in Paris. Feeling very excited, she put the invitations on the mantelpiece and went into the bedroom to get ready for yet another workout session with

Susanna. She decided that afterwards she would call her friend from school. It would be fun to catch up after all these years.

That evening, as Anna and Betsy sat on the living-room sofa sharing a bottle of wine, Betsy told Anna the story of her adult life. It was late, nearly midnight, and Conor and Mícheal were still out. Conor was working on the final details of the Taoiseach's visit the following day and Mícheal was at the press brief-ing. As Anna was alone (again), she had invited Betsy for dinner. She listened attentively as Betsy told her how she had studied interior design and gone to America, where she had worked for a big company. Now she was in Paris to do the interior of a Swedish-owned hotel.

'What about men?' Anna wanted to know. 'Why have you never married?'

'Oh, men,' Betsy sighed. 'I've had a few flings. But I have not yet found a man who will put up with me and my strange habits.'

'Like what?'

'Well, I paint. It's my passion. I have a studio over my flat, and whenever I feel inspired I have to put it on canvas. I often get up in the middle of the night to paint something I have dreamed about. Sometimes I stay up there several days. Most of the time I'm covered in paint stains and reek of turpentine. Not very sexy. Most of the men I've met haven't been able to put up with me for very long. And I haven't yet met anyone that I have been really attracted to. I don't know if I'd cope with living with a man. I'm sure you must understand that. Conor looks like he's hard work.'

'No, he isn't,' Anna protested. 'I don't spoil him at all. He has to look after his own clothes, I only cook when I feel like it, and when he is ill I sleep in another room. If he says stupid boring things at dinners I tell him that he is talking absolute crap, and when he makes a speech I fall asleep.'

'And that works?' Betsy looked at Anna sceptically.

'Eh, well,' Anna stammered, 'most of the time.'

'At the moment I'm not really interested in men,' Betsy said. 'But one day, I'm sure I'll meet a man who'll light my fire. You know,' she continued, 'that Spaniard I was sitting beside at dinner the other night is the kind of man I hate the most. They try their best to get your knickers off and then they dump you when they find someone else.'

'You think he is a bit of a shit?'

'He's an absolute prick, darling.' Betsy beamed. 'I noticed that he is very interested in you.'

'What do you mean?'

'When he heard that I know you from childhood, he started to ask all sorts of questions about you and your husband. He was very disappointed when I said that I had never met Conor. Funny, he wasn't really interested in the story of your life. He just wanted to know about your Irish family. He quickly lost interest when I couldn't tell him anything about them. Strange, wasn't it?'

'Maybe Spaniards *are* strange,' Anna mused. 'He won't get anywhere with me, in any case.'

'That's what he finds such a turn-on. You're a

challenge to him.'

Before Anna could answer, the front door opened, and she heard Mícheal's unmistakable shuffling walk on the marble floor of the hall. He stuck his woolly head through the door. When he saw Betsy, he came into the room with an interested look on his face. Anna sighed and introduced him.

'I love Swedish women,' Mícheal told Betsy as he sat down beside her.

'Really?' Betsy replied lifting one of her eyebrows. 'Do you know anything about them?'

'I have seen all the Ingmar Bergman films,' Mícheal announced. 'There is nothing I don't know about Swedish women. You are mixed-up, depressed, and sexually frustrated. Swedish men can't satisfy you.' He leaned nearer to Betsy. 'You need a real man.'

'And you're one of them?' Anna suggested.

'Indeed I am. I have lots of experience with women.'

'Good or bad?' Betsy smiled, winking at Anna.

'That's none of your business. You look like one of those frustrated career women,' he continued. 'You probably think you are better than men. Your career is just a substitute for sex. I bet you're terrible in bed.'

'Wouldn't you love to know,' Betsy laughed. 'You look a bit frustrated yourself.'

'You're wrong. I'm not frustrated,' Mícheal replied. 'And I have never had to pay for sex.'

'Big deal,' Betsy stated. 'Neither have I. But in your case, I think I would pay. Not to. Have sex with you, I mean.' She took a sip of her wine.

'You wouldn't say that if you knew me. Women

have begged me, you know.'

'Oh, I'm begging you now,' Anna said. 'Please, please. Get lost.'

'OK,' Mícheal grunted, getting up from the sofa. 'You don't know what you're missing.' He shuffled out of the living room.

'Strange man,' Betsy remarked.

'That's putting it mildly.'

'He is so over the top, you'd think he was putting on an act,' Betsy said, looking thoughtful. 'He's like a caricature of a really awful Irishman.'

'He's only like that when he's drunk. When he's sober he's just boring.'

Betsy rose. 'It's getting late. I have a lot to do tomorrow. The hotel job has to be finished by the end of the month.'

'If I can help you in any way, let me know,' Anna offered. 'I don't know anything about interior design, but I speak French, and I can use a computer.' What am I saying, she thought, I have no skills whatsoever. But it might be fun to do something different.

'That's not a bad idea,' Betsy replied thoughtfully. 'I'll call you tomorrow.'

Betsy was only gone a few minutes when Conor arrived home with Sarah in tow.

'Could you make us something to eat, darling? We haven't had time to have dinner,' Conor called from the hall, where he was helping Sarah off with her coat.

Just what I need, Anna thought angrily, having to cook for Moany Maloney at half past midnight. She went into the kitchen and started preparing an omelette, banging the frying pan hard on to the cooker.

'Bring it into the living room, would you, we're so tired,' Conor demanded. 'Sarah's exhausted.'

'Is she?' Anna mimicked to herself. 'The poor darling.' She continued to bash bowls and saucepans as she made an omelette, sautéd mushrooms and made a mixed salad.

She put the food and wine on a tray and brought it into the living room, where Conor and Sarah were sitting (much too close) on the sofa. Sarah was dressed in a light-brown soft suede skirt and frilly cream silk blouse. Her golden blonde hair was cut very short. She didn't look very tired to Anna, who slammed the tray on the table, making everything clatter.

'Careful!' Conor exclaimed. He looked annoyed.

'Enjoy your meal,' Anna snapped. 'I'm going to bed.'

'Don't forget that the journalists are coming here for a drink and something to eat tomorrow after the President's lunch,' Conor reminded her.

'How could I forget a fun event like that?' Anna replied sarcastically. 'Twenty gorgeous men with the same charisma and sex appeal as Mícheal. Any woman's dream.'

'Don't be nervous,' Sarah said. 'I know that it must be difficult for you to talk to journalists. I mean,' she continued, as Anna glared at her, 'you probably don't know much about politics.'

'What makes you think that?' Anna snarled.

'Please, darling, it's late,' Conor pleaded.

'You must be looking forward to the cruise. It

sounds so exciting,' Sarah babbled on in an attempt to change the subject. 'I wish I was going.'

'We're not going. Conor doesn't want to.'

'But you are. He just told me,' Sarah said triumphantly.

'What?' Anna couldn't believe her ears. 'Why doesn't he tell me himself?' She looked furiously at Conor, who had the grace to seem embarrassed.

'I decided this evening. The ambassador wants me to go. He thinks I can make some important contacts with the French officials. And Juan Valverde told me that I would be a great help to him. Sorry,' he added sheepishly.

'Well, yippee.' Anna's voice was dripping with irony. 'Why don't you come too, Sarah? And bring your *cat*.' She marched out of the room, down the corridor into the bedroom and angrily started to close the shutters. Sarah really was the end.

On the other hand ... A slow smile spread over Anna's face. Conor had changed his mind without any persuasion from her. Things were turning out well. Another thought just occurred to her, and she turned and went back into the living room, where Conor and Sarah were giggling over their late supper. They looked, to Anna's eyes, far too cosy.

'By the way,' she started. Conor and Sarah straightened up.

'Yes, darling?' Conor replied.

'You know how Juan is so interested in Ireland and especially Cork? And, God knows why, the Taoiseach?'

'Yes?' Conor repeated.

'Maybe you could get him an invitation to the party at the embassy tomorrow night?'

'Who is this man?' Sarah demanded. 'If he's not Irish or connected to Irish business, there is no way he can come to the embassy. You can't invite just anyone simply because he is your friend.'

'Junior diplomat *and* social secretary, now I know why you're so tired,' Anna remarked with a stiff smile. 'Why can't we invite our friends? It would make the party more fun. *You* could invite your cat.'

'Please, girls, stop sniping,' Conor pleaded. 'Neither of you has anything to do with the invitation list. I'm too tired to think of this now. Sarah, you stick to polishing the speech and planning the reception committee at the airport. And I know you'll do a great job looking after the press people, Anna.' Conor felt that his diplomatic skills were stretched to their limit tonight. These two women were tougher to handle than any politician.

'How difficult can it be to hand out bottles of beer and a few bowls of nuts to some scruffy journalists?' Sarah muttered.

'I think I'll call a taxi for you now, Sarah,' Conor announced very quickly, before Anna could reply. He grabbed Sarah by the elbow and propelled her out to the hall, where he quickly called a taxi. Before Sarah knew what had happened, she was going down in the lift with a promise that a taxi would pick her up 'very soon'.

'Well done,' Anna remarked when he came back into the living room. 'I would never have been able to kick her out that fast. And she didn't even argue.

She must be crazy about you.'

'It was her or you. I knew I had to separate the two of you, or there would have been blood. Probably mine. Since you live here, I unfortunately had to get rid of Sarah,' he said, glaring at her.

Anna knew that if she continued to moan and complain about Sarah, the night would end in a full-blown row. And she did want to try to get Juan invited to the party, as she had promised. She had to do this without making Conor jealous and suspicious. But he was so preoccupied with the events of the following day, that she felt he would accept anything at the moment.

'What about Juan?' she asked, trying to sound casual. 'Can he come to the party? Not that I care,' she added.

'What, darling?' Conor muttered as he shifted through his notes. 'Oh yes,' he continued, 'I think I have a solution. Juan can't come to the party, but as Nolan wants to go out on the town afterwards, I asked Juan to help me organise it. It's actually a bit delicate.'

'What's delicate?'

'Well, Nolan has asked to go to a strip club and to meet some pretty French girls. But we have to keep it from the press.'

'What are you going to do? How are you going to keep it from the press? And what about his security guard?'

'Nolan is going to slip out of the embassy after the party. By that time the official part of the visit will be over, and all the foreign journalists will have gone home. Juan suggested he be taken to the Crazy Horse. The rest will be easy, he said. This is not really my job, but you know what Nolan's like.'

'I know. He could have you fired.'

'Not fired, but sent somewhere a lot hotter than here. I have to make sure he has a good time in Paris, and he doesn't mean at the Elysée Palace with the President of France.'

'No, he means in bed with a French tart and we're not talking dessert.' Anna giggled. 'You make sure he has fun, or it's a posting in darkest Africa. Is that the deal?'

'Exactly,' Conor smirked. 'You're so clever, darling. You really understand diplomacy! In any case, I thought Juan would be the man to take him out. And I would know nothing about it. The press could ask any questions they liked. The whereabouts of the Taoiseach would be a complete mystery.

'But what will you do with his security guard?'

'Get him a tart too. That way, he'll be too busy to worry about the Taoiseach,' Conor joked. 'But seriously, Nolan's security guard has been with him for years. He's used to this sort of thing.'

'So that's all right then,' Anna said. 'It's all taken care of.'

'Mmm, yes,' Conor muttered. 'But there's the Irish press ... Don't forget we have one of them staying here. Where is he now?'

'In bed. He was sloshed when he came in. I'm sure he's fast asleep by now.'

'He must under no circumstances find out about the Taoiseach's little adventure. If this comes out, his wife will find out and Nolan will blame *me*.'

'Never mind his wife, what about Lizzie?' Anna knew on the grapevine that Seamus Nolan had been having an affair for many years with Dublin socialite Lizzie Dobbins, a formidable woman. Everyone knew about it, but no one had the courage to make it public.

'Oh God, yes. She'll kill him.'

'I'd better stock up on suntan lotion,' Anna muttered. 'The sun is very strong in Africa . . .' She did not notice the door to the guest room slowly closing.

CHAPTER 5

It was very quiet when Anna woke up. Everybody seemed to have gone out, the children to school with Assumpta, and Conor and Mícheal to the airport for the Taoiseach's arrival. She would have plenty of time to get organised for the day. She had a long leisurely shower and took her time to get dressed. She would have her breakfast on the terrace before starting the preparations for the journalists' party that afternoon. Anna liked this time in the morning, when she could have breakfast and read the newspaper in peace before the day began properly. Humming happily, she opened the door to the kitchen. Then she screamed, as if she had come face to face with an appalling apparition.

Her heart nearly stopped. It was Mícheal, clean and tidy and dressed in a suit and tie. Even though the ill-fitting brown suit, beige shirt and dark green tweed tie would be considered awful on anyone else, it was a huge improvement on his usual attire.

'What's wrong with you now?'

'You gave me a fright. I thought you were already gone.'

'It takes a long time to get dressed up.'

'You look ...' – she was searching for the right words – '... different!' she ended feebly.

'Thanks. Thought I should smarten up for the Taoiseach.'

'I suppose you will be leaving when the Taoiseach's visit is over,' she continued, trying not to look too pleased. At last they would have their cosy family life back. No more beer cans in the sofa, newspapers on the floor or cigarette butts in the flowerpots. No more nasty comments and innuendoes.

'I have the feeling that you don't like me much.'

'I really don't know what you mean. We have enjoyed having you here. It was a pleasure. Really.'

'Oh? Well in that case maybe you won't mind if I stay on for a bit.'

Anna's eyes widened with fright.

'I have some leave coming up,' he continued, 'and I want to work on my book. I could do it here.'

'I thought you were writing about the west of Ireland. How can you do the research in Paris?'

'I've done all the research I need. I have all my papers with me. It's quiet and comfortable here. A great place to write.'

'But, I don't know if we can keep you,' she stammered. 'We have other guests. They will arrive in a few days.'

'Who would that be?'

Anna tried to think of someone important who might need a room in Paris. 'It's, it's someone from

Foreign Affairs, actually. He's going to, to inspect the embassy.'

'He'll have to stay somewhere else. I like it here. And I get first-hand information about what's going on, as well.'

'Going on? There's nothing in particular going on.'

'That's not my impression. I heard you discussing it last night.'

'Don't be silly! You were drunk last night, you must have dreamed it.'

'I didn't dream that you were discussing the Taoiseach and what he would be doing tonight.'

Anna was really worried now. He must have been spying on them. Hell, if Nolan's little excursion came out they were finished!

'I know about the cake. There's no good denying it.'

'The cake?' Anna asked, mystified.

'The cake you're going to serve the Taoiseach. You're having it baked especially. You must have found out what his favourite dessert is, and now you're going to make sure he gets it, and you and your husband will get extra brownie points from Nolan. You probably think you'll get your husband promoted this way.'

Anna suddenly felt dizzy. She cleared her throat, while she thought of something to say. 'You're right,' she breathed. 'I'd do anything for my husband's career! Please don't tell anyone about this! You can stay here as long as you like if you don't tell.'

'OK,' he grunted. 'But I want a slice of that cake as well. I don't see why that Nolan should get everything, just because he's Taoiseach.'

'All right, I'll try.'

'A big slice?'

'Huge,' she promised.

'Good. Got to go. See you later.' Mícheal walked out the door, slamming it shut behind him.

Anna screamed again. He was like a curse. They would need an exorcist to make him leave. She sighed. She did not have time to think about that now. She had to concentrate on getting everything ready for the journalists' party.

At three o'clock the apartment was full of noise and cigarette smoke. The Irish and French journalists who were reporting on the Taoiseach's visit were busily demolishing the sandwiches Anna had prepared. She was appalled at the way they were putting their cigarettes out on the floor, drinking beer out of bottles and spilling coffee on the furniture.

Mícheal had bumped into some colleagues he hadn't seen for years.

'Hello, Mick,' said one of them, a thin dark man dressed in black leather trousers and a red shirt. 'You're looking good. Have you been working out?'

Anna smiled at the thought of Mícheal in a gym.

'No, but I look after myself' came the reply. He is good at looking after himself at other people's expense, Anna thought.

'You have a great pad here,' the journalist remarked to Anna.

'It's very comfortable. And the hostess is delightful,' Mícheal said, putting his arm around her. His hand on her waist felt sweaty and his breath smelled strongly of beer. She moved sharply away and he nearly lost his balance.

'I have to look after the other guests. Please excuse me.'

'All right, darling,' Mícheal slurred. 'She's more affectionate when we're alone,' Anna could hear him say as she walked away. She gritted her teeth.

An hour later, Anna and Assumpta were clearing up the mess. Mícheal had retired to his room to 'work'. They could hear loud snores.

'I hope he sobers up in time for the party at the embassy tonight,' Anna said, as they lifted the sofa back to its proper place. 'The Taoiseach won't be too impressed if the representative for the *Irish Telegraph* turns up sloshed.'

'He is probably used to that,' Assumpta reassured her, removing a flattened sandwich from a sofa cushion. 'He is supposed to like a drink himself.'

Seamus Nolan was well-known for his fast living. Anna had never met him and she was looking forward to the evening with interest.

Assumpta and Anna had nearly finished the task of putting the apartment back in order when the phone rang. Anna switched off the hoover and went out to the hall to answer it, thinking it was Conor. He might want to tell her what had happened at the lunch.

'Anna?' She recognised Betsy's Swedish voice.

'Hi, Betsy. How are you?'

'I'm not so well. In fact, I'm in awful trouble. The hotel job I'm involved with is running into problems. I'm trying to meet a deadline. The whole job was supposed to be near completion by now, but we are only halfway. I have never had to deal with this kind of workman. Nobody speaks English and my school French isn't good enough to argue with them.'

'I see. It must be difficult.'

'To be honest, I'm going crazy.' Betsy's voice increased in volume.

'I'm sure you can cope. You were always so organised at school.'

'You don't understand. The builders don't turn up until ten o'clock, and then they start the day with a coffee break which nearly runs into their lunch break. The painters are from Sicily, and they just leer at me and say *bella, bella* whenever I give them orders. The plumbers got the plans wrong. The bidets in the bathrooms flush like toilets, and there are no toilets. God knows what the electricians are up to. I'm afraid to turn the power on. In short, HEEELP!' Betsy's tone was jocular, but Anna could hear an undertone of panic.

'What can *I* do?'

'You don't have to do much, just help me talk to these people. I know you speak good French. In fact, I just need somebody to hold my hand.'

'All right. I'll do anything I can,' Anna promised. 'When do you want me?'

'Could you come on Monday? To my office? I will fill you in then.'

'Yes, that's fine. I can be there at eleven o'clock in the morning.'

'Great! Thanks a million.' Betsy hung up.

The Irish embassy was a big private house built in the

middle of the nineteenth century, situated near the Place de la Concorde. Anna arrived there twenty minutes late, because it had taken longer than she had anticipated to settle the children. She had drawn out getting dressed to give Mícheal a head start. She did not want to arrive with him. (Lord knows what he might take into his head to say if they did.) Sitting in a smelly taxi with Mícheal would definitely not be the same thrill as gliding through Paris in a white Mercedes with Juan.

Anna had put on one of her old favourites, a red, and very short, dress. She felt in a festive mood as she pushed open the enormous entrance door. She nodded to the concierge, and proceeded to climb the long curving staircase to the reception area on the first floor.

There was a long queue at the door of the drawing room. The Taoiseach, the Minister for Foreign Affairs, the ambassador and Conor were standing in line greeting the arriving guests. Conor was introducing the guests to the Taoiseach and the minister. He was not particularly good at remembering people's names. In fact he was worse at it than Anna. She could hear him humming and hawing as he racked his brain for the correct name each time a new person came into line. Anna cringed as she heard him make an embarrassing mistake.

'This is Mr Sean O'Hara and his mother.'

'No, my *wife*,' Mr O'Hara hissed.

It took a few awkward minutes to sort it all out. Mrs O'Hara did not look amused. Anna wished she could have been by Conor's side to help him, but the wives of diplomats were not included in this kind of line-up.

When one of the guests paused to chat to the Taoiseach, she peeped at the politicians from behind the broad back of an Irish former rugby player.

Seamus Nolan, Ireland's prime minister, was a short, rather stocky man with thick curly brown hair and piercing blue eyes. His smile was that of a politician, wide and deceptively warm. He must have practised it in front of the mirror, Anna thought.

His dark suit had the widest pinstripes she had ever seen. As she came nearer, she could watch him greet each guest with a firm handshake and that winning smile. When her turn came and she was inches away from him, she felt the charisma of the man. He looked her up and down and, as Conor introduced her, took her right hand in both of his.

'Where have you been hiding this lovely creature, Conor?' the Taoiseach said without taking his eyes off her. She was like a bird frozen in the stare of a snake. She felt oddly attracted to him, the way one is attracted to things that are cheap and nasty but appealing at the same time. He held her hand tightly, looking deep into her eyes with a little smile. 'I have heard a lot about you and I must say I'm not disappointed.'

'You have, I mean, you're not?' Anna stammered.

'I'm looking forward to getting to know you better, my dear. I'll see you later,' he ended with a little wink.

'OK,' she whispered, realising how stupid she sounded. But the man was so intimidating. He gave her hand a final pat and turned to beam his smile on the next guest, a nervous older woman who nearly fainted with excitement. Red-faced, Anna mumbled something and turned to greet the Minister for Foreign Affairs and the ambassador.

'Mrs O'Connor,' the minister said and shook her hand.

'Good evening, minister. How nice to see you again.'

As usual, Robert Sullivan was beautifully turned out. Everything matched. He wore a dark blue suit that fitted him to perfection. His shirt was light blue with a white collar, and his silk tie had a discreet pattern of blue and red. His brown eyes were warm behind his gold-rimmed glasses, and he gave her a little wink. They had met a few times before. The ambassador, a heavy-set man with black hair and dimples, kissed Anna on both cheeks as usual.

Anna continued into the big drawing room. It was beautifully furnished with Irish antiques. The floors were covered with Donegal carpets especially woven to fit the dimensions of the room. Eighteenth-century tapestries adorned the walls, and the mantelpiece of the period fireplace carried an enormous Waterford crystal vase filled with yellow roses. The french windows overlooked a little courtyard with a fountain at the back of the house.

Denise O'Meara, the wife of the ambassador, greeted her.

'Hello, Anna. How did you get on with our esteemed Taoiseach? Did he pinch your bottom?'

'He wouldn't!'

'I wouldn't put it past him,' Denise muttered. 'He is likely to do anything.' Her dark peppercorn eyes flashed and her black curls bounced as she spoke. Her moss-green knitted suit was moulded to her generous curves. She looked cuddly.

'I do miss old TF,' she sighed, 'he had such style.'

T.F. Finnegan, the former Taoiseach, had recently retired. He was a much-loved politician, who had been a father figure to the people of Ireland. He had been a true statesman, with impeccable manners and real integrity. It would be very difficult for any successor to fill his shoes. Seamus Nolan certainly did not do that.

'Do have something to eat,' Denise urged her. 'There is lots of food.'

Anna went into the dining room. It was even bigger than the drawing room. The vast table groaned under the enormous amount of food that had been laid out.

The buffet had been organised by Irish Meats and the Dairy Board. There were several kinds of meat: roast beef, ham and cold chicken. Big baskets were filled with Irish soda bread. There were also heating trays bearing hot food: Irish stew, sausages, a mountain of boiled potatoes, and a huge plate of fried eggs. Three chefs were helping the guests to carve pieces of beef or ham. There was every brand of Irish beer, including Guinness, as well as red and white wine. The china carried the Irish state symbol, a harp, in gold. The silver cutlery was similarly engraved.

A large group of people were already helping themselves with obvious enthusiasm. Anna bumped into Mícheal, who was carrying a plate heaped with food.

'Watch where you are going! I nearly dropped everything.' His look of annoyance turned to satisfaction when he realised who he had bumped into. 'Isn't this a treat! Real food for a change. None of that continental muck served in your house.'

Anna was furious. So the *poulet à l'estragon* and *boeuf bourguignon* that she had taken such trouble with were not to his liking.

'You eat like a bird,' he continued, stuffing a forkful of sausage and a whole fried egg into his mouth. 'Thiff if nutt a time to be fy.'

'I beg your pardon?'

'I said, this is not a time to be shy.' Mícheal had swallowed his enormous mouthful. 'Don't forget about my little treat, OK? As soon as Nolan has had his.' He winked at Anna, turned his back on her, and went over to a round table where some of his journalist friends were already seated.

'Hi, Anna.' Sarah was standing at the other side of the table. 'What a lot of food.' She was carrying a plate on which was a small helping of cold chicken and a piece of bread. 'You wouldn't want to go mad. It is all so delicious, I mean. It would be easy to overdo it. Isn't Denise a marvellous hostess? She must be exhausted with all the work.'

Exhausted telling the servants what to do, Anna thought.

'Conor did a marvellous job with the organisation of the visit,' Sarah continued. 'He is fantastic at this sort of thing. I have told him how great I think he has been. Men need to be encouraged.' Sarah nodded wisely.

'Really?' Anna replied. 'How fascinating. You're such an expert on men.' Sarah reddened. She turned on her heel and disappeared into the next room, where there were tables to sit at. Anna took a small helping of roast beef and some salad. She suddenly didn't feel very hungry.

She joined a table of Irish couples who were living permanently in Paris. They were a fun crowd, mixing Irish liveliness with continental style and sophistication. Irish people were popular in France. French people liked going to Ireland for their holidays, and Irish pubs were beginning to be the in places for young people. It was chic to go to Ireland. When Anna had made this remark to Susanna, she had replied that it wasn't terribly chic to actually *be* Irish.

Conor joined Anna and her friends. He sat down with a plateful of assorted foods from the buffet, sighing contentedly as he drank a slug of beer. At last he could relax. He tucked into the food with relish.

'At last it's over,' he remarked. Between mouthfuls of food, he told his table companions about the luncheon with the French President that day.

'What was the President like?' Anna asked with interest. She thought that Claude-Pierre de Bonamour was a very glamorous man. Tall, with slicked-back black hair and dimples, he had a way of smiling into the camera and into the hearts of females all over the world. Even the Queen of England was said to be smitten.

'He's a real ham,' Conor replied. 'Every time there

is a camera pointed at him, he smiles and waves. Off camera he is a bit of a shit, really. He is very nasty to his own staff.'

'Yes, but a sexy shit,' retorted Anna. Like most women, even the most ardent feminists, she found powerful men extremely attractive.

'That's what makes him a successful politician,' Conor remarked. 'French women are totally taken in by him.'

'You haven't told us anything really interesting,' Anna complained. 'Does he dye his hair? Is it true he's sleeping with his secretary? Was his wife there? What did she wear?'

'I have no idea if he dyes his hair,' Conor replied. 'And he didn't share the details of his personal life with us.'

'Pity,' Anna muttered, disappointed.

Dessert was now being served in the dining room. A new buffet was being laid out with a variety of puddings and cakes. There were big bowls of trifle, several big apple tarts, chocolate cakes, lemon meringue pies, deep dishes of whipped cream, and what seemed like gallons of custard. After dessert, you were supposed to help yourself to cheese and biscuits from the big cheeseboard where an array of delicious Irish cheeses with names such as Gubeen and Jigginstown were displayed. Anna could see Mícheal taking a helping of each dessert. He had eaten enough to feed a family of five, she thought.

'This is the first time I have enjoyed a meal since I arrived,' she could hear him say to another guest.

'Thank God we are getting rid of that idiot,' Conor

sighed beside her.

'That's what you think. He told me today that he is thinking of staying on for a bit.'

'Oh, no, I don't believe it! I can't just throw him out. He is well-known as a journalist and could cause me endless trouble.'

'That's not all,' Anna added. She went on to tell Conor about the 'cake' for the Taoiseach and how Mícheal was looking for a piece of it. Conor thought this was very funny.

'You'd better come up with a piece of cake for him, or he won't be happy.' He chuckled into his beer. At that moment one of the Taoiseach's aides came up to Conor and muttered something into his ear.

'Darling, the Taoiseach wants us to join him,' Conor announced. 'Let's go.'

The Taoiseach, the ambassador, the minister and the rest of the official party were having dessert at a round table in the small dining room, away from the other guests.

'Conor and Anna,' Nolan exclaimed as they entered. 'Anna, come and sit here beside me.' He indicated with his spoon the empty seat on his left. Trembling with nerves, Anna sat down. A maid served her a slice of strawberry cake. The Taoiseach smiled at her, and, still eating his cake, turned to speak to the ambassador who was sitting on his other side. Anna listened to their conversation with half an ear, and nibbled at the cake. The room was stuffy and rather dark. There was a din of voices discussing the events of the day.

She looked at the Taoiseach and wondered idly if

he permed his hair. The curls did not look natural. Maybe it was a wig? And was that a real tan? His face had the orange tinge you get from applying fake tanning lotion. Anna wondered if he was that colour all over. And what was that smell? She didn't recognise the scent he had obviously sprayed rather generously on himself. He glanced at her and gave her a little smirk. She looked away, embarrassed, and pretended to admire a painting on the opposite wall.

Suddenly, Anna felt something on her knee. Not another dog, she thought, but remembered that the O'Mearas didn't have a dog. Oh no! It was someone's hand. Was Nolan feeling her up under the table? It must be a mistake. He had probably lost his napkin, and was looking for it. No, the hand wandered higher. It went under her skirt. She felt a wave of panic sweeping over her. What was she going to do?

She looked across at Conor, who was happily talking about gardening with Mrs O'Meara. She tried to give him a sign, but he didn't see her. The hand was just above her knee. She shot a sideways glance at Nolan, who was still talking to the ambassador, and eating dessert with his right hand. There was no sign of his activities under the tablecloth, but the hand was still feeling her leg. She felt sick and humiliated. She wanted to protest, but was afraid to. He would probably pretend she was making it up. Conor would be embarrassed, his career on the line.

Coffee was being served. Yes, that was it, coffee! Anna took an empty cup from the tray that the maid was holding out to her, grabbed the coffee pot, and instead of pouring the warm liquid into the cup, pretended to miss. The coffee hit her lap and the wandering hand. 'Oh!' she exclaimed, jumping up, dabbing at her skirt with her napkin. 'I'm so sorry.' Nolan had quickly jerked his hand away, and pressed his napkin to it. She could see that the top of his hand was a little red. No one seemed to have noticed what he had been up to.

'Are you all right, my dear?' the Taoiseach enquired, looking totally innocent. Anna had to admire his cool manner.

'Yes,' she replied, 'it's just a small stain.'

'But it must have burned you.'

'Just a little. It was worth it,' she muttered as she sat down again, this time pulling her chair as far away from him as she could. Everyone started talking again, and no one paid attention to Anna, who was feeling weak and very angry.

'I thought Swedish girls liked a bit of attention,' Nolan muttered into her ear.

'Not that kind,' she hissed back with an angry look.

He glanced at his watch. 'Time I was off. Someone is waiting for me. I'm just going to slip away. Goodbye, my dear.' He gave her hand a squeeze, nodded to the ambassador and, accompanied by his security guard, quickly left by the door that led to the stairs. Robert Sullivan had also risen, and was taking his leave of the ambassador and his wife.

'Anna, let's join the others,' Conor said, when the minister had gone. He sat down briefly on the chair that Nolan had vacated. 'It all went very well, and now Juan will look after the rest of the arrangements. I can relax and enjoy the party, at last.'

'I want to go home,' she said in a small voice.

'Why? You know I can't go until the last guest has left. Are you not well?'

'I feel terrible. That creep felt my leg under the table,' she whispered angrily.

'Who?' Conor asked, sounding less than moderately intelligent.

'Who do you think? The Pope?' she snapped back.

'You mean, you mean ...' he stammered into her ear.

'That's right! Our esteemed prime minister! The leader of the country and the slimeball of Irish politics!' Anna was trying to think of the worst names she could call him.

'But,' Conor protested, 'I saw him. He was talking to the ambassador, and ...'

'Eating cake,' Anna filled in. 'And feeling my leg under the table with his other hand. Fantastic skill, when you think about it.' She was beginning to feel better.

'So that was why you spilled the coffee.'

'It was the only thing I could think of. You certainly didn't notice a thing! The subject of Mrs O'Meara's compost heap was far too fascinating.'

'I'm sorry, darling,' Conor pleaded, putting his arm around her. 'It must have been horrible for you.' He knew that it had not been Anna's fault, but he secretly hoped that the Taoiseach had not been too annoyed. 'I'll take you home, if you want,' he offered.

'No. It's all right. I feel better now.' She looked down at the big slice of cake she had barely touched. 'There's something I must do.' She picked up the plate and walked out of the door and across the drawing room. When she reached a table where Mícheal was still eating, she put the cake down in front of him. 'There you are,' she said. 'There's the little treat I promised you.'

'That's it?' he asked. 'This is the special dessert? It doesn't look very special to me. Has Nolan had his?'

'He certainly has.'

'Right,' Mícheal replied, and proceeded to devour the cake. His beard was soon speckled with whipped cream and cake crumbs. Anna left to join her friends.

The ambassador had put on some dance music. He asked Sarah to dance. She looked delighted. Maybe she thought it would earn her extra merits in the staff report or even a promotion? But Anna knew that the ambassador would ask every woman in turn, because he was a polite and considerate man. No one would be left out.

Suddenly, everybody was dancing. Anna was on the floor with nearly all the men in turn. Even Mícheal invited her to dance a rock-and-roll, which he was surprisingly good at. His sandals flew on the polished floor and his face became shiny with perspiration. Anna was past caring. She had drunk rather a lot of wine and was having a wonderful time. She loved to dance, and the music carried her back to her youth and the parties she and Conor used to go to when they first met. The ambassador danced with her twice, which earned her annoyed looks from Sarah.

Conor and Anna danced a much-applauded samba. He was a marvellous dancer, with surprising rhythm and suppleness for such a big man. They made a handsome couple, dancing in perfect harmony that came from many dancing sessions together. Sometimes they would put on a record when they were alone and dance together in the living room just for fun. When the music stopped, Conor bowed and handed Anna a rose from a nearby vase.

Breathless and smiling, she sank down on the nearest sofa. Conor asked Sarah to join him for the waltz. His change of partners was not a good move. Sarah was awkward and hesitant. She stepped on Conor's feet several times and in no way came near Anna's perfect motion. The other guests joined them on the dance floor, or resumed their conversations. The spell was broken.

As the evening wore on, there were more people sitting down drinking than dancing. The music stopped. There was a short lull in the conversation, until somebody stood up to sing. It was Thomas O'Shea from the Trade Board. He had a beautiful baritone voice and it was a joy to hear him sing. Anna knew the evening had entered another phase. This was 'party tricks time', when everybody would take their turn to sing, dance or recite poetry. One by one, the guests rose unbidden to do their turn. Anna was always amazed at the talent most Irish people possessed. If they couldn't sing, which was unusual, they could at least tell a funny story with fantastic comic timing, or dance with great gusto. Anna didn't feel she could compete in any way.

When nearly everybody had performed, somebody remembered Anna.

'Come on, Anna, it's your turn,' somebody shouted.

'Sing a Swedish song,' called Thomas.

'Dance again!' shouted another voice.

'Show us your knickers,' suggested Mícheal, who was sitting on the floor surrounded by beer cans.

Anna sang a Swedish lullaby a little out of tune.

'What was it about?' asked Sarah when she had finished. 'It sounded a bit sad.'

'Probably something rude,' Mícheal suggested. 'I would stick to dancing if I were you.' He staggered to his feet. 'I'll sing a *real* song,' he announced, and, swaying in time with his own voice, began singing the first verse of 'Danny Boy'. Tears started rolling down his cheeks as he sang.

'Oh, put a sock in it, Mick,' someone shouted. 'Sing something cheerful!'

Mícheal hiccuped loudly, blew his nose and started into a rude song. After a brief silence, the assembled company started to talk among themselves. When Mícheal realised he was losing his audience, he sang louder.

Conor got up and took him by the arm. 'Shut up, you fucking idiot, or I'll knock your block off,' he growled.

'You just don't appreciate a really good song,' Mícheal complained. But he stopped and sank down like a deflated balloon. 'Any more beer?' he enquired.

It was four o'clock in the morning, and the guests were beginning to take their leave. Mícheal had disappeared. Anna was grateful they did not have to take him home. Sarah had also left. Conor and some of the other diplomats were trying to get the last stragglers to leave. Anna helped tidy up and put out the lights. When the reception rooms were empty and reasonably tidy, they could finally go home.

The sun was rising over the Arc de Triomphe as they reached the Place de la Concorde. Paris was waking up. Anna and Conor decided to walk home even though they were very tired. Hand in hand, they walked up the Champs-Elysées. The streets were deserted and bathed in pink light. There was a delicious smell of newly baked bread and coffee. The newspaper stalls were opening up. The girls in the flower shops were placing pots of flowers on the pavement and the owners of all the small shops were washing the pavements outside their premises. Some early risers were already walking their dogs. Everything seemed fresh and clean.

Half an hour later, they reached their building.

'I'm going to sleep for a week,' Conor sighed as they got out of the lift and entered their apartment. 'I'm absolutely wrecked.'

All the shutters were still closed, and the apartment was in darkness.

'What's that noise?' Anna asked and stopped taking off her coat.

'What noise?' Conor listened intently. 'I can't hear anything.'

'There it is again,' Anna whispered. 'Shh, can't you hear it?'

They could now both hear somebody moaning and groaning loudly.

'It's coming from the guest room,' Conor exclaimed. 'Maybe Mícheal is sick! It wouldn't surprise me after all he ate and drank.'

'If he throws up on the carpet, I'll kill him,' Anna exclaimed angrily. 'I've just had it cleaned.' She marched down the corridor with Conor in tow and threw open the door. It was now clear that the noise was coming from the bed. Anna switched on the ceiling light. The bed, which was covered with a heap of clothes and newspapers, was moving in a strange way. Then everything stopped. Not one, but two heads emerged from under the sheets. Anna gasped, staring at the woman beside Mícheal.

CHAPTER 6

Anna could hear Conor gulp behind her as he looked at the blonde head beside Mícheal's grizzly one.

'Sarah,' he whispered. Sarah gave a little squeal and looked back at Conor with big blue eyes. She pulled the sheet up to her chin, then higher still, until she disappeared completely. Not a sound could be heard from beneath the bedclothes.

'Is there no privacy in this house?' Mícheal shouted. 'Get out!'

He clambered out of bed, and before Anna could look away, she saw that he was naked, except for his orange socks. He suddenly realised that he had nothing on and snatched a cushion from a chair to cover his private parts. The cushion had 'Home Sweet Home' embroidered on it in pink. Anna, who had made it herself, was furious.

'We thought you were hurt,' Conor tried to explain as he and Anna backed out of the door.

'Someone *will* be hurt if you don't clear off!' Mícheal advanced threateningly still holding the cushion against his crotch. Anna quickly switched off the light. Conor closed the door.

'Now where were we, my love?' they could hear Mícheal say through the door.

Anna rushed into their own bedroom where she collapsed on the bed, laughing hysterically.

'I don't see why it's so funny,' Conor exclaimed. 'Poor Sarah. She must be so drunk that she doesn't know what she is doing and that pig is taking advantage of her. I'm going back to rescue her.' He turned on his heel to go back out, but Anna threw herself across the bed, grabbed his jacket and held on tight.

'Stay here, you fool. Couldn't you tell that she was enjoying it? I bet she hasn't had that kind of fun in ages.' Anna started laughing again. Conor looked unhappy, but he stayed. He started to undress with a gloomy look on his face.

'How are we going to face them in the morning?' he wondered. 'Sarah will be mortified.'

'She will be gone by the time you get up. And when you meet her in the office on Monday, just don't mention what happened. You can be sure she won't.' Anna was exhausted. All she wanted was to sleep and not worry about Sarah and Mícheal.

Conor was trying to get into his pyjamas, but he was so tired that he only managed to get the pants on. He fell into bed and was instantly asleep. Anna put on her nightgown, got into bed, pulled up the covers and switched off the light.

'Are we there yet?' Declan asked impatiently.

'We're only five minutes away from home, you stupid eejit,' Lena snapped at her brother.

It was a week after the embassy party, and Anna was driving the big car through the Saturday midday traffic. They were on their way to the Château de Bailleul in Normandy, and it would take them at least two hours to get there. Conor was asleep beside her, and the children and Assumpta were together in the back seat. The traffic would ease up once they were out of Paris.

Soon, the French countryside was rolling past the windows. It was lovely to be out of the city. Although Anna was tired, she was looking forward to the weekend. Luckily last week had been less hectic than the week before. They had had a quiet weekend to recover from the excitement of the Taoiseach's visit. There had been no sign of Sarah the next day and Mícheal had been going around with a smug look on his face.

Anna had called into Betsy's office the following Monday to see if she could be of any help. She had found more of a mess than she had expected. Most of the workmen were either standing around talking, or drinking coffee. The Sicilian painters were indeed the worst problem. They were taking advantage of the fact that Betsy both spoke terrible French and was obviously intimidated by their macho behaviour.

When Anna walked through the half-finished lobby of the hotel, some of the Sicilians started to whistle and make obscene gestures.

'*Bella signora!*' one man shouted. Someone touched her breast and another man pinched her bottom as she walked past. Furious, she made a two-fingered gesture at them as she went in through the nearest door, which she was hoping would lead to Betsy's office. When she came in, she found Betsy, surrounded by pink toilet bowls, screaming into the phone.

'No,' she shouted in English, 'I did not order twelve pink toilets with gold seats. I wanted twenty in white. They were not supposed to be pink *or* in my office! If you don't come and take them away now, and give me what I want, I'll cancel the order.' She paused as she listened to the very loud and angry voice at the other end. 'I don't give a shit what it says on your bloody invoice. It's a mistake. Can't you get that through your thick head?' She paused again as the voice screamed at the other end. 'And the same to you.' Betsy yelled and hung up. The phone rang at once. Betsy lifted the receiver and banged it down again.

'Bloody hell,' Anna exclaimed.

'You can say that again,' Betsy sighed. 'That moron said he thought I wanted pink because I'm a girl. What do they think I'm doing, building Barbie's dream house? Thanks for coming. Sit down, and we'll have some coffee.'

'OK,' Anna said and sat down on one of the pink toilets, as there was nothing else to sit on. 'Those workmen are pretty scary,' she remarked, massaging her bottom. 'I'll be black and blue tomorrow.'

'Tell me about it,' Betsy replied glumly as she filled a cup with black coffee from a thermos and handed it to Anna. 'Sexual harassment with a capital S.'

'What a mess. This place will never be finished!'

'Thank you for being so optimistic.'

'They have obviously never worked for a woman before,' Anna remarked. 'Maybe you should complain to their boss.'

'I have, but he just told me I was cute and asked me to go out with him.' Betsy groaned. 'What am I going to do?'

'Maybe you should. Is he rich and good-looking?'

'Please,' Betsy protested. 'Be serious. I'm trying to work here, not catch a man.'

'OK, sorry. I just thought . . .'

'You didn't,' Betsy snapped. 'Try to come up with a solution instead. What would you do if you were me?'

'If I were you?' Anna mused. 'I don't know. I suppose I'd pack it in.'

'You're a great help. I can't give up. There must be a way. Couldn't you speak to them? My problem is that I haven't enough French to tell them off.'

'You must be joking. I'm even scared to go back out there again! Can I climb out the back window?'

'You used to be so brave! Can't you think of something? I was so sure that you would be able to communicate with them in some way.'

'How do you communicate with apes?' Anna demanded. 'You see, it's not a language problem. It's about hormones. Those creeps have an overload of testosterone. When they see a woman, they only think of one thing, and it has nothing to do with building. What we need is another ape. Someone who can scare them into doing what they're told.'

'I don't know any apes.'

'I do.'

'You do?'

'Yes,' Anna replied. 'Sexy as hell, but an ape in sheep's clothing. Let's call him and see if he can come and scare the shit out of the bastards. Where's my address book?'

Juan was at his desk looking at a detailed map of Cork city and the surrounding area. He looked at the coastline around Kinsale with interest. There were some aerial photographs of the town in a pile on the desk. What a perfect spot, he thought. I wonder if the Irish are ready for another Spanish invasion?

The phone rang. Juan picked up the receiver.

'Juan Valverde.'

'Juan? It's Anna.'

'Darling Anna. It seems such a long time since I have seen your lovely face. I long to see you again. Hearing your soft voice makes me . . .'

'Yes, I know,' Anna interrupted. 'But I'm calling you about a little problem I'm having. Maybe you could help?'

'You know that I'd do anything for you.'

Anna told Juan about Betsy's unfinished building, and about the sly Sicilians and their sleazy boss.

'Please, Juan, could you come over and shout a bit? We need an a—, I mean a man who isn't afraid to bark. Someone who's nasty and aggressive.'

'And you immediately thought of me? I'm flattered!'

'Well, no, I mean . . .' Anna stammered. Then she became annoyed. 'You know very well what I mean. Will you help us or not?'

'Darling, calm down. I'll be there straightaway. Just give me the address.'

Anna told him where the hotel was. 'Thank you,' she added. 'I knew you wouldn't mind doing us a favour.'

'Of course I don't mind. But there's something I would like you to do for me in return.'

'If you sort this out, I'll do anything,' she replied.

'Really? Anything?' Juan teased. 'That sounds promising.'

'Oh, for God's sake, stop bullshitting and come over here.'

'OK. Straightaway. I'll fix the bastards. Just remember, Spanish bullshit is the best there is.'

'I believe it.' Anna hung up. 'Problem solved,' she announced. She went to the window, opened it and climbed out into the street. 'Let me know if it worked.'

The next day a delighted Betsy was on the phone. 'How can I thank you? Juan was marvellous. He made mincemeat out of those little creeps. They are working like ... like ... Sicilians! And he sorted out the pink toilets as well. I think this job will finally be a success. You must come and see it. You wouldn't believe your eyes.' Betsy sounded happy and relaxed.

'So you are changing your mind about Juan? Maybe he isn't as bad as you made him out to be.'

'He still isn't my type. He is great to work with, but I don't want him in my bed.'

'Absolutely.' Anna did not want Juan in Betsy's bed either.

'Don't *you* get involved with him, Anna. He's

nothing but trouble.'

'I can look after myself.' Anna was fed up with single women giving her advice on how to handle men. First Sarah (and look how she ended up) and now Betsy.

'You really saved me,' Betsy continued. 'I couldn't have done it on my own. You know something? I could do with some help here. How about giving me a hand in the office for a bit?'

'Why not? I'd like that. It would be more fun than arranging flowers. Especially if you pay me.'

'Of course I'll pay you,' Betsy promised. 'Conor won't mind?'

'He'll love it.' Anna had no idea what Conor would think of her working.

The rest of the week was taken up by a lot of exercise (those spare tyres just had to go), the children's end-of-term exams, and renewed (and unsuccessful) efforts to get rid of Mícheal. Anna spent Friday afternoon packing for the weekend in the country.

She was wondering who would be among the guests at the château. She was sure Juan would be, he seemed to be invited everywhere, being the perfect guest: elegant, polite and fun. Monique had told Anna that she and Jean-Pierre were going. Anna had been looking forward to the weekend ever since she received the invitation. It would be such a wonderful break from big-city life. You could go riding or walking in the beautiful park, swim in the lake, or play tennis on the tennis court on the back lawn. There would be a formal dinner that evening which required a bit of dressing-up. Anna was hoping that she would be able to fit into the dress she had brought.

At last they came to the big entrance gates. A long avenue lined with beech trees led to the front of the château. It was a beautiful three-storey building with a magnificent double staircase leading up to the front door. Their hosts were coming down the staircase to welcome their guests. The Comte and Comtesse were both in their seventies. Despite their age, they looked youthful and fit, the kind of good-looking older couple who advertise vitamins for the elderly in glossy magazines. The Comtesse wore her grey hair short. She was casually dressed in light blue linen trousers and a white cotton blouse. The Comte had a panama hat on his balding head and wore beige chinos and a navy Lacoste tennis shirt.

'Welcome, welcome,' they both exclaimed as they arrived at the bottom of the staircase. They spoke excellent English with just a trace of an accent. Lena and Declan were kissed soundly on both cheeks, at which Declan made a face as if he wanted to be sick.

After Anna and Conor had unpacked and settled into their spacious bedroom, which was full of lovely old furniture, Anna went downstairs to join the rest of the guests for afternoon tea. She didn't bother to change out of her white trousers and blue shirt – their hosts had assured them that everyone would be dressed very casually.

Conor wanted to listen to the news on his small portable radio. He listened attentively to the Irish radio stations wherever he was, as if Ireland was always in the grip of a national disaster, political crisis, imminent civil war or some other catastrophe. He had brought piles of work with him in his battered old briefcase. If anyone was taken unawares by events, it wouldn't be Conor!

The Comte had invited the children and Assumpta to see the horses. He and Declan had taken to each other in a big way. Anna could hear Declan asking innumerable questions as the party moved off. 'Is this castle haunted? 'Cause if it is I want to see the ghost.'

A dozen people or thereabouts were gathered on the terrace outside the drawing room. It was a beautiful place with views of the rose garden, the tennis court and the lake, and as Anna stood by the stone parapet of the terrace with a cup of tea in her hand she felt as if she had been transported to another century. Big hundred-year-old oaks shaded the lawn. Horses grazed in the paddock beside the lake. She was miles away and barely heard her hostess as she was introducing one of the guests.

'Anna? May I introduce Señor Carlos Sanchez?' Anna turned around and shook hands with a fat bald man. He had a big white moustache.

'A pleasure, *madame*,' he said and bowed. When he smiled, Anna could see that one of his front teeth was made of gold. The hostess turned to greet Juan, who had just joined the group. He kissed the Comtesse on the cheek before she left them to supervise the maids who were serving tea.

'I see you have met my old friend Carlos.' Juan put his arm around Anna's waist and smiled into her eyes. He was wearing jeans and a white polo shirt and looked absolutely divine, as usual. He'd look sexy in anything, she thought.

'Juan!' she exclaimed. 'I didn't expect to see you here.' She tried to appear cool.

'I'm here because I knew you were coming,' Juan replied. He turned to the other man. 'Anna has just moved to Paris,' he explained. 'Her husband is an Irish diplomat.'

'I see,' Carlos replied. 'I would very much like to meet him, *madame*. I love Ireland.'

'So does Juan,' Anna replied.

'He does?' Carlos asked.

'Yes, you know I do, Carlos,' Juan exclaimed with an impatient look at his friend.

'Of course. How silly of me.'

'Carlos is in France on business,' Juan explained, 'so I thought he would enjoy a weekend in the country.' He moved his hand to the small of her back. It was a light touch, but it burned Anna through the thin cotton of her shirt.

'It is very hot, *madame*,' Señor Sanchez remarked. 'Maybe you would like a cold drink?' He moved off to the table further down the terrace where glasses of various cold drinks had been set out. He came back with a tall glass of orange juice which Anna gratefully accepted. But it was not the weather that was making her feel warm.

Conor was standing in the door leading out to the terrace. He was looking for Anna. He glanced at their hosts who were talking to a young French couple, ignored Susanna and her husband who had just arrived, nodded at Monique and Jean-Pierre, and finally spotted Anna with her two Spanish admirers.

'Hello, Juan,' Conor called as he walked across to

join them. He shook hands with Juan and his friend as Juan introduced them.

'Mr O'Connor,' Carlos said, 'how nice to meet you. I have just come back from a visit to your beautiful country.'

'Really? What part of Ireland did you visit?'

'Conor,' Juan interrupted, 'I'd like to show Anna the rose garden. Do you mind if I take her away for a moment?'

'Not at all. Go on, darling, have fun,' Conor said in a tone one would use to a child, and waved his hand as if to shoo them away. He turned to Carlos to continue their conversation.

Juan walked Anna down the staircase that led to the rose garden. 'Let's admire the roses.'

'I didn't know you were interested in gardening.'

'More than I am in business.'

'Business? What business?'

'Oh, I don't know. Carlos loves talking business,' Juan replied airily.

'What business is he in?'

'Building. He builds hotels.'

'Where? In Spain?'

'Here, there and everywhere,' Juan replied. 'But enough about him. Let's enjoy the garden. I love beautiful flowers. Just look at these magnificent roses.'

'They're lovely,' Anna agreed.

'My father grows roses in his garden. The soil there is perfect. But you need the right fertiliser as well. Do you know what we use in Spain?'

'Lots of bullshit?'

'Very clever,' he laughed plucking a red rose from a

bush and handing it to her. '*Mignonne, allons voir si la rose ...*' he quoted from an old French poem. 'Seize the day, that is my motto. Enjoy the moment.' He looked up at the blue sky, breathed in deeply and then out again. 'What a beautiful day, what a lovely place, and what enchanting company. Right now I feel good.'

How could one not feel good on such a day? They walked along the path to the lake, where Lena, Declan and Monique's two girls were playing. They were trying to make small flat stones skim over the surface of the water. Juan picked up a stone and showed the children how to throw it. The stone skipped one, two, three and four times before it sank.

'Wow!' Declan shouted. 'Do that again!' His eyes were wide with excitement and Juan smiled down at him. He picked up another stone and proceeded to teach the boy how to throw it. The other children gathered around to watch. At that moment, Anna could have sworn that Juan was no older than about ten. She smiled, shook her head and walked away. Nobody noticed her leaving.

'Aren't you ready yet? We'll be late for dinner.' Conor was standing at the open door of the *en suite* bathroom dressed in a dark blue suit, white shirt and red silk tie with a design of horses. He looked handsome but irritated. Anna was putting on her make-up, but was not yet dressed. She had had a nap and a long, leisurely bath. Assumpta, Monique's Swedish au pair, Eva, and the four children were having their dinner in a small dining room just off the kitchen.

'You go on down. I won't be long,' Anna replied. She wanted to get dressed on her own. The black chiffon dress she was going to wear was hanging on the front of the old wardrobe. Maybe it was too small? Anna hadn't worn it since last summer and had meant, but forgotten, to try it on. Conor left to join the others for a drink in the drawing room.

When Anna put on the dress, she noticed that it wasn't too tight at all, but even a bit loose at the waist. Hooray! The exercising and dieting had trimmed her waist and flattened her stomach. Her arms too had considerably less flab on them. She could even see some muscle definition. The only problem was that the dress was very low-cut, and she was showing more cleavage than she wanted. She tugged at the neckline to make it come up a bit more. Maybe nobody would notice. She would laugh and talk a lot to draw the attention away from her bust. Yes, it would be all right . . . She sprayed on some perfume, and gave her hair, which she was wearing secured with a black velvet hairband and loose down her back, a last brush.

Anna glanced at her watch and, realising she was late, ran out of the room. She arrived breathless at the bottom of the stairs in a cloud of black chiffon and Chanel No. 5. Juan, impeccably turned-out from his wavy dark hair to his polished Gucci loafers, was waiting for her in the hall. He took in her dark auburn hair shining in the light of the chandelier, her creamy skin and bright blue eyes. He noticed that she had lost weight off her arms and waist, but not off her full bosom. Her now thinner face revealed her wonderful cheekbones and delicate chin. Not bad, he thought.

'I wanted to escort you in, *madame*,' he joked and offered her his arm.

She took it and looked up at him with a smile. 'What a gallant gentleman.'

'Interesting dress.' His eyes were directed at her neckline and his voice was teasing.

'You are as bad as those bloody Sicilians. I was going to thank you for your help the other day, but I won't now.' She let go of his arm and went into the drawing room on her own, where she helped herself to a glass of champagne and joined the first group of people she saw. It was Susanna and a French couple who lived nearby. They were looking at Susanna in confusion as she spoke to them in English. Susanna's accent was nearly perfect, but her choice of expressions was often completely off the wall. For example, she seemed to think that 'piss off' was an upper-class way of saying that someone was leaving. 'Must piss off now, darling,' she would say, or, 'the ambassador pissed off early from the party last night.'

'Why won't somebody tell her it's wrong?' Anna had asked Conor once. 'Wouldn't you think her husband could correct her?'

'She wouldn't believe you if you told her,' Conor had replied. 'And it's too funny to make her stop. Her husband stopped listening to her years ago out of sheer self-preservation.'

Anna went across the room to join Conor. He was talking to a young French girl who had arrived with her parents. She was explaining that they were both well-known artists.

'Zey have exposed zemseleves twice,' she told him.

'Really?' Conor replied. Anna crazily imagined the couple stripping in front of a large audience. Conor was awful. He always took particular pleasure in French people massacring the English language, and he never tried to help them.

'They are so snooty about foreigners speaking French,' he would say, 'they deserve to keep making mistakes without being corrected. They should get the same ridicule as they give us.' He always looked at the person talking to him with polite interest, letting them get more and more entangled. 'So, you always rape the carrots for the soup?' Anna had once heard him say to a woman who was explaining a recipe at a dinner party. It was obvious that she was trying to find the word for 'grate', which is *raper* in French. He had looked at her, rapt and without as much as a snigger. 'Anna,' he had called across the table, 'you have to *rape* the carrots for this soup!' It was his own small revenge on the French.

More champagne was being served. The last guests, a couple from a neighbouring estate, had not yet arrived. If they don't come soon, Anna thought, everybody will be on their ear.

At last the door opened to admit the latecomers, friends of the Comte de Bailleul and his wife. They looked much older than their hosts and had none of their youthful vigour. Conor was being seated beside the old lady.

'You will have to cut up her meat,' Anna whispered to him. He smiled feebly at her in reply.

The guests were invited to move into the dining

room for dinner. It was a big oak-panelled room whose walls were lined with paintings of the host's ancestors. The doors were open to the mild evening air, and there was a faint smell of roses, candles and good French cooking.

Anna was seated between Señor Sanchez and the elderly baron who had arrived so late. She looked nervously down at her neckline. Juan was right. It was very revealing.

'Maybe this will help?' Carlos picked a red peony rose from the display in the centre of the table and handed it to Anna. She gratefully took it and tucked it into her cleavage. It did hide some of the exposed flesh. In fact, it helped a lot. Anna smiled at her table companion.

'Thank you so much. How did you know?'

'I could see that you were uncomfortable.'

'You are a very astute man, Señor Sanchez.'

'Please, call me Carlos. All beautiful women do.'

Anna was charmed. What a nice man. They continued a conversation that was at the same time friendly, amusing and informal. Carlos told her about his interest in Ireland and how he was particularly fascinated by Kinsale, the lovely old fishing town on the south coast of Ireland.

'There was a Spanish invasion there in the early seventeenth century,' he said.

'I know, but the English managed to beat them. There is a lovely old fort there. It was built after the visit of the Spanish Armada. Probably to make sure they didn't try it again.'

'You know a lot about it.'

'I love Kinsale. My husband's parents live there.'

'So he told me. The fort is an interesting place. It's right on the waterfront. It would be perfect for . . .'

A sudden bark from the old baron sitting on Anna's other side interrupted them. 'Your husband is very young to be hard of hearing,' he said.

She was startled – it was the first time he had uttered a word since the beginning of the meal. She glanced across the table at Conor who seemed to be listening to the old baroness with an expressionless look. A thin white flex ran from his right ear to his suit pocket. I don't believe it, she thought, forgetting Carlos and their conversation, he is listening to the bloody radio. Conor was really going too far this time! The dinner was coming to an end. She would give him hell!

The guests filed out of the dining room to take coffee and liqueurs on the terrace and to enjoy the warm evening air. Anna hurried ahead of Carlos, still talking about Kinsale, the old baron, muttering about some wartime memory, and Juan, trying to make her stop to chat. She caught up with Conor at the door of the terrace. He still had the earpiece in his ear and a vacant look in his eyes.

'Take that thing out of your ear at once!' she hissed at him.

'What, darling? Are you having a good time?' he muttered. Anna yanked at the flex, and the little earpiece popped out of his ear.

'That hurt!'

'Have you lost your mind? How can you be so rude!'

'Oh come on, the old bird didn't notice. She is totally gaga. At the end of the dinner, she opened her handbag, took out her handkerchief and blew her nose. Then she took *my* napkin that I had put beside my plate, put it into her bag and left the hanky still sitting on the table. I didn't know what to do.'

'There is no excuse for what you did. Why do you always have to listen to the news? Is there a political crisis or something?'

'As a matter of fact there is,' Conor said, looking important. 'There is a huge row brewing in Cork. Something about the plans for a hotel. I don't have the details yet, but I know it involves a foreign property developer and a historic building. I could have found out the whole story if you hadn't yanked my ear off.'

'That doesn't sound like a big crisis to me. How can they get planning permission to build a hotel in a historic building?'

'You never know. But that's not all. The Taoiseach is in real trouble. Lizzie has decided to spill the beans. She is going on national television to tell the nation all about their affair. He'll lose the next election for sure.'

'I don't believe it for a moment. The Irish voters forgive sexual misbehaviour very easily. In fact, they admire it. I bet the Taoiseach will score even higher in the opinion polls after this.'

'You think you know everything. Wait till you see, there will be a new government, or I am a monkey's uncle.'

'You're a bloody twit. Put away that radio, or the earpiece will go somewhere very uncomfortable.'

Anna glared at him and turned her back to join some of the other guests who were helping themselves to coffee on the terrace. Conor walked back into the drawing room looking furious. She saw him join Jean-Pierre by the fireplace. They will talk European politics until dawn, Anna thought.

It was a heavenly night with a full moon and a black sky full of twinkling stars. Anna, standing at the end of the terrace, looked up entranced. The moon seemed close enough to touch. A phrase from *Peter Pan* came into her mind: 'second star to the right, and then straight on till morning'. She wished she could fly away to Never-Never Land like Peter and Wendy, away from Conor and his radio, Mícheal, Sarah, the embassy and all the annoyances of diplomatic life. She sighed deeply.

An arm encircled her waist tightly from behind. Someone dropped a kiss on her bare shoulder. She leaned back against a strong body and felt the heady scent of Hermès cologne. She knew who he was, but did not care.

'Look at the moon,' he whispered into her ear. His breath was warm and his lips touched her hair.

'Mmmm . . .'

'When there is a full moon, you can make a wish.'

'Really? Then I wish . . .' but she couldn't think of anything, except that the moment would not end.

'Be careful what you wish. It may come true.'

'I'm not afraid.'

'Good.' Juan held her a little tighter. 'Do you remember I asked you to do me a small favour?' he murmured into her ear. 'In return for helping your friend, I mean.'

'Yes?' Anna could hardly breathe. Juan's arms around her waist, his hot breath on her neck, and the feel of his muscular body were making her dizzy.

'It's just a small thing, really. But it would mean a lot to me.'

'I'll help you if I can,' she replied, not caring what the favour was. She felt totally in his power.

'Could you help me deliver a letter?'

'A letter? You want me to go to the post office? To post a letter?'

'No, silly woman,' he laughed. 'I want you to deliver a letter to someone in Ireland. In person. It's too important to post in the normal way.'

'Oh I see. But why don't you ask Conor? He can put a letter in the diplomatic bag for you easily.' Anna received and sent all sorts of things in the daily diplomatic bag. She would sometimes receive packages marked 'top secret' that contained nothing more exciting than a pair of socks, some black pudding and a birthday card from Conor's mother.

'Not the diplomatic bag,' Juan exclaimed. 'That's far too public. No, I need someone to deliver a personal letter to the prime minister.'

'The prime minister?'

'Yes, the tea-shop, or whatever it is you call him.'

'The Taoiseach? But how can I . . .'

'Stop repeating everything I say, and listen,' Juan muttered, sounding impatient. 'I know that you and Conor are going to a dinner in Dublin next week for the visit of the French Minister of Foreign Affairs.

Seamus Nolan will attend, of course.'

'Of course.' Anna knew that she sounded as stupid as she felt.

'Right. What I want you to do is slip my letter to Nolan during the dinner. He knows you'll have it, and he will make sure that there will be an opportunity for you to meet him. He has taken a liking to you, you know.'

'He has? How wonderful,' Anna remarked. 'Lucky me.'

'I know, I know. But,' Juan continued, running his hands up her bare arms, 'will you do this for me, Anna darling?'

'But I don't understand. What's in the letter? Why can't you . . .'

'Shhh,' he interrupted, 'don't ask questions.' Was she going to be difficult? He had feared that Anna would not be easy to fool.

'Why?' she insisted. 'I want to know what this is all about.'

'It's something to do with Spanish–Irish relations. We want to deal with Seamus Nolan directly, without involving other government ministers or civil servants. I won't bore you with the details, but under the circumstances doing it this way is better.'

'It's something political?'

'Sort of. I know you're not interested in politics, but will you do this one thing? For me? And for Ireland? You're an intelligent woman. I know you can handle this very discreetly.'

'Do you really think so?' Anna asked, flattered.

'Absolutely.'

'In that case . . .' she began.

'Thank you, darling! You won't be sorry,' Juan purred, as he touched her neck with his lips. 'And, darling, just one more thing.'

'Mmm?'

'Don't tell anyone about this. Not even Conor.'

'Why?' Her body stiffened in alarm. 'I don't want to lie to Conor.'

'It wouldn't be lying. Just not telling. That's not the same thing. It's just better if he doesn't know about it for the moment. Seamus Nolan will be very grateful for this. It could be very good for Conor's career.'

'Oh. Well, that's different.' Anna relaxed into his arms again. She knew that Conor would never ask a politician for favours. This way he would improve his career prospects without even knowing it. And when he was promoted, it would all be thanks to her.

'I won't tell him a thing,' she promised.

'What's that noise?' Juan enquired suddenly.

'What noise?'

'That crackling sound. Like thunder. But the sky is clear. There! Did you not hear that?'

There was indeed a strange sound coming from the lawn, hissing and crackling. Anna recognised it at once, and moved away from Juan.

'It's Conor's radio.'

'His radio?'

Conor was coming up the steps, his small radio in his hands. He was looking down at it, frowning. 'Terrible reception in this place. I can't get RTÉ.'

CHAPTER 7

Sunshine flooded the garden. It was only half past eight in the morning but some of the more energetic guests were already having their breakfast at small tables set out on the terrace. Anna, Conor and their children were among them. Anna had felt that it was too beautiful a morning to stay in bed and the children had been impatient to go downstairs. They had been promised that they could go riding with their father. Both Lena and Declan were good riders. They had spent several summers at pony camp in Ireland. The Comte de Bailleul had a fine stable of horses to provide his guests with good mounts for any type of riding. Anna did not ride and was nervous of horses. She left the riding to Conor and the children.

It promised to be a hot day. Anna was enjoying a big cup of *café au lait* and some freshly baked French bread with butter and apricot jam. Declan was munching on a croissant and Lena was noisily slurping a bowl of hot chocolate. Conor was reading a French Sunday paper.

'I want to ride a big horse,' Declan exclaimed. 'Not a pony.'

'You will ride whatever you're offered,' Conor corrected him.

Juan arrived looking handsome and relaxed in buff-coloured breeches, highly polished leather boots and a blue cotton shirt. He was accompanied by Carlos, who looked surprisingly fit in his riding clothes. The two men went around kissing all the ladies' hands. Juan winked at Anna as he bent over her hand.

'You're not riding?'

'I can't ride. I don't think I would like it. I'm frightened of horses, really.' She didn't mind admitting it. She was going for a walk and then maybe a swim in the lake.

The guests who were riding moved off to the stables. Susanna was doing stretches on the lawn with a group of people she had forced to come running with her. 'We'll do seven kilometres,' Anna could hear her say to the reluctant-looking company. They moved off along the path by the lake. Anna was looking forward to a few restful hours. Nobody was going to bother her. She had not been alone like this for a long time.

'All alone?' Juan stood in front of Anna on the terrace where she was sitting in a deckchair reading a book. It was half past eleven and she had had a wonderful morning. She had walked for over an hour with Monique in the park, gone for a refreshing swim in the lake, and was now relaxing under a big umbrella while she waited for Conor and the children to come back.

'Alone, but not lonely.'

'You look happy.' Juan helped himself to some orange juice from a jug on a nearby table, flopped down in an adjoining deckchair, propped his feet up on the stone wall of the terrace and closed his eyes to the sun. 'Mmmm, wonderful.'

'Where are the others? Have they finished their ride?'

'They're still out there.' He flicked his hand vaguely in the direction of the woods without opening his eyes. 'They wanted to jump logs. I decided to quit. It's too hot, and I had a hopeless horse. I did us both a favour by coming back.' He turned his head and gave her a lazy smile. His eyes were barely open. He yawned and fell into a light sleep. I have a strange effect on men, Anna thought.

She looked at his sleeping face, his long eyelashes, perfect nose, beautiful mouth and strong chin. His long legs looked even longer in breeches and riding boots. She knew that his laziness was only an act. His lean, athletic body was the result of twice-weekly polo matches, regular swimming sessions and tennis games. He is a truly gorgeous man, she thought. Then she felt suddenly sleepy. She closed her eyes and dozed off.

Anna woke ten minutes later and turned her head to smile at Juan. She was startled to come face to face with Susanna. Was this a nightmare?

'Your boyfriend pissed off.'

'He's not my boyfriend. We're just friends.'

'Friends my eye! I have noticed how you flirt with him. I wonder what your husband thinks about it.' Susanna squinted at Anna with a spiteful look. 'Isn't this a wonderful break,' she continued. 'It beats entertaining at home. It's great to have someone else do the work.'

'What work? You always have an army of hired help when you give a party.'

'Yes, but there is a lot of work supervising them. And you can't let them leave before you have counted the silver.'

She was interrupted by the children's arrival on the terrace. They bounced up the stairs, followed by Conor and Carlos.

'Mammy, Mammy!' shouted Declan. 'Mr Sanchez took us into the forest, and we jumped logs. Mr Sanchez jumped a huge fence, but Daddy wouldn't let us follow.'

'Did Daddy jump the fence?'

'No, he said the horse was tired.' Conor looked embarrassed and Anna laughed.

Lena looked at Anna curiously. 'You have a flower in your hair, Mammy.'

'Oh.' Anna put up a hand to find a rose tucked into her hair by her left ear. Juan must have put it there while she slept.

'How strange,' Susanna muttered from her chair. 'How did that get there?'

'Time to wash up for lunch,' Anna announced in a loud voice. 'Come on, kids, let's go!' She rose from her chair and ushered the children through the french windows and up the stairs.

Conor followed. He chatted to her about their ride as they climbed the stairs to their room. He told her how well Carlos rode despite his age and size. 'He's a truly magnificent rider. And a very nice man. He is so interested in Ireland. He's going there next week. I told him to call on my parents, as he's going to be in Kinsale for a few days.'

'Is he going there on holiday?'

'No, business, he said. He explained what he was doing, something about a hotel but I didn't hear it all, because I had to help Declan with his horse. I'm sure we'll find out about it in due course. My father will be pleased to meet him. He loves showing visitors around Kinsale.'

'I know. He should have been a tourist guide.'

'So, what did you do?' Conor asked.

'Oh, nothing much. I went for a walk and a little swim. Then I sat on the terrace and listened to a lecture by Susanna on how to control the servants. She counts the silver after every dinner party to make sure they haven't nicked any of it!'

'Lovely woman,' Conor remarked. 'Working for her must be such a treat.'

Conor drove them home in the gathering dusk. Anna was dozing beside him, full of sunshine, good food and fresh air. It had been a wonderful weekend. A lunch of cold meats, salad, cheese and bread had been laid out on tables under the big oaks in the garden that day. Anna had taken the children swimming after the meal, while Conor snoozed in a deckchair. When they left, Susanna was ahead of them as they waited to thank their hosts and say goodbye.

'Have they counted the silver yet?' Conor muttered into Anna's ear. 'She may have stashed some of it into that huge tote bag of hers.'

They arrived home just as it was becoming dark. Loud music could be heard as the lift brought them up. It seemed to come from their apartment.

'Oh no!' Anna had been worried about leaving Mícheal alone for the weekend. And now her worst fears were confirmed.

The door to the apartment was wide open. Irish music was coming from the stereo, and what sounded like a huge crowd could be heard laughing and talking in the living room. A blonde woman dressed in a tight red leather skirt and skimpy T-shirt was coming into the hall.

'Hi!' she said and, turning towards the living room, 'More guests, honey.' She was obviously American and certainly not top-drawer. 'Don't you just *love* Mick's place?'

'Mick's place?' Conor's voice was thick with anger. But Anna was pleased. He will have to throw the creep out now, she thought with glee.

Mícheal came through the door with his arms around two equally scantily clad women. 'You're back! I'm giving a small brunch party. I didn't think you'd mind. There is plenty of food left.'

'Brunch? It's eight o'clock in the evening!' Conor shouted. 'If you don't get everybody out at once, I'll call the police. And you can leave as well. I'm sick of you.' He grabbed Mícheal by the front of his pullover and raised his other hand balled into a fist. Goody,

Anna thought irrationally, a fight. She was waiting for the impact of Conor's fist on Mícheal's nose. He put up his hands to avert the blow and suddenly pulled against Anna with a jolt. She woke up and found herself still in the car which had come to a sudden stop at a traffic light.

Anna blinked, and slowly realised that it had only been a dream. Mícheal would still be there when they arrived home.

A few minutes later they were going up in the lift. Loud Irish music could be heard from their apartment. The front door was open, just as in Anna's dream. It gave her an eerie, *déjà vu* feeling, and her heart beat a little faster. Maybe her dream would come true? But the place was deserted. The music was coming from the empty guest room. Mícheal had obviously forgotten to switch off his tape recorder.

A plate of cold sausages and chips was on the floor beside the unmade bed. Anna sighed as she picked it up and brought it into the kitchen, where she found more unappetising evidence of the meals cooked by their guest during the weekend. She felt suddenly a bit sorry for Mícheal. He must be very lonely, she thought. Nobody really loves him. She still wanted him to leave. But she would kick him out in the nicest possible way.

The rain was beginning to fall as Anna emerged from the Métro station on her way to Betsy's hotel. It was Monday morning, and the lovely late spring weather had been replaced by dark clouds and a chilly wind.

Anna was wondering what Betsy would ask her to do. Conor did not know about Betsy's offer of part-time work, but Anna was sure that it would not bother him in the slightest. She would only work while the children were in school. Working with Betsy would be a welcome change from her humdrum weekday existence.

The atmosphere in the lobby was very different from the previous week. There was a tremendous noise of hammering, sawing and drilling, and a strong smell of fresh paint. Great progress had been made, and Anna could now imagine what the hotel would look like when it was finished. The workers glanced at her as she walked past, and one of them winked, but that was all.

'What a difference,' Anna exclaimed as she entered the office. 'It's going to be finished on time.'

'I hope so,' Betsy replied. 'But it's great! Nice to see you so early,' she added. 'Have some coffee before we start. I have good news. The owner of the hotel has agreed to let me hire a part-time assistant. I will even be able to offer you a salary.' She mentioned a sum that seemed very generous to Anna.

'So what exactly do you want me to do?'

'I have to be away from the office quite a lot. We're still trying to agree on some of the furniture and choose the curtains and carpets. That means visits to interior design shops and other suppliers. I need you to answer the phone and take messages. There are two lines. You can get me on my mobile if there is anything urgent. Here's the number. Check the e-mail every half-hour. If invoices start arriving, you will have to file them according to my system. It's written down on a piece of paper that I stuck up on the noticeboard. Several deliveries are due this morning. Here is the list of what they are and where they're to be put. And you have to keep an eye on the painters and carpenters.'

'What?'

'I know, I know. We had trouble with them at the start. Don't worry. They know they will get Macho Man back if they play up. Of course, it might make your day less boring if he calls around from time to time. A little sexual harassment a day keeps the doctor away. Anyway, must fly. See you later.' Betsy gathered up her filofax, handbag and mobile phone, and was gone.

Anna took off her jacket and rolled up the sleeves of her shirt. She sat down at the desk and lined up pencils and pads to use for receiving messages. She switched on the computer. She was ready for her first day at work. My new career has started, she thought, feeling excited.

Nothing happened for about half an hour. Then the phone rang. Anna eagerly grabbed the receiver to answer.

'Hello?'

'Is that *Les Petits Pains?*' a woman's voice asked.

'You must have the wrong number.' Anna sighed and hung up.

She checked the e-mail on the computer. There were no messages. An hour later, absolutely nothing more had happened. Anna checked the e-mail again. Not a thing. She turned on the menu and saw that there was a game programmed in the computer. It was Tetris, a game for eight-year-olds. Anna switched on the game, and was soon completely absorbed. When she had scored 50,000 points five times in a row, she became bored. She stretched and yawned. She was feeling terribly sleepy.

To keep herself awake, she tried to remember the last time she had been this bored. Was it when they had to listened to a speech given by the President of the European Commission that had lasted over an hour? Or when they had attended the opening of parliament in the Hague and the Queen of the Netherlands had delivered her address to the nation, in Dutch of course? Maybe it was the time when she had been sitting beside that English literary agent at dinner?

He had told her about all the authors he had signed to his London agency and the contracts he had secured for them. She had found it so hard to concentrate on his long-winded, self-congratulatory tirade that she had started to do her shopping list in her head. When he paused and looked at her expectantly, she had been totally confused. 'Half a dozen eggs and ten loo rolls,' she had stammered. 'I beg your pardon?' he had said. Red-faced, she had muttered something about trying to remember a poem. That had only started him off again. He kept talking about his successful agency until she wanted to scream. That was definitively the most tedious dinner companion she had ever had. Thinking about him made her feel sleepy again.

She got up from her chair and started to walk

around the room to wake herself up. She stopped in front of a mirror. God, she looked dull. She started to make faces at herself. She smiled. I do show a lot of gum when I smile, she thought. She frowned. No, that was worse. How about a little smirk? And if I turn up my nose just slightly at the tip, I look a bit like Michelle Pfeiffer. The door opened.

'Having a problem?' Betsy had come back.

'No, I just got something in my eye.'

Betsy gave Anna a suspicious look. 'And in your nose as well, by the look of it.'

'Yes, well, it's hard to explain.'

'Please, don't even try. Any calls?'

'No, not one.'

'That's strange. I called an hour ago, and this line was busy for at least half an hour.'

'Really? How odd!' Anna didn't want to tell Betsy that she had called her mother and that they had discussed the love lives of the British royal family and the latest gossip about the rich and famous.

'Maybe there is something wrong with the phone?' Betsy suggested.

'Or a kink on the line?'

'There'd better not be another one. I need the line free for incoming calls.'

'I don't think there will be any more problems.'

'It's nearly lunchtime. You can go home now if you want.'

'Thanks.' Anna gathered up her things.

'See you tomorrow.'

Anna had mixed feelings about her first day at work. It had been really, really boring. Working in an office was not as exciting as she had thought it would be. Of course, working in Betsy's office did not involve any contact with other people. The only attractive thing about it was the generous salary Betsy had mentioned. But money was not everything.

Anna spent the rest of the day trying to catch up. She hadn't realised how much she had to do in a normal day. She also had to organise her trip to Dublin at the end of the week. She would have to skip exercising for a while. Susanna would give her hell and Monique would not be pleased, but it was impossible to fit in everything. Maybe she should tell Betsy she had changed her mind about working?

Conor arrived home as Anna was trying to cook dinner and help the children with their homework at the same time. There was no sign of Mícheal.

'Are you not ready yet?'

'For what?'

'The reception at the British embassy. I tried to call you all morning to remind you.'

'Oh shit. I forgot.' The card had been sitting on the mantelpiece for over two weeks. She had not paid attention to it.

'Do you think you could concentrate on getting ready, if that's not too much to ask.' Conor's voice was icy.

'But I gave Assumpta the day off, because she will have to work at the weekend when we go to Dublin, and I haven't organised another babysitter.'

'We are too big for babysitters,' Declan piped in. 'We can mind ourselves.'

'Find a babysitter then, and get ready, for God's

sake!' Conor shouted. 'You really are the end, Anna! You couldn't organise yourself out of a paper bag.' He marched angrily into the bedroom to shave and change.

The front door slammed at that moment, and Mícheal stuck his head in the door of the kitchen.

'Happy family life, how touching. It's moments like these that make me thank God I'm single.'

'And married women thank God every day they are not married to you.' Anna had decided that the velvet gloves were coming off as far as Mícheal was concerned.

'Have you found a sitter yet?' Conor shouted from the bedroom.

'Nn ...' Anna started to say, but changed her answer as she looked at Mícheal. 'Yes. I have the perfect sitter.'

'Who?' Conor called.

'Mícheal!'

'Are you mad? He can't be trusted with children.'

'He's right,' Mícheal stammered. 'I have no experience with children. They scare me.' He was backing out of the kitchen with a frightened look on his face.

Anna advanced on him with a cheery smile. 'Our children won't bite. We'll be back in two hours. They will be perfectly behaved if you feed them and read them a story before bedtime. They'll love having you mind them, won't you children?' The children nodded wordlessly, their eyes big. 'Anyway,' she continued, 'this is the perfect opportunity to pay us back for our hospitality!'

'OK then. But don't be long. And I refuse to kiss

them goodnight or read bedtime stories,' Mícheal grunted.

Anna quickly changed into a black jacket and skirt, her constant standby for emergencies. She pinned up her hair and clipped a pair of gold hoops into her ears. A little powder, some mascara, a touch of blusher and she was ready.

'We won't be long. Two minutes in the micro-wave, and the dinner is ready. Have fun! Bye darlings,' she chanted to a still-stunned Mícheal and the two children. She and a sullen Conor swept out of the apartment and into the lift.

The British embassy was packed with people. Conor turned his back on Anna and joined a group of diplomats who were discussing the imminent Irish presidency of the European Union. Anna looked desperately around for a familiar face, Monique, Teresa or, hopefully, Juan. But the only person she knew was Sarah.

'Hi, Anna. How are you? And Conor?'

'Great, thanks.'

'And how are the children? Tina and Dickie?'

'Lena and Declan,' Anna corrected. 'They're fine. Mícheal is minding them tonight.'

'But Mícheal hates children! How did you get him to do that?'

'You wouldn't understand. It's a female thing.'

'Oh.' Sarah looked confused. She knew she had been insulted but not quite how.

Anna chatted half-heartedly with a few diplomats' wives and nibbled on some of the canapés, which consisted of cold sausage rolls and meat balls on sticks.

She could see Susanna chatting animatedly to an unfortunate group of ambassadors' wives. Conor had finally had enough and joined her to say goodbye to the host and hostess. They drove home in silence.

When they came into the living room, they found Mícheal fast asleep on the sofa with a teddy bear in his lap. Declan was watching a French pornographic film on television and Lena was tripping around dressed in one of Anna's dresses and high-heeled shoes.

'Some babysitter he turned out to be!' Conor grunted. He disappeared into the bedroom without a second glance. Anna was left to sort out the children and the now snoring babysitter. At least the children are still alive, she thought to herself. She ushered the children into their room, got them into bed and said goodnight.

'He was a really good babysitter,' Declan declared. 'We could do what we wanted and he didn't even notice. But he cheated when we played cards. I saw him put two up the sleeve of his jumper. But I won anyway. We don't need Assumpta any more. We could keep Mícheal. And he's a boy.'

'I prefer Assumpta.' Lena yawned. 'She takes care of us much better. Babysitters shouldn't have beards.' She yawned again and gave her mother a hug.

'Beards are cool. I'm going to grow one when I'm older,' Declan announced. He snuggled into his bed and was asleep in an instant.

Anna put out the lights in the children's rooms. She decided to leave Mícheal on the sofa. He could stay there all night for all she cared. He probably always slept in his clothes, anyway. She went out to the kitchen to clean up the mess that Mícheal and the children had made, and to cook Conor a light supper. She sighed as she remembered his anger. And he doesn't even know about my job, she thought.

Conor came into the kitchen with the Irish newspapers. He had not had a chance to look at them yet and was going to read them while he ate.

'Where were you this morning?'

'I was at Betsy's office. She asked me to help her with some work.'

She was about to tell him that she hadn't enjoyed it much and was thinking of not continuing, when he snorted, 'Work? You? But you can't do anything! Is she mad?'

'I'm not a complete moron, you know. Betsy has offered me a part-time position as her assistant. I'll be working in the mornings while the children are at school. Don't worry, nothing will change. I'll still run the house as before.' She decided not to tell him that the job was only for two months.

'You bet nothing will change. You're not doing it. And that's final. I'm not going to eat fast food heated up in the microwave just so that you can play the career woman.'

'You're very picky, for someone who was brought up on tinned spaghetti and baked beans,' Anna snorted.

'Are you insinuating that my mother is a bad cook?' Conor demanded.

'Cook?' Anna snorted. 'Anyone who crunches crisps on top of a bowl of soup from a packet and calls it *croutons* doesn't deserved to be called ...' She stopped. 'But we're not arguing about your mother. This time,' she added.

'You can't manage the things you are supposed to do as it is!' Conor shouted. 'How are you going to find the time for everything?'

'I'll ... I'll ... make lists.' Sarah always made lists and Conor had mentioned to Anna what a good idea this was. 'I thought you loved independent women. You're always praising Sarah.'

'But she's not a woman.'

'What?'

'I mean she isn't my wife. I never think of her as a woman in any case.'

'I'm sure she would be delighted to hear that. Why don't you tell her tomorrow?' Anna's tone was scathing. 'I just want to do something more interesting than arranging flowers and buying groceries,' she explained. She would never admit to him how boring she had found the morning. 'I want a career of my own. I might get into interior design this way.'

'Interior design!' Conor snorted. 'Ha. You could start by picking up your clothes in the bedroom. That would be great interior design.'

'It's easy for you to sneer. This is only a start. When the hotel is finished, I can look for another job. I will have experience and references then.'

'Experience! Of what? Lifting a phone and switching on a computer? That will get you very far. That's what you want to neglect your family for?'

'I won't neglect anyone. Can't you understand that I just don't want to spend the rest of my life playing golf and bridge. And I don't want to end up as one of the ladies who lunch.'

'Golf? Bridge? Lunch? You hate cards, you have never been near a golf course and these days you don't eat lunch because you're always on a diet.' But the fight had gone out of Conor. He was tired and just wanted to eat and read his papers. He didn't really think that Anna would stick it out for long. She was easily bored. 'I suppose it's not as bad as that time when you tried to get your silly novel published,' he remarked.

'It was not silly! It just takes a long time to get a novel published.'

'Yeah. Forever *is* a long time.'

'I don't want to talk about that now.'

'OK. Let's drop it. I just want to read the papers.' He unfolded the paper and started to read. 'Bloody hell!' he shouted.

'I don't care what you say. I'm going to keep my job.'

'It's not about your stupid job. Look at this,' Conor yelled and waved the *Irish Telegraph* in front of Anna. 'It's about that hotel. It's in Kinsale. They're going to build a hotel in the fort. I don't believe it.'

'In Charles Fort? But that's impossible,' Anna replied. 'It's a listed building and a very popular tourist attraction. Who's stupid enough to think that they can get planning permission to build anything there? It must be a bunch of silly Americans. They'll try anything.'

'No,' Conor replied, studying the newspaper, 'it's a bunch of silly Spaniards, actually. Sanchez Construction, it says.' He looked at Anna, his eyes wide. She stared back.

'Sanchez Construction,' they said in unison.

'It couldn't be . . .' Anna whispered.

'Oh, yes, it could,' Conor replied, studying the paper. 'Carlos Sanchez, the head of the construction company, revealed plans for a three-hundred-bedroom hotel and marina at Charles Fort in Kinsale,' he read. 'It is the perfect spot for a luxury hotel which will cater for yachtsmen from all over the world. It will turn Kinsale into a luxury resort like Marbella and St Tropez. How bloody awful.' He shuddered.

'Marbella with Irish weather,' Anna snorted. 'Rain and gale-force winds. And that's only in July.'

'Shut up and listen,' Conor snapped, and continued to read aloud. 'Mr Sanchez is confident that planning permission will be granted. This scheme will create hundreds of jobs in the area, both during construction and when the hotel employs staff, which he assures will all be local. We are negotiating with members of the county council at the moment, and are hopeful that they will realise what a huge boost this development will be for Kinsale, said Mr Sanchez. He maintains he is on very friendly terms with a member of the county council.' Conor turned pale. 'I bet he is,' he whispered.

'What? Who?'

'My father,' Conor replied. 'I told Carlos to call on him. I phoned Dad last week and told him that Carlos would arrive and to give him a good time. But I didn't mean, I didn't know . . . Oh God.'

'But your father can't give them permission to

build on his own,' Anna tried to reassure him. 'The county council will never agree. The government won't allow it. It's right in the middle of Nolan's constituency. He'll make sure it won't happen.'

'A lot of people seem to believe it will. There are demonstrations in Kinsale. Look.' He showed Anna the front page of the paper where she could see a photograph of demonstrators carrying placards bearing inscriptions such as HANDS OFF OUR FORT and SPANISH VANDALS CLEAR OFF!

'I'm going to phone my father right now.' Conor rose and went into the hall. Anna could hear him dial, and a short discussion followed.

'What did he say?' Anna asked when Conor came back into the kitchen.

'He wasn't too upset. He said that Carlos was a very nice man, but a bit unrealistic. Dad had tried to explain to him that his scheme was impossible. In any case, the construction company have sent in their planning application. It will be refused, of course. In the meantime, there is a huge protest campaign in Kinsale. Dad thinks it's a storm in a tea cup. In fact, he seems to enjoy the excitement.'

'Carlos was trying to tell me about this during the dinner at the château, but he was interrupted,' Anna said.

'And he mentioned it to me but I didn't listen,' Conor added.

'Well, it has nothing to do with us,' Anna remarked. 'It will all be forgotten in a few days.'

'I hope so. I don't want to have my name involved with this row. If Nolan thinks I had anything to do with a scheme to destroy a historic site in his beloved Kinsale, it'll be bad for my career.'

'Don't be silly. It won't come to that.' And very soon your career will improve no end, thanks to me, she thought.

'I suppose you're right.'

'What about my job then? Are you going to keep making a fuss about it?'

'I'm fed up with you and your bloody job. But OK,' he sighed. 'If you must. You won't be able to keep it up for long.'

'Just watch me!'

The next morning Conor found Anna at the kitchen table writing lists. She was dressed in a light blue linen suit and had put her hair up, which she hoped made her look cool and businesslike.

'Good morning. Here's your list.' She handed him a piece of paper with half a dozen items on it.

'My what?'

'Your list. Everyone will have to do a few extra chores while I'm working. Those are yours.'

'You must be joking!' Conor exclaimed, glancing at his piece of paper. 'Collect dry cleaning? Bitcher?'

'Oh, sorry, it should be butcher,' Anna said. 'You have to pick up the meat for tonight's dinner.'

'Lay table, check homework,' he continued. 'What *is* this? Have you gone completely bonkers? I haven't time to do all this!'

'You have to make time,' Anna replied. 'If every-one did just a few little things ...'

'Forget it!' Conor interrupted and threw his list on the floor. 'If you can't manage your job and the running of the house, you shouldn't be working.'

'It's just a little reorganisation,' Anna replied. 'But if you don't want to do it, it's your problem. Pity about that suit, though.'

'What do you mean?' Conor asked.

'Well, since I'm not going to collect it, you'll never see it again if you don't get it yourself. I wonder what they do with clothes that are not picked up . . .'

'All right,' Conor snarled. 'I'll get it.'

'You might as well get the meat too, as it's next door,' Anna directed. 'Or maybe we should try a vegetarian diet?'

'OK,' Conor snapped. 'But that's it. I'm not doing another thing and that's final.'

'Thank you, darling,' Anna smiled.

'Look! I've got things to do!' Declan ran into the kitchen waving a piece of paper. 'It says, Pick up your toys and do your homework. I even have to lay out my clothes in the evening for the next day. It's called 'ficiency, Mammy says! It doesn't say anything about having fun or watching TV,' he continued, looking worried. 'Does that mean it isn't allowed?'

'Of course not, sweetheart,' Anna reassured him. 'The lists are just meant to help you organise your day. And it's called *e*fficiency.'

Assumpta and Lena were studying their lists in silence. They looked glumly at each other. Their haphazard, carefree life seemed to be at an end.

'Make your bed. Empty dishwasher,' Lena read. 'But I always do it anyway, and you say what a good girl. Why do I need a list?'

'It's just to remind you. And you *are* a good girl.'

Assumpta just looked at her piece of paper and sighed. Anna was disappointed. She had been up since six o'clock that morning working on the lists. She thought they would all be delighted. She had even been tempted to give Mícheal a list. There would have been just two items on it. 'One. Pack. Two. Leave.' But she had not been quite brave enough.

'Where is your list?' Conor asked Anna.

'I don't need one. I know what to do. One. Go to work. Two. The usual things.'

'If anyone needs a list it's you,' he remarked. 'I have never met anyone who forgets to do so many things.'

'Yes. Whatever,' Anna said vaguely. 'I have to go to work now.' She got up from the table. 'If you are wondering what to do, just look at your lists. Byeee.' She didn't see the glum looks directed at her departing back, or feel the mutiny in the air.

Anna was trying to answer both phones at once when she heard a knock on the door.

'Come in. Please hold,' she said into each receiver. The computer made a strange sound and the screen went blank. Someone came into the room. She lifted her eyes and looked into Juan's face.

'Working? You look sweet playing the little career woman.' He smiled at her.

'I'm not playing. If you have come to waste time, you can leave. I have a lot of work to do.' She wasn't going to tell him that this was the first time she had done anything at all in the office for several days.

'I just came to check on the workmen.'

'Well, that was kind. I'll tell Betsy you called.'

Anna turned her attention to the two calls. 'As you can see, I'm very busy,' she said when the last caller had hung up. 'Maybe it would be better if you came back later.'

'I like watching girls at work.' He sat down on the edge of her desk and folded his arms. A little smile played on his lips. The phone rang again. Anna nearly jumped out of her skin. She wasn't used to this much activity. It was a representative from a Swedish textile company who was supplying the upholstery fabric for the sofas and chairs. The conversation continued for about twenty minutes. Anna tried to keep her voice businesslike while Juan attempted to make her laugh by pulling faces. He finally tickled the back of her neck with the end of a pencil. She managed to end the call without losing her cool, but she was angry.

'That was unbelievably childish. How dare you disturb me like this! Please go.'

'Oh, come on, darling, you can't be enjoying this. Let me take you to lunch.'

Anna had to admit to herself that going to lunch with Juan would be far more pleasant than sitting doing this mind-bogglingly boring job.

'I enjoy it enormously, as a matter of fact,' she replied. 'And I'm good at it. Now, if you'll excuse me, I have work to do.' She switched on the e-mail and tried to ignore him.

'OK, darling. Maybe another time. You'll soon get bored. But you do look cute behind that desk. I did come here for another reason though.'

'Yes?'

'I want to give you the letter for Seamus Nolan.'

He took a white envelope from his breast pocket and handed it to Anna. 'Put this somewhere safe. You'll give it to Nolan during the dinner in Dublin on Saturday.'

'How do I do that?'

'It's all arranged. At the end of the dinner, when they are serving coffee, you go to the ladies' room. Stay there exactly five minutes. When you come out, Nolan will be outside. Alone. Just give him the envelope and go back to your table.'

'That's it?'

'Yes. That's all you need to do. Thank you so much, darling Anna.' Juan smiled, caressing her cheek with his finger. 'I really appreciate your help. Now, put that letter away and don't lose it. And not a word to anyone. Remember, this little favour could be the turning point in your husband's career.'

Anna put the letter into her handbag. She had a strange feeling about it, and she looked up at Juan, her eyes worried. He smiled back in a way that made her heart melt. I just wish he wasn't so bloody gorgeous, she thought.

CHAPTER 8

'Please take a seat, *madame*, Monsieur Adolphe will join you in a moment.'

Anna sat down nervously in the chair offered to her. She was in Carita's, the most fashionable beauty salon in Paris. She had decided, after a lot of pressure from Monique, to cut her long hair. She had been given the day off by Betsy, who would be in the office herself all day and could deal with the phone calls.

Anna had been in Dublin with Conor the previous weekend to attend the official dinner for the French foreign minister at Iveagh House, which housed the Department of Foreign Affairs. It was a wonderful evening and she enjoyed catching up with some of her friends among the Irish civil servants and their wives. She had bought a new long dress in Paris because her old one did not fit her. It was too big! She celebrated with a lovely creation from the boutique around the corner from their apartment.

The formal dining room at Iveagh House, once the ballroom, had been restored to its former splendour. Conor and Anna sat at a table with some of his colleagues and several young politicians. There was a lively discussion about a wide variety of subjects including, of course, the big row about the proposed development in Kinsale. It was generally agreed that it would never be built.

'The Taoiseach won't allow it,' Sean Murphy, one of the Irish diplomats, remarked. 'He'll be in enough hot water as it is when Lizzie's book comes out next week.'

'Lizzie is on the warpath,' Mrs Murphy agreed. 'She will destroy him.'

'I don't believe that,' Noel Grogan, a young Fine Gael politician retorted. 'That man is indestructible. He'll just shrug it off and carry on as before.'

'I saw an artist's impression of the hotel in the *Irish Telegraph* last week,' Sean announced. 'It's pretty horrendous. It looks like a huge Spanish hacienda with Moorish columns and arches. It will be called Hotel Sanchez del Mar. They are proposing to build a huge marina in Summer Cove as well. It will be a bloody mess.'

'But it won't be built,' Conor stated. 'Take my word for it.'

'I wouldn't be so sure,' Noel argued. 'Those awful apartment blocks on the hills above Kinsale were built despite the protests of the local population. It must have been some kind of fiddle.'

'Fine Gael was in government at that time,' a Fianna Fáil politician stated.

'That had nothing to do with it,' Noel Grogan protested.

'The Taoiseach is a Liberal Socialist,' Conor said.

'He wouldn't allow this to happen.'

The discussion turned back to the coming revelations of Lizzie Dobbins and her affair with the Taoiseach. Everyone, including members of his own party, seemed to be looking forward with great glee to see Seamus Nolan embarrassed.

Once the meal was over, Anna's role as messenger went off as planned. She excused herself to 'powder her nose' when the coffee was being served, and the Taoiseach was waiting for her in the deserted corridor when she came out of the ladies' room.

'Good evening, my dear,' he said with a smile. 'You look particularly lovely tonight.'

'Thank you,' she replied nervously. 'I have the letter here.' She took an envelope out of her evening bag and handed it to him.

'Excellent, dear girl. I am most grateful.' He put a hand on her shoulder.

'It was no problem,' she stammered, as she broke away from him and ran down the corridor.

'I won't forget this,' Nolan called. 'You'll be rewarded in a very special way.'

Anna was shaking as she came back to her table. She downed a large brandy offered to her by a waiter, and felt a little better. Phew, she thought, I'm glad that's over.

Now, in the beauty salon, she looked around to see if the famous Adolphe was on his way. She was looking forward to having her hair done by this so-called genius. But there was no sign of him. Monique had warned her that she would have to wait. But it was actually nice just to sit and do nothing for a change.

Life had been rather hectic lately.

Anna had been working for two weeks and was used to her new life. She still found the work boring, but she had started taking a book or a magazine with her to the office, and sometimes she used the many idle moments to write long letters, do her nails, pluck her eyebrows, or do other little grooming jobs. If I keep this job I'll soon be as polished as Monique, she thought.

The few hours she spent in the office were the most relaxing of the entire day. The rest of her time was taken up with housework, child care and entertaining. Conor seemed content. Maybe he was a bit too content? Anna found it suspicious that he was so meek. He did not blow up in his usual way when things went wrong. Not even the evening she forgot that the ambassador was coming to dinner.

'Mammy! There is someone coming into the building who looks just like the ambassador,' Declan had told her, looking out the window.

'What?'

'Anna, I told you I had invited him last week,' Conor said. 'His wife is away for the weekend. You said it was fine. Weren't you listening?'

'Oh, God. I'm sorry.' She swallowed nervously while she tried to find a solution. 'He'll be here in a few minutes. Give him plenty to drink while I throw something together.'

It had been all right in the end, but the dinner, mainly consisting of stew from the freezer that she quickly microwaved, was far from the tasty meal she usually served. The ambassador looked surprised, but politely chewed the tough meat and ate the vanilla ice cream with chocolate sauce from a bottle.

'Is it hard to cope?' Conor had asked gently (too gently!) as she tidied up. He didn't help her. It wasn't on his list.

'No, it's fine,' she had replied, trying not to sound too exhausted. Why didn't he lose his temper as usual? It was making her nervous.

'*Bonjour, madame*. What can I do for you?' Anna was startled out of her reverie. Adolphe was standing behind her looking at her long hair with delight in his eyes. He was a handsome man in his early fifties. He wore his blond hair in a pony tail and he had an earring in his left ear. His tall, thin body was dressed entirely in white. Adolphe was the king of French coiffure, the most sought-after hairdresser this side of the Atlantic. No fashionable woman in Paris would go to an important event without consulting him. 'He is an absolute genius,' Monique had said. It had taken her three weeks of pleading to get an appointment for Anna. So how could she refuse to go? In any case, the famous ball at the Opéra Garnier was taking place that evening. It was the perfect opportunity to have her hair done. Anna wanted a change. Her long hair seemed too old-fashioned and girlish. She was ready for a more sophisticated look.

'You may do what you want.'

'*Oui, madame*,' Adolphe replied and, turning to his assistant, a dark, rather beautiful girl, shouted, '*On coupe!*' He grabbed Anna's hair in both his hands and lifted it off her neck and shoulders. His eyes lit up.

'You will be stunning. Believe me.'

After two hours of shampooing, conditioning, cutting and many cups of strong coffee, a startled Anna looked at herself in the mirror. A new face she hardly recognised looked back.

Adolphe had cut her hair into a short bob. The expert cut had released her natural curls, framing her face and making her eyes look enormous. The short hair revealed her fine cheekbones and delicate chin. Her neck looked long and graceful and her shoulders could finally show her excellent posture.

'Now, shake your head.' Anna shook and her hair danced around her face and settled again into the same perfect shape.

Her eyes shone. 'I will tell everyone that it was you who cut my hair.'

'There will be no need. They will know.' His conceit did not shock her. He was right. Who else could have achieved such a miracle?

It had stopped raining by the time the taxi bearing Anna and Conor arrived at the Opéra Garnier. The wet pavements reflected the street lights and the flood-lit opera house. A huge crowd had arrived to watch the many celebrities who had been invited to the ball, and it gave Anna a thrill to walk up the red carpet to the steps in front of the enormous building.

Inside, Conor and Anna walked arm in arm up the long curving staircase. Conor looked at Anna with pride. She was stunning tonight. She wore the new dress with the red velvet bodice and ballerina-length black taffeta skirt. She had black patent leather pumps on her tiny feet. He loved her new short hairdo, and her now thinner figure reminded him of the lovely girl he had fallen in love with twelve years ago.

Anna felt like a different woman with her new look.

The reactions had been mixed when she came home.

'Mammy! You look so pretty!' Lena had exclaimed.

'I don't like it,' grunted Declan. 'You don't look like a mammy any more.'

'It's gorgeous.' Assumpta smiled.

Anna knew that Mícheal was going to say something rude. She was not disappointed.

'Looks a bit butch, if you ask me,' he grunted. He had seemed resentful of the fact that she was working. He had been left very much to his own devices these last few weeks and showed his displeasure in snide remarks like 'How's life in the fast lane?' or 'Have you been fired yet?' She tried to ignore him, but she knew that there would be a showdown one of these days.

The Opéra foyer was teeming with people. Champagne was being served before the performance. The Paris Opéra Ballet were performing *Giselle,* one of Anna's favourite ballets. Tonight, one of her friends from ballet school, Pierre du Perrier, was dancing the main male part. He had recently been appointed principal dancer with the Paris Opéra company and was one of Europe's biggest stars. Anna and Pierre had become close friends when he had taught some classes at her ballet school. He had been very sympathetic during her struggle to become a professional dancer, never once pointing out that a tall girl with fat thighs was not prima ballerina material. He was gay, but wanted to keep it quiet, so Anna had pretended to be his girlfriend. Conor had been in on the secret, and the three of them had had great fun, once Pierre realised that Conor was interested in Anna and not Pierre. Anna knew that the dancers had been invited to the dinner and to dancing after the show. She was looking forward to talking to Pierre about old times.

'Anna! You look *très chic*.' Monique was looking at her with satisfaction. 'I knew Adolphe would do a great job.'

'You don't look too bad yourself.' In fact, Monique looked wonderful, dressed in a silver-sequinned dress that shimmered as she moved. Her hair was dressed in short curls all over her head. She was one of the most elegant women there.

The Opéra Garnier is one of the most beautiful theatres in the world. As Anna sat waiting for the performance to start, she looked up to admire the famous ceilings by Chagall, the Venetian chandeliers and the gold leaf decorations. The musicians were tuning their instruments and the theatre was slowly filling up with elegant people. Anna and Conor had fun trying to recognise famous faces. The seat beside Anna was still empty as the lights dimmed and the curtain slowly rose. The music started and Anna was lost in an enchanted world.

As the sad story of Giselle unfolded, Anna became more and more moved, partly by the story and partly by the dancing. Pierre du Perrier was truly magnificent in the part of Loys, the count who pretends to be a poor country boy to win Giselle's heart. He deserved to be hailed as the greatest dancer since Baryshnikov. Anna's heart sang as she watched him, and she felt a twinge of longing. She realised how much she missed the ballet. Not the hard slog, the hours at the *barre,* the disappointment of not being good enough or the endless dieting, but the dancing. Oh, the dancing! Her eyes filled with tears and she started to sniff. As usual, she had forgotten to bring a handkerchief. She touched Conor's arm.

'Shhh!' He looked at her with irritation.

'Have you got a hankie?' she whispered.

'No. Be quiet!' he hissed back. He wasn't going to offer her the pristine white handkerchief that decorated the top pocket of his new tuxedo. Anna tried to wipe away the tears with her hand. She sniffed again.

The person on the other side of her handed her a dazzlingly white handkerchief. It smelled of Hermès cologne. Anna wiped her eyes and blew her nose discreetly. She turned her head to thank the latecomer, and Juan looked back at her with tenderness in his eyes. He took her hand, kissed it and held it until the end of the ballet.

The curtain was lowered for the last time. There had been more than ten curtain calls as the audience rose to their feet and clapped, shouted and whistled their appreciation. The Parisians loved a good performance, and this one had been outstanding. Conor had forgotten his irritation and beamed at Anna. 'Wasn't it fantastic?'

'Wonderful,' she agreed. But she didn't mean the ballet. She looked around, but Juan had gone to find his table for the dinner. Slowly, Conor and Anna followed his example.

There was a big noticeboard in the foyer displaying the table plans. Anna found her name between those of Pierre and Juan. Conor was to sit opposite her between Monique and one of the principal female dancers. He would enjoy that, Anna thought. She would have fun catching up on old times with Pierre. Hopefully, Juan wouldn't feel too left out. No, he had a famous actress on his other side.

'Anna! My darling.' Pierre was pushing through the crowd to get to her. He wrapped his arms around her in a warm hug. Then he let her go and took a good look at her. '*Magnifique*. Absolutely gorgeous. You haven't changed a bit. And I love your hair.' His brown eyes flashed as he grinned happily at her. 'And Conor. Darling Conor.' He kissed Conor on both cheeks.

'Steady!' Conor protested. But he was pleased to see Pierre, who looked wonderfully fit in a tight tuxedo and frilly shirt. His skin glowed, and hours of gruelling dancing didn't seem to have tired him in the least. He put his arms around Anna and Conor and marched them over to one of the round tables.

'I managed to change the seating plan so we could sit together. You have some kind of Spanish yo-yo on the other side.' At that moment Anna caught sight of Juan, who was not looking amused.

Pierre, Anna and Conor were enjoying themselves

talking about their years together in Stockholm. Pierre and Anna gossiped about well-known dancers, and Pierre filled her in on what had happened to all of them. Anna tried to involve Juan in the conversation at the start. But she soon forgot him in her excitement. She didn't notice that he was becoming more and more annoyed. He hardly touched his meal, and barely spoke to his neighbour on the other side. He just sat there, playing with the cutlery and staring angrily straight ahead. Monique suddenly noticed his face. Oh-oh, she thought, the little boy is being ignored. She tried to catch Anna's eye, but to no avail. Anna and Pierre had their heads together giggling at a photograph Pierre had brought.

The members of the orchestra were beginning to tune their instruments. Pierre looked up. He whispered something to Anna. She nodded, looking nervous. Pierre rose from the table and walked over to the leader of the orchestra. As he returned to his place, they started playing a slow tango. Pierre smiled and held out both his hands to Anna. She took his hands and rose slowly to her feet. They started to dance. She was tense at first, as she felt the many eyes on her, and she missed a beat.

'Forget the people. Just relax and feel the music,' Pierre muttered. 'Look into my eyes. Remember how I taught you to dance the tango.'

Anna remembered, and the years rolled back. Anna and Pierre danced the tango in perfect rhythm. The music increased in volume and speed. The dancers followed faultlessly, unsmiling, their eyes locked together. The guests were hypnotised. This was magnificent.

The music stopped suddenly and Pierre and Anna were rooted to the spot in a deep tango dip. Anna was bent back and Pierre leaned over her. They were eye to eye, nose to nose. A wild applause suddenly erupted. Anna and Pierre straightened up and hugged each other, laughing and breathless. They bowed. The music changed to a more modern tune, and the floor slowly filled with dancing couples. Anna sank down on her chair still panting and smiling. Conor threw her a kiss. Pierre asked Monique to dance.

'Phew! That was exhausting! But fun.' Anna smiled at Juan, who didn't smile back.

'You never told me you could dance like that,' he muttered.

'You never asked.' She was trying to joke away his bad mood. She had drunk rather a lot of wine and the dancing had made her feel euphoric. What was the matter with Juan? He looked so sour. It must be something Spanish, she decided.

Juan had a hard look in his eyes. The skin around his nostrils was white and a muscle twitched in his jaw.

Juan had been taken aback by Anna's transformation. Her job, her new hairdo and her trim figure told him that she was becoming more confident and independent. She was no longer the pretty housewife who would fall for him like a ripe plum. She didn't even wear Chanel No. 5 any more, she wore Shalimar. That she was becoming something different both annoyed and excited him. He had played the game of flirting with her in order to make her deliver that letter. And he knew he had to keep her sweet so that he could use her again, if he needed to. But he was becoming more than a little attracted to her. Used to the undivided attention of most women, and annoyed by her obvious delight in the company of the dancer made Juan forget to play his part in the scheme he was involved in, forget to thank her for delivering the envelope to Seamus Nolan, forget even to be the cool, aloof man of the world. At that moment he was just a red-hot Spanish male who was being ignored.

'I love to dance,' Anna continued. 'Don't you? Why don't you ask me to dance?'

'Certainly not.' Juan rose from his chair and walked towards the exit without a second glance. Anna looked at his departing figure with confusion. He had never been so rude before.

'He looks like a man scorned.' Monique settled into the chair that Juan had vacated. 'Or a little boy whose favourite toy was stolen.'

'What do you mean?'

'Women don't ignore Juan Valverde,' Monique explained. 'They usually throw their knickers at him. This is a new experience. And he doesn't like it. He is totally obsessed with you at the moment. He looked positively homicidal all through dinner. I wouldn't have been surprised if he had taken out a gun and shot both you and Pierre. Terrified I would have been, but not surprised.'

'But Pierre is gay. I thought everybody knew. He came out last year. He lives with another man.'

'Really? What a waste.' Monique sighed.

'I know. But everybody loves Pierre. He keeps his

private life very private. And he is the best friend a girl could have.'

Despite Juan's abrupt departure, Anna continued to enjoy herself. She danced with Conor, who twirled her around the room in a wild rumba, with Jean-Pierre, with some of the other male dancers, and even, to her surprise, with Patrick Daly, the Canadian ambassador, who had been sitting at another table.

'Would you like to dance?' he had asked. 'That is, if you don't think it's a form of sexual harassment.'

'I'm surprised you even want to speak to me,' she replied.

'I don't. I want to dance. Now, be quiet and let's have a go.'

He was a terrible dancer. 'This is fun,' he said, twirling her around the dance floor, bumping into Jean-Pierre and Monique, who gave Patrick annoyed looks. 'Oops! Sorry,' he exclaimed and stepped on Anna's foot, making her wince. He held her so tightly she could hardly breathe, her face pressing into his chest. He twirled her around again, narrowly missing a big urn filled with flowers. Around and around they twirled, faster and faster.

Anna was so dizzy she was beginning to feel nauseous. The room spun so she could no longer see where they were. 'Please,' she gasped, 'please stop. Let me go!' The music ended. Patrick suddenly stopped twirling and let go of Anna. She stumbled, and would have fallen if he had not caught her by the arm. 'Oh my God,' she panted, holding her hand against her heaving bosom.

'Wow! That's what I call dancing,' he beamed,

wiping his damp forehead with a handkerchief. 'What did you think of that, eh?'

'You're dangerous!' Anna gasped, when she had caught her breath.

'I knew you'd be impressed.'

Anna and Conor didn't arrive home until five in the morning. Anna smiled happily as she undressed. The evening had been truly wonderful. She frowned slightly, remembering Juan's bad mood. It had shown her a side of him she neither understood nor liked. She got into bed and snuggled close to Conor, who was fast asleep. She felt suddenly lonely.

A week later, Anna was running up the street in the rain. They were having a dinner party that evening and she had forgotten to buy the half-dozen items without which, according to Conor, the party would be a flop; they included toothpicks for the olives, paper napkins, tiny chocolate mints to go with the coffee (which nobody drank) and bread rolls, thousands of bread rolls. Conor never helped with any of the preparations, but there were certain things he insisted they must have. Bread rolls were one. Nobody really took more than one, Anna had observed, but if they didn't offer bloody bread rolls to their guests every ten seconds, Conor felt they were bad hosts. So here she was, with a huge bag of fresh rolls that were becoming soggy in the rain.

They had invited fourteen people, most of whom were what Anna called 'the usual suspects'. She had asked Pierre, who was at a loose end because his partner was out of town, Patrick Daly, whom Conor

– against Anna's wishes – wanted to introduce to Betsy, Sarah, because Conor insisted, and Mícheal because she couldn't lock him in his room.

Juan, whom Anna hadn't seen since he had stormed out of the Opéra Garnier, had also been invited, because Conor wanted to keep a good contact with the Spanish. (Little did he know that Juan knew less about Spain's foreign policy than did Sarah's cat.) It would be a fun evening.

The children had left to spend a few weeks with their grandparents in Sweden. Anna had put them on a plane that morning feeling very lonely. She knew they would have a good time, and that they would forget about her within minutes of their arrival.

That evening at five minutes to eight, Anna was running around the apartment placing little bowls of nuts on the tables, tidying away newspapers and switching on lamps. Conor did what he usually did just before a party: he was drinking a large gin and tonic and telling Anna that nobody would come. She ignored him. Mícheal had just stuck his wet and woolly head through the door and asked what he should wear. Anna told him to wear a pullover. His suit would put the guests off their dinner, she decided.

She was wearing a short black knitted dress that looked demure from the front with long sleeves and a high neckline, but plunged to her waist at the back. Her very high-heeled strappy shoes made her wobble a bit, but they showed off her legs. She wore no jewellery except for a pair of long dangling earrings made of turquoises set in silver.

'How do I look?' she asked Conor, pleased with herself.

'You look fine,' he replied without taking his eyes off the television screen.

'You mean you like me naked with my hair dyed green?'

'It's lovely, darling.' Conor didn't look up.

'Conor,' Anna screamed. 'Look at me! For once, pay attention!'

'Calm down! What's the matter now?'

'Just look at me! Do ... you ... like ... it? Try to concentrate on me for only a brief moment!'

'But you always look well. What's different?' Conor looked at Anna with confused eyes.

'Never mind.'

Mícheal came in to the living room dressed in a pullover Anna had never seen before. It was a navy V-neck with a design of trout and reindeer in bright yellow across the front. He wore a white shirt and a yellow knitted tie. His corduroys had been pressed and his sandals looked as if they had been polished. He did not look as messy as usual.

'That's an interesting pullover. Is it new?'

'My mother knitted it the year before she died. She combined an Irish and a Scandinavian pattern. I only wear it on special occasions. There are matching socks.' He pulled up one of the legs of his trousers to reveal blue socks with smaller reindeer and trout around the edge at the top.

'How unusual.' Anna smiled. She was relieved that he looked less weird than usual. At least this pullover was clean.

She went out to the kitchen to check that everything was in order for the party. The menu consisted of foods that required the least possible amount of cooking: smoked salmon, leg of lamb – which if it was undercooked would be typically French and if it was overcooked very Irish (either way, it couldn't go wrong) – followed by cheese, and sorbet for dessert.

There was a marvellous ice-cream shop around the corner where they made delicious sorbets in the most artistic shapes. Anna had asked for the sorbet to look like a huge pear. George, the French waiter who always helped out at their parties, was just taking the sorbet out of its box to put it in the freezer. Assumpta was cutting up the vegetables for the main course and Thelma, the Filipino waitress, was slicing the salmon.

'Is everything OK?'

Thelma and Assumpta nodded, but George looked worried.

'*Madame*, just look at the sorbet!'

'What's wrong with it?' Anna turned to look at the shape that had just come out of the box. 'Oh, my God.' The sorbet didn't bear any resemblance to the pear she had envisioned. It looked like a huge bottom.

'Yes, *madame*,' agreed George. 'It's a leetle bit rude.'

'What are we going to do? It's too late to try to get another dessert. All the shops are closed.' Anna was looking at the bottom with rising panic. Why did things always go wrong when she had a party? she thought, fighting tears.

'We can try and cut a bit out of it to change the shape slightly,' Assumpta suggested. 'It won't look as elegant as it should, but at least it will not look so, ah, suggestive.'

'Yes. I think it's the only solution. See what you can do, George. I'll be in to check on it later. I have to go back, the guests will arrive any minute.'

Sarah was the first guest to arrive, and she headed straight for Mícheal.

'How are you?' she asked him shyly. 'I haven't seen you for a long time.'

'I've been busy,' he replied. 'I haven't time for trivia at the moment.'

'Trivia?'

'Yeah, well, a man's got to work, you know.' Mícheal took a slug of beer which made him burp. Sarah looked at him adoringly. His unsavoury habits only seemed to make her more attracted to him.

'You have to tell me what you are working on,' she exclaimed. 'It must be very interesting.'

'It's very academic. Not something you would understand.' He looked down at Sarah in a pretentious way. She was looking unusually attractive, he thought, dressed in a long dirndl skirt and peasant blouse. She had changed from her normal career woman's style in order to impress him. She was even wearing Birkenstock sandals. He liked the gypsy look that she had been trying to achieve.

'Doesn't Sarah look strange?' Conor whispered to Anna.

'Really weird,' she muttered back. 'Isn't she a bit old for the milkmaid look? And she treats Mícheal as if he was the answer to a woman's prayers.'

They were interrupted by the arrival of more

guests. It was Jean-Pierre and Monique, who looked as if she had been poured into her very tight thin-strapped blue dress. 'So, where is he?' she panted, her eyes darting around the room.

'Who?'

'Your house guest. You said he'd be here.' Oops, Anna thought, Monique hasn't met Mícheal yet!

'Come on,' Anna said, 'I'll introduce you.' Together they walked over to the french windows that led to the terrace, where Sarah was still chatting to Mícheal.

'Mícheal? I want you to meet Monique, who's a great friend of mine.'

Mícheal turned around and stared at Monique. 'Hello,' he grunted, his mouth full of cheese straws. 'Howerya.'

Monique didn't reply, but stared at Mícheal in fascinated horror.

'Cat got your tongue?' he asked. 'Great dress,' he added, 'pity it shrank, he, he.' His laugh ended in a cough, which made him spray beer and bits of cheese straws on his pullover. Monique winced and took a step back. Sarah slapped Mícheal on the back. 'The beer went the wrong way,' he spluttered when he could draw breath again.

'I'm Sarah Maloney,' Sarah volunteered and shook hands with Monique, who was still looking a little dazed.

'Oh, hello,' Monique stammered. 'Excuse me. I have to . . .' She sidled away from Mícheal and walked over to where Anna was greeting Betsy, who was looking fantastic in a pair of black baggy drawstring trousers and a yellow halter neck top.

'Very funny,' Monique snapped, grabbing Anna by the arm. 'Incredible, you said. Unforgettable!'

'Well,' Anna said, 'he is.' She turned to Betsy. 'This is Monique. She is trying to recover from her first encounter with Mícheal.'

'The thinking woman's nightmare,' Betsy replied, shaking hands with Monique. 'I'm Betsy. You look as if you need a drink. I know how you feel. I had an encounter myself with the man from the wild and woolly west.'

Monique shuddered. 'He's like something from a horror film. Love your shoes, by the way. Blahnik?'

'Yes,' Betsy replied, 'how clever of you.' They were friends for life.

'I think Mícheal's great fun,' Betsy remarked 'You never know what he's going to say next.'

'I'm glad you think so,' Anna said. 'You're sitting beside him tonight. I had to put him between you and Sarah. She's weird enough to find him attractive and you're the only other woman who can talk to him without getting sick, screaming or hitting him.'

'OK,' Betsy replied. 'Who's that man?' she asked, looking toward the hall door, which had just opened to admit Patrick Daly. 'Nice.'

'That's the man on your other side,' Anna answered and started to walk to the door. 'But I think you'll prefer Mícheal,' she added over her shoulder.

'What does she mean?' Betsy asked Monique, who just shrugged her shoulders.

Juan arrived, looking sleek in his dark suit. He kissed Anna's hand and uttered a few polite words, his eyes hard. He's still in a snot, she thought, and he is sitting beside me tonight. Hopefully he will just sulk. Nobody will notice.

Pierre was the last guest. He bounced into the room in his usual theatrical way, crushing Anna to him in a warm hug. 'Sorry I'm so late, but the rehearsals ran on and on.'

'Don't worry, darling,' Anna reassured him. 'If you don't mind skipping the drink, we can go into dinner now.'

'Why does that Spaniard look at me as if he wants to hit me?' Pierre asked Anna as they waited to go into the dining room.

'He thinks we are having an affair.'

'We could have one if you want.'

'Stop it, you tart. It's not funny.'

'You bet it's not. He looks positively dangerous to me. Why don't you put him out of his misery and tell him the truth?'

'I think I'll let him stew a bit longer.' Anna smirked.

Anna had placed Patrick Daly on her right as the guest of honour and Betsy on his other side. Juan, as the second most senior diplomat, sat on her left with Monique as his neighbour. She kept a close eye on Betsy and Patrick. She was sure Betsy would heartily dislike Patrick and the patronising way he had with women. She felt a little guilty about having landed Betsy with him. Anna chatted with Patrick for a few minutes over the smoked salmon before she turned away to give Betsy a chance. She looked at Juan with trepidation.

'I was extremely flattered by your invitation,' Juan began. 'I didn't think you would want to be bothered with a Spanish yo-yo now that you have taken up with an old flame.'

'I don't know what you mean. And you haven't thanked me for doing you that little favour. It wasn't easy.'

'Thank you,' he said stiffly. 'I'm most grateful. In any case,' he continued, darting an angry look in Pierre's direction, 'it's obvious what's going on, even if your husband doesn't seem to notice.'

'That didn't worry you before.' Anna was becoming angry.

'I have also noticed the great change in your appearance,' Juan continued, ignoring her last remark, 'due to the rekindled passion in your life, no doubt. Is that a new dress? Very sexy.'

'This old thing?' She had bought it the day before especially for this party (and especially for Juan).

'You look confident. But I know you're not.'

'I'm not?'

'No, you're not. Your life is in a bit of a mess, isn't it? You can hardly cope with your job, your husband ignores you, and you are bored with diplomatic life. On top of that, you're reliving an old romance. You are trying to manage an emotional high-wire act. Be careful, you might fall.' His eyes glittered dangerously in the gloom of the candlelight dining room.

'Will you catch me if I do?'

'You don't need me. There seems to be someone else more than willing to help.'

The dinner progressed smoothly. Anna never tried

anything really complicated at these dinners, and she laughed away any disasters. Tonight everything seemed to be going well. George was now offering round the big platter with the expertly carved rather rare lamb and beautifully arranged vegetables. Thelma followed with the sauce boat. Everything looked fine.

'Keep the bread rolls coming,' Anna whispered to George as she was served. He nodded with a smile. She looked down the table at Conor, who had the wife of a senior French official on his right. They seemed to be having an animated conversation. All the other guests were tucking into the food with enthusiasm.

'Lovely meal, Anna,' Pierre called from further down the table. He lifted his wine glass to her as if in a toast.

'That is the most handsome man in Paris,' Monique sighed on the other side of Juan. 'Pity one couldn't have a fling with him.'

'Because he is in love with Anna?' Juan enquired.

'No, you fool. He's gay.'

'How stupid of me!' he exclaimed, slapping his hand to his forehead.

Anna tried to check on how things between Patrick and Betsy were progressing. Patrick had seemed charmed with Betsy as they were introduced, and she had responded to his wide, admiring smile with a blush. Maybe they would get on, after all. But no. Patrick was looking annoyed as Betsy snapped some-thing at him and turned to her other neighbour, Mícheal. Patrick was looking morosely down at his plate. Anna was not surprised that Betsy was looking so angry. He would annoy the knickers off anyone.

It was time to serve the dessert. Anna was hoping that George would have been able to change the ridiculous shape of the sorbet. She hadn't had a chance to check it before dinner. Assumpta opened the double doors to admit George carrying the big silver platter with the dessert. Anna craned her neck to see what it looked like. The guests were now all busy talking to each other. There was a din of animated conversation around the table.

Anna looked at the sorbet. Her heart sank. George had indeed tried to cut out a bit of it in an attempt to alter the suggestive shape. But it looked even worse. The bottom now had a pair of thighs that were set wide apart. It looked like something out of the *Kama Sutra*. Anna's eyes widened and she glared at George, who gave a Gallic shrug and a look which said 'I did my best.'

'Wow! That's what I call a perfect pear.' Juan's voice was light and full of laughter. 'Is it supposed to be a work of art?'

Anna turned and looked at him with alarm. 'Do something. Quick!' she pleaded under her breath.

Juan rose from his chair with a spoon and fork in his hand. His broad back hid the awful-looking dessert from the rest of the company. He cut a few pieces out of the pear, changing it into a more abstract, geometric shape. Anna sighed with relief, noting that none of the guests had noticed what happened, except Mícheal.

'Did you model for the pudding?' he called to her

across the table. As nobody seemed to know what he meant, Anna simply ignored him.

'Thank you. That was a terrible moment,' she whispered to Juan. He took her hand.

'I was a brute before. Forgive me?' She could only nod in reply. 'And I am most grateful for what you did in Dublin,' he added, lifting her hand to his lips.

The dinner was coming to an end. Patrick clinked his glass and made a short speech, thanking the hostess for the meal. He managed to sound annoyingly super-ior when he talked about her 'efforts in the kitchen', and 'the pretty table'. Anna was fuming as she tried to look pleased. She rose to give the signal to their guests to take coffee on the terrace.

It was a wonderfully mild evening and the guests were soon admiring the views over Paris. The lights of the Eiffel Tower could be seen glinting far in the distance. The stars twinkled in the black sky and a soft breeze played with Anna's hair as she brought around chocolates. George was serving brandy and liqueurs from a big tray. She looked around for Patrick and Betsy, hoping they would have sorted out their differ-ences. Patrick was talking to Conor in the living room, and Betsy was sharing a joke with Mícheal on the terrace.

'What happened?' Anna asked Betsy.

'You mean with that, that Canadian twit? That pompous know-it-all?'

'He is the Canadian ambassador, after all.'

'I don't care who he is. He has no manners. He's an opinionated oaf.'

'That's right,' Mícheal cut in. 'All those North

Americans think they rule the universe. Time they learnt a lesson. They're all gay, anyway. And they're drug addicts.'

'You're very prejudiced for a journalist,' Betsy smirked.

'That's not prejudice. I'm just stating a fact. Bloody Canadian queer.'

'Yeah,' Betsy agreed, 'that's why he hates women. He must be.'

'No, no.' Anna exclaimed. 'Stop it. He's not gay. He's been married. His wife left him not so long ago.'

'I don't blame her,' Betsy stated.

'What did Patrick say that made you so angry?' Anna asked.

'Everything. When I told him I was an interior designer, he said it was *sweet* and *a lovely hobby* for a pretty girl like me. It was downhill from then on.

'Oh God.' Anna giggled.

'I told him that I'm related to Charles Lindbergh, the aviator, you know? He then proceeded to tell me that Charles Lindbergh was a Nazi sympathiser!' Betsy's face was red with anger. 'When I didn't believe him, he said he was going to send me a book on the subject to prove the point. Then he said he felt sorry for women who put their careers before relationships. He said, I bet you think you can have a baby on the Internet. I said no, but maybe he could try to get a personality there. I'm sorry, Anna, the man annoyed me. He also had the nerve to ask me for a date.'

'What did you say?'

'I said I would rather have dinner with Boris Yeltsin!'

'Lovely.' Anna laughed.

'How can he behave like that and still get women to go out with him?'

'He's an ambassador,' Anna explained. 'Women think he's sexy because of his job.'

'But he doesn't seem to know that women have careers or even brains. Where has he been the last thirty years? On a desert island?'

'He's been on diplomatic postings,' Anna replied. 'If you spend long enough only meeting diplomats, you lose touch with the world of normal people.'

'I hate that man.' Betsy declared. He's so pompous. He has no sense of humour either.' That was a mortal sin in Betsy's book. 'He is the kind of man who says, I'm a cereal killer, over the Rice Crispies and expects you to laugh! And he's dressed like an accountant.'

'How do they dress?' Anna wanted to know, looking across at Patrick's dark suit, white shirt and discreet tie.

'Boring.'

'Conor thought you'd be perfect for him.'

'Only if he wanted him murdered.'

The guests were beginning to take their leave. Anna watched as Patrick said a rather stiff goodbye to Betsy.

'Maybe we'll meet again?'

'I hope not,' she replied, shaking his hand limply. She turned to Mícheal. 'Bye sexy,' she laughed, giving him a hug.

'Get off me,' he protested, pushing her away,

but looking pleased all the same. 'It must be my beard,' he said to Sarah. 'It's a real turn-on.' Sarah fumed.

'I'll call you,' Patrick insisted in Betsy's ear.

'Fuck off,' she muttered between her teeth.

'Those two are made for each other,' Juan, who had overheard the exchange, muttered into Anna's ear. 'Goodbye, my sweet.' He placed a kiss, as light as a butterfly, on her lips in the darkness. It burned like fire.

She stayed on the terrace long after the guests had departed. Mícheal had retired to his room and Conor had disappeared into the study to write a report about a conversation he had had with the official from the French foreign office.

Why was she so attracted to Juan? He was a male chauvinist, arrogant, selfish and curiously childish for a man of forty. But he was divinely handsome and the attention he paid her was very flattering. He made her feel young and beautiful. Conor made her feel guilty that she hadn't washed his socks. Juan didn't know or care if she had vacuumed under the beds, remembered to buy yoghurt, or made sure he had enough clean underwear for the following week. She had no idea who washed Juan's socks or underwear. She had never even seen his underwear. She didn't know if he wore any. The mystery of his personal life was exciting. And what about the chemistry between them? It made her dizzy.

All the lights suddenly went out.

'What are you doing?' Anna exclaimed.

'Oh, are you still out here?' Conor said,

annoyed. 'Why don't you go to bed? What's the matter with you? I have to get up early tomorrow. Can't you think of somebody else but yourself, for a change?'

Oh, yes, I can, she whispered to herself.

CHAPTER 9

'Haven't you finished packing yet?' Conor was closing his small suitcase and looking at Anna with irritation. They were preparing to leave for the cruise.

Anna was trying to cram a pair of white shorts into her already overfull case. She had bought a lot of clothes for the cruise at the special sale Monique had brought her to. They had come out of the warehouse exhausted, scratched and bruised, but with armfuls of designer outfits.

'That was the worst sale I've ever been to,' Anna panted, pushing her hair out of her eyes. They were recovering with a glass of cognac at a nearby café.

'I know.' Monique sighed as she inspected her scratched arms. 'But wasn't it worth it? What did you get?'

Monique had told Anna to grab anything in her size and colour, and Anna didn't really know exactly what she had ended up with. She looked into the big holdall she had brought to put her loot in. 'I hope there is something here I can wear, since I paid a bit more than I had planned.' She pulled out a pair of white trousers. 'Yves St Laurent. That's a start.' The trousers were followed by two T-shirts by Versace, one white with gold embroidery, the other one a deep cerise. 'So far, so good. But what am I going to do with these?' She was holding up a pair of pink pedal-pushers and matching bolero top from Delacroix.

'But they're Delacroix, darling. It doesn't matter that they're hideous. In this case it's the label that's chic. Not the garment.' Monique sighed, exasperated. Anna would never really understand fashion.

The rest of the clothes in Anna's bag were wonderful bargains. She had been lucky enough to grab a navy backless linen dress from the Chanel collection, two pairs of shorts, a light-blue silk blouse from Dior, a red swimsuit from Guy Laroche, and a number of scarves and belts from other designers. Monique had not been so lucky this time. Her bag contained items that Anna would label as serious fashion mistakes.

'When am I going to wear these?' Monique muttered to herself as she examined a pair of gold lamé flared trousers.

'How about the Australian bush?' Anna laughed. 'They would frighten any wild animal.'

'*Tais-toi!*' Monique exclaimed and threw the trousers at Anna. 'At these sales you can't always be sure to end up with clothes you can actually wear. It's a bit like playing roulette.'

'Russian roulette, you mean,' Anna added. 'I would rather shoot myself than wear those. Why did you go for the gold lamé anyway? It isn't really your style.'

'I saw that bitch Jeanne la Chienne eyeing it. I didn't want her to have something she really wanted.'

The lady in question was one of the best-known hostesses in Paris. She was disliked by most women because she flirted with their husbands, gossiped about their love affairs, and stole their dinner guests. Men loved her. A good-looking woman of a certain age who would flatter a man until he fell into her bed, Jeanne la Chienne was the queen of Paris society.

'Anyway, I can sell them to her for twice the price later. If I tell her they are the only trousers of that style in town, she will kill for them. Did you notice how stretched her face was? That's the third face-lift she's had in five years. Her eyebrows nearly meet her hairline.'

Monique and Anna launched into a conversation about the other women who had been at the sales and about which of them had had cosmetic surgery and other rejuvenating treatments. It had been a fun day.

Anna turned to Conor as she finally managed to close her suitcase. 'We have plenty of time. The plane doesn't leave until five o'clock.'

They were taking an Olympic Airways flight to Athens. Then a car would pick them up at the airport and bring them to the yacht which was moored in the harbour of Piraeus.

'I don't know why you have packed so many clothes,' Conor grunted. 'I'm only bringing a pair of shorts, a couple of T-shirts, a suit, a few shirts, some underwear and swimming togs.'

'And a mobile phone, a radio, fifteen newspapers

and a couple of folders with documents,' Anna added. 'All of which you will put into my hand luggage, leaving me laden down while you skip on the plane with your hands in your pockets.'

Conor didn't understand why women needed to buy new clothes all the time. He thought that if you bought an outfit, it should last until you died or it fell apart, whichever came first. The fact that fashion changed each year was something that had never really registered with him. 'Why don't you wear that nice blue dress?' he would ask her. 'It's really lovely.'

'You mean that dress that's twelve years old and makes me look like a pregnant camel?' she would reply. 'I'm sorry, darling, but I threw it out.'

Anna tidied the flat and checked the kitchen for any leftover food. Assumpta had gone to Ireland to spend her holiday with her family. Anna went into the empty guest room. They had finally got rid of Mícheal. Just as she was beginning to believe that he would stay forever, she had stumbled on a piece of information about Mícheal's life that she could use against him. Speaking to an English journalist at a party, she had asked about Mícheal.

'Mike, you mean?'

'Well, Mícheal, really. He's so Irish.'

'Irish, my eye! He is no more Irish than you or I.'

'You must be mistaken!' Anna couldn't believe her ears. 'He speaks fluent Irish, he cries his eyes out when he sings "Danny Boy" and he positively lives in that Aran jumper.' You couldn't be more Irish in Anna's eyes.

'I know him well. His real name is Michael

Higgins. His father was a clerk in a solicitor's office in Fulham.'

'But his mother . . . She was –'

'Polish. Came from Krakow.'

Anna's eyes looked as if they were about to fall out of her head. 'But, but,' she stammered, 'why the charade? Why pretend to be Irish?'

'He thought he would have more success as a journalist if he pretended to be an Irish scholar. He went to Ireland fifteen years ago, grew a beard, donned a pair of sandals and stopped washing. Now he's trying to cash in on the trend by writing a novel about his supposed childhood in the west of Ireland. As for speaking Irish, weeell . . . How could you tell? Do you speak it?'

'No.'

'There you are then. He has probably learnt enough to manage. Very few could challenge him on that. And doesn't everybody cry when they hear "Danny Boy"? It makes me very weepy, and I don't even know what it's about.'

'But his mother . . .' she said again. She found it hard to believe this strange story.

'It was very sad about his mother. Ended up in a home.'

'Why? What was wrong with her?'

'Obsessive knitter. Couldn't stop. It was like a drug.' He shook his head sadly.

Anna's head was spinning. It was the strangest story she had ever heard. She found it hard to believe. But it did explain Mícheal's strange behaviour. He was trying to be typically Irish. She suddenly felt elated. This could be a way to get rid of Mícheal!

She was able to put her idea to the test the following evening. She had come home tired from work, exercise and some last-minute shopping. Mícheal was sitting in his favourite place, the sofa in front of the television. He was surrounded by beer cans, and the living room stank of beer, cigarette smoke and sweat.

'Would you mind not turning my home into a pigsty,' she snapped as she opened the windows. 'And when are you leaving? You have overstayed your welcome by about fifty years. I've had enough!' She shouted the last words angrily.

'You'd better change your tune. I can make life very difficult for you, you know. I could write an article about a certain Irish diplomat. I could tell the public how you live in style on the taxpayer's money. And how your husband has arse-licked the politicians to get himself to the top. Maybe the readers would also be interested in how a certain diplomat's wife flirts with her Spanish boyfriend? I have heard your lovey-dovey conversations on the phone. And I saw the huge bouquet of flowers he sent accompanied by a little card.'

Juan had sent an enormous bunch of flowers to thank Anna for the dinner. She had torn up the card which said 'To my lovely Anna with thanks from Juan.' Mícheal must have read it before she did.

'I could also report how you and your husband suck up to the Taoiseach. I believe that there was more than dessert involved in the "special treat" he received when he was here. And what about this favour you were supposed to have done someone in Dublin?'

'I have no idea what you're talking about.' Oh my God, she thought, he can't have found out about the letter.

'Your telephone conversations are very interesting. That extension in the guest bedroom has been more than useful.'

'So you're a spy and an eavesdropper.'

'I'm a journalist.'

'Same thing.'

'Well, I know what I would call you. I think Lizzie Dobbins would love to hear about your flirt with the Taoiseach.'

'What?'

'Yeah, I know all about it. Someone who was at the dinner in Dublin heard Nolan promise you a special reward.' He rose from the sofa and put his hands on her shoulders, staring into her eyes. 'I bet you're a right little raver behind that straight-laced façade.'

Furious, she took a step back, which made him nearly lose his balance. 'Get away from me, you drunken pig.' She no longer cared what he thought. She just wanted him out of her home. 'How dare you come here and spy on us! It's disgusting.'

'Who are you to criticise anyone?' Mícheal slurred angrily.

'At least I don't pretend to be something I'm not,' Anna snapped back.

'Like what?'

'Like Irish,' she retorted triumphantly. For a moment, there was complete silence.

Mícheal's face was white and his eyes nearly

popped out of their sockets. 'Well, fuck me,' he whispered.

'No, thanks.' There was a long silence.

'How did you find out? I suppose you're going to tell everybody.'

'Not if you leave at once. Then it will just be between you and me.'

'That's blackmail. It's against the law.'

'Look who's talking.' Anna didn't know if impersonating an Irishman was a crime but she thought it should be. And he had also been black-mailing her.

'Could I not stay just one more week?' Mícheal looked pleadingly at Anna.

'No. Absolutely not. You leave tonight or I'll tell the world.'

'Who are you going to tell?'

'Well,' she mused, 'we could start with your news-paper. They would be very interested to know that you are not the great Irish scholar they are always boasting of having on their team. Then how about the Department of Foreign Affairs? And Sarah. I wonder how she will take the fact that her romantic Irish caveman is a nerd from west London? That your poverty-stricken parents did not struggle to survive in a thatched cottage in Connemara? And that you did not go to the village school and learn to read and write through Irish? How will she react when she hears that your childhood was not a country version of *Angela's Ashes?*'

'You wouldn't tell her?'

'I would. In fact, it will be great fun.' Anna smiled

at the thought of giving Sarah this piece of news. 'There are a lot of other people who would love to know about you,' she continued. 'What about your publisher? And your agent? Maybe I should have my own website?'

'But I can't leave tonight. I have nowhere to go,' he whined

'You can sleep on the street, for all I care. Join the tramps under the bridges. You look just like them anyway.'

'Maybe Sarah would put me up,' Mícheal muttered. 'In fact, that's not a bad idea,' he said, his face brightening up. 'I'll call her at once!' He started to walk out to the hall to use the phone.

'No! Don't call her. Give her a surprise. Just arrive,' Anna suggested. 'Sarah loves surprises.'

'Good idea,' Mícheal replied with a happy grin. 'She is probably lonely in that big place of hers.'

Sarah had a beautiful flat with views over Notre-Dame. It was furnished with leather chairs and sofas, teak bookcases and white Indian rugs, just perfect to spill beer on, Anna thought. And how would Jonathan, the cat, like it? Sarah's organised life would be seriously disrupted. Things were really turning out well, for once. She was getting rid of Mícheal and at the same time making trouble for Sarah. It was nearly too good to be true.

An hour later, Mícheal was lugging his enormous suitcases out the door. Anna carried a big cardboard box with his papers and laptop into the lift. She would have carried Mícheal and his suitcases as well, just to get rid of him.

'Well, goodbye,' he said. 'Promise you won't tell now.'

'My lips are sealed.'

'I hope you mean that.'

'Scout's honour.' Anna held up a hand in a mock scout's salute.

'Ha!' he retorted angrily. 'Not from you!' He grunted as he heaved the two cases into the lift. Anna closed the door. She did a little dance in the hall.

'Yes! Yes!' she yelled. She felt dizzy with power. Mícheal's reign of terror was over. And she had done it all by herself. She wasn't too worried about his threat of reporting what he had picked up on the phone. Who would believe him?

Conor had been amazed when she told him a some-what edited version of the story, and very impressed with her achievement. 'Well done!' he exclaimed. 'He was beginning to get on my nerves.'

'On *your* nerves?' Anna snapped 'You were never home long enough to even notice him! *I* had to clear up after him and listen to his never-ending com-plaints. *I* had to look at him every day and put up with his disgusting habits! *You* didn't even have the guts to make him leave!. *You* were too worried about your precious career. Never mind what I had to suffer.' She was angry and tired, and not in the mood to humour Conor. The evening had ended in a very frosty goodnight, and it had been days before they made up.

A week later, Conor had apologised to Anna and they were on better terms.

'Sarah is behaving very strangely these days,'

Conor told her.

'Oh? In what way?'

'She has started coming to work late looking tired and dishevelled. She still wears the strange clothes and the Birkenstock sandals. And she seems to have stopped shaving her legs. I could nearly swear that she doesn't have a shower very often.'

'It must be Mícheal. Sarah's in love.'

'With that ... that ...? It's not possible!' Conor looked incredulously at Anna and, also, curiously hurt.

'Some women really go for the caveman look. Somebody as organised and boring as Sarah is probably incredibly turned on by a dirty, sweaty, rude man. They must be having wild sex every night. That's why she's looking so wrecked. Or maybe she has masochistic tendencies.' Anna was enjoying herself.

'Oh, please! Enough of that pop psychology! Where do you get it? Women's magazines? It's absolute crap,' Conor retorted.

'I don't care about Sarah. If she and Mícheal are happy, why worry? At least we'll never have to put up with him again.' Anna considered the subject closed.

'Ladies and gentlemen, this is your captain speaking. Welcome on board flight OL 215 bound for Athens. The flight will take approximately two hours and fifteen minutes, and ...' The voice droned on in the loudspeaker just above Anna's ear. The plane had just taken off from Charles de Gaulle airport. She didn't listen to the rest of the usual announcements, but turned her attention to the magazines she had brought: the latest issues of *Hello!*, *Howerya!*, *Image* from Ireland and the French fashion bible *Elle*. Conor was sorting through some documents beside her in search of the *Irish Telegraph* of that morning. Anna opened *Howerya!* magazine.

'Look at this,' she exclaimed. '*Lizzie reveals all*. And there are pictures as well.'

'Please,' Conor pleaded. 'Don't show me. I don't want to look at that woman with nothing on. It will put me off my lunch.'

'No, she's not naked. It's just a photo of her and Nolan on holiday in the Caribbean. They are wearing swimsuits.'

'Nearly as bad.'

'Yeah, you're right,' Anna agreed as she studied the photograph. 'She was quite heavy even then.'

'What an enchanting couple,' Conor remarked as he glanced at the picture.

'Her memoirs are being serialised in *Howerya!* This should be interesting. Look,' Anna continued, 'a picture taken in New York. She's wearing a mink coat here. I'd love to know how he could afford all the holidays and expensive gifts.'

'So would the Revenue Commissioners, I'm sure,' Conor grunted, opening his newspaper.

'Jesus Christ!' he exclaimed.

'What, darling? Are you feeling sick?'

'Yes. And so will you when you see this.'

'Are they naked in the *Telegraph?*'

'No. Look.' He held the newspaper in front of her

eyes with shaking hands, indicating the front-page headline: *Costa del Fiddle? Planning permission granted for Spanish hotel in Kinsale.*

'It's not possible,' Anna exclaimed. 'Is it a mistake?'

'No, it's true all right. How can it have happened?' Conor looked at her in panic. 'Where's my mobile? I have to call my father.' He started to rummage around in the big black bag Anna used as hand luggage.

'You can't use your mobile during the flight. It's not allowed.'

'I have to get off. This is an emergency. I have to go home.' Conor was babbling hysterically. He looked like a cornered rat, eyes staring at Anna and sweat beginning to run down his forehead.

'Conor!' Anna grabbed his hand, then said slowly, 'Take a deep breath and calm down. You can't do anything about this now. We are ten thousand feet in the air. We will be landing in Athens in two hours. Your father is on holiday in Kerry. I'm sure he has nothing to do with this. Read the article. Maybe there's an explanation there.'

Conor took a deep breath. 'OK,' he sighed, 'you're right.' He was looking calmer as he picked up the newspaper and started to read.

'It says here that the county council decided to agree to the hotel because of the many jobs it would create in the area, and the money that would be spent by wealthy yacht owners. The government are pushing it in a big way. They may even give the bastards a grant. There are rumours of bribes to ministers. This is absolutely scandalous.'

'When did they decide to give them planning permission?' Anna asked.

'Yesterday.'

'While your father was away. Very clever. They probably thought he might put up a fight.'

'You're right. Some of the other members of the county council were away as well. How convenient.'

'Have there been protests from the locals?'

'Protests? More like riots. They have thrown eggs at the county council building. And they have been camping in the fort for days. Some people have even chained themselves to the gates. I would do the same if I was there. Kinsale will be ruined, Anna. It's a disaster.' Conor looked angrily at her. 'What the hell are we doing on this stupid trip? It's all your fault.'

'Why is it my fault?'

'You were insisting that we went.'

'Now, hold on a minute,' Anna replied angrily, waving away the air hostess, who had just arrived at their seats with lunch in plastic containers. '*You* were the one who decided that we should go on this trip. *You* didn't even tell me of your decision. I had to learn it from Sarah.'

'Yeah. Maybe.'

'What happened to sorry?'

'OK. Sorry,' Conor muttered. 'It was Juan Valverde and the ambassador who both convinced me to come. You don't think Juan has something to do with this hotel thing, do you? He seemed very chummy with that Sanchez creep.'

'Juan?' Anne asked. 'No, I don't believe it. He and Carlos were just friends. Juan knows nothing about business.' She sighed. She was becoming tired of the whole subject. She loved Kinsale and was as upset as Conor about the proposed construction. But at the moment she just wanted to enjoy her holiday.

'This is a catastrophe for Ireland,' Conor complained.

'I know,' Anna replied, 'but there's nothing you can do right now. Can't we forget about it for a while?'

'How can you say that? Those Spaniards are destroying my town. Doesn't it upset you?'

'I don't care if they nuke the place! Will you stop moaning? Can't we just try to have a holiday? You can worry about it when we come back.'

'You don't realise how serious this is.' Conor was sounding hysterical again. 'All you can think of is your bloody holiday.'

'What can I do about it?' Anna snapped. 'Tell me, and I'll do it. And then, shut up.' They stared angrily at each other for a moment.

'I suppose you're right,' Conor muttered, finally.

'I *am* right. You need a break, Conor. You're beginning to get stressed and frantic. I think you should try to relax and enjoy this trip. It's only for a week, anyway. This cruise could be great for your job. I'm sure you'll meet some people from Brussels. You can probably write lots of reports about conversations you'll have with them about the European Union. You can find out what's going on in Kinsale when you come back.' Anna thought that Conor would stop being upset if his thoughts were turned in a different direction. She was right.

'That's true,' he said, his face brightening. 'But I'll phone Dad when we arrive. Now where's lunch? I'm hungry.'

'We are about to land at Athens airport. Please fasten your seat belts and raise your seat to the upright position,' the air hostess's voice called through the loudspeakers. Anna looked down to see the sprawling city of Athens and the mountains beyond. It was a beautiful evening with a pink sky from the setting sun. The rest of the flight had been uneventful, except for the slight flap when Conor had complained to the air hostess that she had forgotten to give them lunch. A bad-tempered discussion followed, which resulted in a lunch box for Conor, but nothing for Anna, who had to satisfy her hunger with half a bar of chocolate she found in her handbag. Then Anna had read while Conor slept with a bunch of documents on his lap.

'I'm going to work all through the flight,' he had announced importantly, 'so don't disturb me with chat.' Ten minutes later, he had been fast asleep.

'Wake up, Conor. We have landed.'

'I wasn't asleep,' Conor protested, blinking and screwing up his eyes. 'I was thinking.'

'Oh, yeah, I know. Come on, we have to get off now.'

They walked down the steps into the hot evening air. It was at least thirty degrees, and Anna was already feeling overwhelmed by the heat. A big black limousine was waiting on the tarmac to take the O'Connors, Monique and her husband and Susanna and her husband, who had all been on the same flight, to the yacht. Most of the other guests had already arrived. Their bags were taken care of, and they swept through the gates without having to show their passports or go through customs. Six heavily armed security guards on motorcycles followed the huge car through the city. So this is how the other half lives, Anna thought, as she enjoyed the cooling effect of the air conditioning.

It was dusk as they arrived at the harbour of Piraeus. A motor launch was waiting at the quay to take them to the *Agamemnon*, whose bulk they could see in the distance. Conor had made several unsuccessful attempts to contact his father on his mobile, but there had been no reply.

'Look,' Conor exclaimed, as they entered the lobby of the ship. 'There's Betsy. What is she doing here?'

'Oh, didn't I tell you?' Anna replied. 'She was asked to act as hostess on this trip by the owner. They know each other from the time Betsy did the interior of the ship. She couldn't pass up an opportunity to go on a cruise like this.'

'Bloody hell.'

'What's the matter? Don't you like Betsy?'

'I do, but I like Patrick Daly more. Don't you know he's going to be on the trip as well?'

'Oh, no!' Anna exclaimed. It's bad enough when they're in the same town. What is it going to be like when they're on the same ship?'

'Maybe they'll fall in love?'

'Not bloody likely. She hates him.'

They were interrupted by Betsy.

'Hi. Did you have a good flight?'

'Great, thanks. You look very efficient,' Anna said, admiring the navy linen suit with the ship's emblem embroidered on the breast pocket. 'And what a lovely tan. Where have you been?'

'In my bathroom with a bottle of fake tanning lotion. But don't tell anyone,' Betsy laughed. 'Pavlos gave me this suit to wear. It was especially made for me by Chanel. I thought a tan would be the perfect accessory. Now, let's get you settled in. You're in stateroom twenty-four.' She showed Conor and Anna on a little map how to get to their quarters. 'I hope you'll be comfortable. You have to be back in the lobby in an hour, when the launch will take you to the yacht club for dinner.'

Anna couldn't believe the opulence of the ship's interior. She stared wide-eyed at the exquisite furniture, beautiful carpets and curtains in soft colours in the salons and staterooms they passed. One small salon had a circular white sofa with blue and white cushions scattered on it. It was surrounded by marble pillars carved with an intricate leaf design. Another salon had a gold piano in the middle of the floor.

'Close your mouth,' Conor hissed at her. 'You look as if you have never been on a ship before.'

'Not one like this. And neither have you.'

'Yes, but try not to look so gobsmacked! How about a little sophistication? Ah, here we are.' They had arrived at their stateroom before Anna had a chance to retort.

Their air-conditioned living quarters consisted of a small salon, a big bedroom curtained and carpeted in a lovely duck-egg blue, and an elegant white marble bathroom with stacks of fluffy towels and every kind of toiletry any well-groomed man or woman could wish for. The large bathtub looked very inviting to Anna, who would have preferred just to have a good soak and retire for the night to the enormous canopied four-poster bed.

Instead, she had quickly to unpack, shower and change for dinner. She chose a cerise silk camisole top and short black Thai silk skirt. A string of pearls and very high-heeled strappy evening sandals completed the outfit. She looked in the mirror and silently blessed Adolphe, who had trimmed her hair again before the trip. Glossy auburn curls framed her lightly tanned face. Her eyes were intensely blue, and a few freckles had appeared across the bridge of her nose. She would have to be careful with the hot sun during the trip. Conor was wearing a dark blue linen jacket, white shirt and grey trousers.

The guests were already boarding the launch as Anna and Conor appeared in the lobby. They were the last to board. Anna carefully climbed down the steep steps into the smaller boat. A strong hand grasped her elbow.

'Don't break one of those lovely ankles.' Juan, dressed in a cream linen jacket, light blue shirt open at the neck and blue jeans, helped her into the launch. His wolfish grin glowed in the gloom. Only Juan could look so devastating dressed like that, Anna thought.

A coach took them from the harbour to the yacht club, which was situated on a cliff high above the coastline. Tables had been set out on the vast terrace under the black starlit sky. A light breeze from the sea cooled the guests as they were served champagne before the meal. Betsy and a man called Nikolaos, with a last name nobody could pronounce, who was Pavlos Patmos's closest associate, greeted the guests. But where was Pavlos Patmos? There was no one there who looked even remotely like a multi-millionaire.

Anna noticed that Patrick Daly, who had just arrived, was trying to talk to Betsy. He seemed to get a frosty reply which made him look glumly away. He turned to Anna.

'Hello, Anna, nice to see you. I don't know what's wrong with that woman.'

'What happened?'

'I just said that I was happy to see her again and that she looked lovely.' Betsy did indeed look her very best. She had changed from her uniform into an off-white short linen dress whose straps crossed over her tanned back.

'I can't find anything wrong with what you said. What was her reply?'

'She just stared at me and told me to piss off. She said she didn't know that I was going to be on the ship and she wouldn't be here if she had.'

'What did you say to that?'

'I complimented her on her charming welcome and asked if she had greeted all the guests in this way. But then I thought I would try to make peace by being nice, so I told her I liked her name and that I once had a dog called Betsy.

That's when she became even more cold and angry.'

'I don't blame her,' Anna snapped. 'I wouldn't like being compared to a dog.'

'But I loved that dog. I loved her more than anything. Even my wife. I cried when Betsy died.'

'But not when your wife left you?'

'No,' Patrick exclaimed, looking confused. 'Why would that make me cry? The marriage was a terrible mistake.'

'You're a true romantic,' Anna declared.

The guests were invited to take their seats for dinner. Anna found herself sitting beside Nikolaos. Conor was at another table with Monique, Jean-Pierre and a man from the European Commission. Juan was opposite Anna, squashed between two full-bosomed Greek ladies. He looked curiously small, and he directed a pretended frightened grin at Anna.

'Between a rock and a hard place, eh?' he joked. The ladies, who only spoke Greek, giggled in unison.

Anna turned to the handsome man beside her. 'I didn't quite catch your name?'

'Just call me Nick,' he replied. 'All my friends do. And I hope you and I will be friends.' He smiled at her, his teeth white in his dark face. He had black hair, greying at the temples, and his eyes were very dark under thick eyebrows. He was a suave, elegant man who knew how to make a woman feel attractive. He wanted to know all about Anna, where she came from and how she had met Conor. They were soon on very friendly terms.

Anna looked across at Juan, who was trying to cope

with the two Greek women, who looked as if they wanted to eat him. He took out a handkerchief and mopped his damp brow. Cool, collected Juan was for once a little lost.

The conversation was interesting and lively. The food was light and delicious, consisting mainly of fish and beautifully cooked vegetables. The Greek white wine that was served all through the meal was cool and crisp, perfect for such a warm night. At the end of the meal, the conversation turned to horses. Nick was a keen rider, and Juan was a real expert when it came to horseflesh.

'Polo is a dangerous sport,' Nick remarked. 'Are you not afraid of breaking something?'

'I'm less afraid of horses than women,' he replied, looking across the table at Anna. 'A horse can only break your bones. A woman can break your heart. That is a thousand times more painful.'

'I see,' murmured Nick, looking from Juan's face to Anna's blushing cheeks. 'Interesting, very interesting.' The Greek ladies giggled again.

After dinner the guests were brought back to the yacht, where coffee and brandy were served on the top deck. The ship swayed slightly in the swell of the sea and the water clucked against the hull. The stars glimmered in the black velvet sky and little pinpricks of light could be seen on the deck, where some of the men were smoking cigars. Anna leaned against the railing looking up at the stars. The light wind felt delicious on her bare arms and shoulders, and her hair was moving softly around her face.

'How did you get on with medallion man?' Juan

was standing beside her with a glass of brandy in his hand.

'It's only a small medal,' she replied. 'And Nick is very charming.'

'Like a grinning crocodile. He would have you for breakfast. Phew,' he continued, 'those two mamas nearly did me in. They both gave me the numbers of their cabins. Pretty scary. Can I get you a drink?'

'No, thanks. I have had quite enough to drink already.'

'A glass of water? A bunch of grapes? A bowl of cherries? A box of chocolates? Or,' he whispered into her ear, 'a small aircraft to take us both away from here?'

'I don't want to go anywhere.' She looked around for Conor. He was in deep conversation with Jean-Claude Bonhomme, a high-flyer from the European Commission. Anna knew that Conor had been hoping to meet this man. He would be there until dawn, given a chance. Then he would spend several hours writing a report about their conversation. Conor could not pass up an opportunity like that. It would earn him a hundred thousand brownie points from the Department. He seemed to have forgotten about Kinsale for the moment.

'If a bunch of terrorists arrived to steal you away, he wouldn't notice,' Juan muttered. 'He might just complain about the noise.'

'Don't be silly. He is just very interested in his job. Unlike some, I might add.'

'I'm very interested in my job. I just know when to take a break.'

'By the way,' Anna began, 'I would like to ask you something.'

'Go ahead.'

'How much do you know about your friend Carlos's work?'

'How do you mean?' Juan asked with a bland expression on his face.

'Did you know he was planning to build a huge, horrible pile of a hotel in one of Ireland's most beautiful coastal towns?'

'I'm not interested in architecture.'

'This is not architecture,' Anna remarked. 'It's rape and destruction.' She was becoming carried away. 'It's, it's vandalism of the very worst kind, and just for money.'

'Come on, sweetheart, don't get excited,' Juan pleaded. 'At least not about that.' He put his hand on her shoulder and ran it down her arm. 'It's such a lovely night. A beautiful girl should not worry about business and building projects.'

'You haven't answered my question,' Anna protested, moving away from his disturbing nearness. Why can't I breathe when he touches me? she wondered. Why can't I think straight when I hear his voice?

'OK. I'll answer. Carlos is a very old friend. I knew he had some kind of project in Ireland, but I didn't know the details. What's the problem anyway? Aren't the Irish delighted with all this foreign investment?'

'Not when it involves destroying a historical site and ruining a stretch of beautiful coastline.'

'But when it's built the row will be forgotten,' Juan

remarked. 'And everyone will be rich: the Irish, the Spanish and Mr Nolan.'

'Mr Nolan?' Anna asked, confused. 'Why will *he* be rich? What's he got to do with this?'

'Nothing at all,' Juan soothed, moving closer again. 'I just meant that he would profit with the rest of the population.'

'There's something funny going on.'

'Darling, darling, let's forget about it. It has nothing to do with either of us, believe me.' Juan put his arm around Anna's shoulder, but she broke away.

'I smell a rat,' she persisted.

'And I smell your perfume,' he whispered in the dark. 'Come here.'

Anna knew she should not stay. She didn't trust him, and she trusted herself even less.

'I'm going to bed.' She walked down the steps to the lower deck to say good night to Betsy. Juan followed, a hand under her elbow. She didn't need assistance, but she didn't try to shake him off. When they arrived at the bottom of the steps, he pulled her closer.

'Sweet dreams,' he whispered, his mouth in her hair. Then he was gone.

Anna stood in the dark for a while, unable to move. Suddenly angry voices disturbed the calm.

'Come on, honey, give me a break.' It was Patrick's voice.

'Leave me alone. And I'm not your honey!' Betsy snarled.

'Why are you so hostile? Don't you like men?'

'I love men!' Betsy replied angrily. 'Real men, who

don't patronise women. Men who can accept the fact that women have brains.'

'That's a little far-fetched, sweetheart. Women weren't meant to have careers. We all know that. Why don't you relax, and just enjoy being a woman. A lovely, sexy woman at that.'

'Do you know what I'd enjoy?' Betsy spat. 'I'd enjoy watching you drown. Very slowly.'

Patrick laughed. A slow, mocking laugh. 'You're so cute when you're mad.'

Anna could hear a rustle and then Betsy's furious voice. 'Don't touch me! I'll call the captain, you slime-ball. Can't you see how much I loathe you, you big, thick, ignorant ... you boring ... Canadian!' she finally snarled at him.

'Betsy?' Anna called out. 'Are you all right?'

'I will be as soon as I get rid of this creep,' came Betsy's voice.

'OK, honey,' Patrick drawled. 'Don't get hysterical. I'm going. Good night!' Anna could hear him walk off into the night.

'Bastard,' Betsy muttered.

'What did he do?'

'He told me I was beautiful. Then he ... he ...' Betsy started to sob.

'My God!' Anna exclaimed. 'Did he try to ...?'

'He put his hand on my shoulder.'

'That's it?'

'Well, yes,' Betsy stammered. 'What did you think?'

'You were practically crying rape.'

'Sorry,' Betsy whispered. 'I overreacted. It's just

that he upsets me so. Oh, I don't know what's wrong with me. This really good-looking man, wealthy, single, and not gay, is chasing me. And I try to run away. So, he's a little macho? I should be able to handle that. I'm in denial. That's my problem. I'm trying to deny my female side.'

'You were too long in America. That's all,' Anna declared, confused by Betsy's sudden psychological analysis. 'Patrick is certainly not what you'd call perfect. I find him absolutely deadly. But maybe he has a positive side. We know he likes dogs. He does patronise women though. That's his biggest problem.'

'No. He's an ambassador,' Betsy said. 'That's his biggest problem.'

'Why?'

'Honestly, Anna. Twin sets and pearls, bridge and coffee mornings. Getting drunk on sherry at ten in the morning and ending up having an affair with the gardener.'

'What?' Anna asked. 'Why would you turn into the Queen of England?'

'But I would. It's living death for a woman to be married to an ambassador.'

'That was fifty years ago,' Anna replied. 'It's not like that now. But you don't have to marry him. He probably just wants a roll in the hay, anyway.'

'I'm not going to hang around him to find out,' Betsy declared. Then she changed the subject. 'What have you been up to? Snogging Juan in the dark?'

'Well, no. We were just . . .'

'Talking? Be careful, Anna. Don't play with fire,'

Betsy warned.

'Why not? It's fun.'

'But is it safe? Juan won't stop at flirting. I know his technique. He will slowly turn your head by being very romantic. He will flatter and flirt with you, touch you and give you little kisses, until you are putty in his hands. Then he will want to sleep with you and, if you do, there will be great passion for a while. He will finally get bored and turn to another woman. Conor will leave you and take the children. You'll be all alone.'

'Why do you always expect the worst?'

'Because that way I'm never disappointed.'

'Two Swedish beauties. That's more than a man could wish for.' Nick had strolled up to the railing where Anna and Betsy were standing. 'Are you talking about me?' He put his arm around the two women. Anna found his touch a bit cloying. He smelled of cigar smoke and brandy.

'No, Nick,' Betsy replied. 'You're not always at the top of the agenda.'

'And why not? Do Swedish women not like Greek men? That's not what I've heard.'

'Whatever you've heard, it's all lies,' Betsy retorted.

'What about free love? I thought Swedes were all for that.'

'It's a myth invented in the fifties to sell Swedish movies. And love is never free,' Betsy stated.

'But Dutch women love it,' Anna said as Susanna strolled past them. 'Why don't you ask Susanna?'

'Really?' Nick asked, lifting one eyebrow. 'I have never heard that.' He went over to Susanna who had stopped to put her coffee cup on a nearby table.

'Hello,' they heard him say. 'We met earlier. May I call you Susanna?'

'No.'

'But I love tall Dutch women! And I have heard so much about you.'

'Really? What have you heard?' Susanna's tone was softer.

'Well,' he said, putting his arm around her. 'It's like this . . .' They walked away and Betsy and Anna could no longer hear what Nick was saying.

'What have we started?' Anna giggled.

'Nothing,' Betsy replied. 'Don't worry. She's six feet tall and has a black belt in Karate. Nick only comes up to her shoulder. I'd worry more about him than her, to be honest.' She yawned. 'I must make sure everybody has everything they need. Then I'll go to bed. I'm so tired. Good night, darling.' She kissed Anna on the cheek and started to move around the guests.

Anna walked past a group of men which included Conor, Jean-Pierre and Susanna's husband, deep in conversation, across the deck to the door that would bring her to the long corridor leading to her state-room. She passed Susanna sitting on the edge of a deckchair talking to Nick, who was leaning over her and whispering something into her ear which made her giggle. Nick looked up and winked at Anna as she left.

She felt tired, annoyed and worried. She was now certain that Juan had a lot more to do with Sanchez Construction than he had let on. But it was impossible to get anything out of him, and the way he made her feel did not help. She took a deep breath, enjoying the soft air. The stars still twinkled in the sky and she could see the lights from the harbour in the distance. The ship was beginning to move in the black water. They would be arriving at Delos in the morning.

CHAPTER 10

Anna woke with a start. The noise of the ship's engines had stopped. The sun was streaming through the curtained portholes. She glanced at her watch. Nine o'clock. She and Conor had overslept. They were supposed to board the launch that would bring them to the small island of Delos right now. She shook Conor, who was still fast asleep beside her. God only knows when he went to bed, she thought. There had been no sign of him when she had finally switched off the light.

'Conor! Wake up. We've overslept.'

'Wh ... what?' Conor looked at her, bleary-eyed. 'Oh shit,' he exclaimed when he looked at the watch Anna held in front of his eyes. 'Get up. Get dressed. We'll miss the launch.'

They both leaped out of bed and hastily washed and dressed. Conor pulled on a pair of beige cotton trousers and a dark green polo shirt. Anna pulled a comb through her hair and grabbed a pair of white shorts and one of the Versace T-shirts. She stuffed a swimsuit, Conor's trunks and two towels in a canvas bag. They would not have time for breakfast.

They raced through the corridor and down the stairs to the lobby. The launch was just pulling out. Conor ran up to the railing and waved his arms over his head. The launch stopped and reversed engines. It returned slowly to the yacht, but the swell of the sea was too strong to use the gangway. Conor and Anna had to jump from the yacht to the launch in one big leap.

'Ballet training is useful sometimes. That was a wonderful *grand jeté*.' Juan grinned at her from the bridge of the launch. He was dressed in white shorts and tennis shirt. She decided to try to resist him from now on. Betsy's words last night had shaken her up a little, and she was sure that he had been lying about his involvement with Sanchez Construction. But when she looked at Juan she couldn't help but admire his deep tan, broad shoulders and strong legs. Just looking won't do any harm, she thought. She put on her sunglasses to hide her eyes.

'Did you sleep well?' Nick asked her.

'A bit too well. That's why we nearly missed the launch.'

'Your husband didn't leave until the small hours of the morning. There was a big Euro-discussion on deck.'

'Euro-bore, you mean.'

'That's it.'

'And how did you get on with . . . eh . . .'

'With the lovely Susanna?' He grabbed her arm and led her out on the small deck where they wouldn't be overheard. 'You were pulling my leg last night, weren't you? That woman would put off an army. She spent all evening telling me how much money they were saving by coming on this trip. She had it down to the last cent. Free love indeed. It would be very expensive.' Nick shook his head. 'Anyway, she is too tall for me. It wouldn't be making love, it would be mountaineering,' he chuckled good-naturedly. At least he didn't get angry, Anna thought, relieved.

It was a lovely day. They sped past small islands sticking up out of the sapphire-blue sea. The wind whipped Anna's hair around her face, and the hot sun and sea salt stung her skin. She was feeling hungry and thirsty and she was hoping they would be able to have at least a cup of coffee when they landed.

Delos, a small island situated near the much bigger island of Mykonos, had remains of houses from ancient times. Anna was fascinated by the remarkable mosaics and surprisingly well-preserved statues and reliefs. The small museum was full of tourists who were peering at the artefacts and other remains that had been dug up by archaeologists. Anna was amazed to discover the level of sophistication and culture the items revealed. It was difficult to imagine that such a civilisation had existed so many thousand years ago.

After a few hours on Delos, the launch took the group to Mykonos where it was intended they would swim and later have lunch at a small taverna. They had to walk half a mile from the little harbour to the beach.

Anna was feeling very strange. The heat and the long fast had made her weak and dizzy. Her mouth was dry from thirst. She was lagging behind the rest of the group as they descended a hill that led to the beach. The view of the hills, the bay below, and the blue sea was lovely, but she hardly noticed it. Conor was walking far ahead, talking to the man from the European Commission.

'Anna? Are you all right?' Juan put his arm around her and peered into her face with a worried look.

'I just feel a bit weak. We had no breakfast because we overslept. And I'm so thirsty.'

'We'll soon be at the beach. I'll get you some water when we get there. In the meantime, here is some breakfast.' He reached up and pulled some odd-looking fruit from a small tree.

'What are those?' she asked, looking at the wrinkled, purplish-brown fruit with suspicion.

'Fresh figs. Here, just break them open.' He opened one of the figs to reveal the flesh inside. She took a small bite. It was delicious. When she had eaten three figs, she felt instantly better. The juices the figs contained had raised her blood sugar and quenched her thirst a little. She looked gratefully at Juan. He was such a wonderful man. She forgot her resolution of that morning, and smiled sweetly at him.

'I think you just saved my life.'

'I couldn't let a lovely woman go hungry and thirsty.'

When they arrived at the beach, Anna joined the other women who were changing into their swimsuits in the small changing room that belonged to the taverna. Anna knew that her slimmed-down figure looked well in the red swimsuit she had bought at the sales. Betsy had convinced her to come to a gym near the office on her lunch break.

'I hate gyms,' Anna had protested. 'It's so boring to work out with weights.'

'But it's very effective. Come on, give it a try. You'll like this gym. There are good-looking instructors in tight T-shirts who give you advice, and no Dutch women who shout at you.'

Anna had gone to the gym with Betsy and worked out three times a week. She still did not enjoy it much, but she had to admit that there were great rewards.

Now Susanna was standing next to Anna in the changing room. 'You don't look bad, Anna, considering you don't come to my classes any more,' she announced. 'But there is still some flab on your thighs, and your stomach will never be quite firm.' She was putting on a small thong bikini that left very little to the imagination.

'What's that on your thigh?' Betsy asked, peering at the back of one of Susanna's legs.

'What? There's nothing on my thigh.'

'Yes, yes there is. Is it a mosquito bite? Or, could it be ... Anna! Come here and take a look at this!' Together they examined Susanna's thigh with dead-pan faces. They looked at each other and nodded. 'What do you think?' Betsy asked. 'Is it ...?'

'Yes.' Anna murmured. 'The big C.'

'What's that?' Susanna shrieked.

'Cellulite,' Betsy announced. 'Definitely. No doubt about it.'

'What,' Susanna yelled. 'It couldn't be! Not cellulite.'

'Yes,' Betsy continued. 'It's most certainly cellulite.' She nodded, pretending to look concerned.
'You'll have to have major liposuction when you get
back. It's the only way to get rid of it.'

'I don't have any cellulite!' Susanna shouted. 'It's
not possible.' She grabbed a towel and tied it around
her waist to hide her hips and thighs and stalked out
on to the beach. Anna and Betsy collapsed, laughing
hysterically.

'That was very cruel,' Monique remarked with a
grin.

'I know,' Betsy laughed, 'wasn't it great? Now we
don't have to look at her perfect little ass for the rest of
the day.'

Anna sat on a towel in the sand watching Betsy
swim. She was feeling much better. Juan had brought
her a big glass of water and some olives. Conor was
having a beer at the small bar with some of the other
men. She was planning to go for a long swim just
before lunch. Betsy waved at her from the water. She
was quite a long way out, but Anna knew that Betsy
was a good swimmer. She had been school champion
several years in a row.

Betsy was floating on her back looking up at the
blue sky. The water was surprisingly cold, but it was
a relief from the intense heat. She felt relaxed and
happy. The cruise was going well and everyone was
content. Pavlos would be pleased. He was coming
aboard the ship to greet his guests on the last day of
the cruise. She waved to Anna on the shore, and
started the long swim back. It was nearly time for
lunch. Suddenly, there was a movement in the blue

water. Someone was swimming very fast towards her. She saw that it was a man, and that he was an excellent swimmer. He was beside her only moments later. He grabbed her arms.

'Hang on, I've got you.'

'Wh ...' Betsy gurgled, her mouth under water. What was he doing? He proceeded to turn her on her back, and, with his arms under her armpits, dragged her, swimming on his back, to shallow water. It was Patrick. He heaved her over his shoulder and carried her on to the beach.

'What are you doing? Put me down!' Coughing and spluttering, she beat her fists against his back and tried to kick him. 'Let me go! Leave me alone!'

He put her down on the sand. 'You could be a bit more grateful. I just saved you from drowning.'

'I wasn't in trouble.'

'You weren't? But I saw you wave for help.'

'I was waving at Anna. If you weren't so incredibly stupid, you would have realised that. Now, leave me alone. Don't ever come near me!' Betsy was shouting angrily, her face red.

'Do excuse me!' he exclaimed. 'I'll never again try to save you. Even if you really are in danger.'

'I wouldn't want you near me if I was dying.'

Patrick grabbed her by the arms and looked down into her face. She couldn't get away. 'Now, listen, you silly, snooty woman,' he snarled. 'I haven't done anything to you. If you weren't so self-centred and conceited you would realise that I really like you. I have been trying for weeks to get you to at least say hello. But you are too stuck-up to pay me the slightest attention or to give me a chance to show you what I'm like. Who are you waiting for, Prince Charming? Aren't you a little too old?'

Betsy was furious. She lifted her hand and slapped his face.

'You vicious little bitch,' he exclaimed, putting a hand to his cheek.

'You were asking for it! If you were trying to make an impression on me, you've failed.'

'You certainly made one on *me*.'

'Good.'

'You have very strong feelings for me. You can't deny that, honey.'

'That's right. I hate you,' Betsy yelled.

They stared into each other's eyes. They were panting both from anger and the strenuous swimming. He has very long eyelashes, Betsy suddenly thought. And his hair curls at the back of his neck.

Patrick suddenly grabbed her by the shoulders and kissed her. Betsy struggled to resist, but when she felt his lips on hers, her legs turned to jelly. What a kiss it was. She had never been kissed like that. It made her dizzy, and she was sure she could hear music. Fireworks went off in her head and her knees buckled.

'Am I making a better impression now?' he enquired.

'I'm not sure,' she replied. 'Maybe you could try it again?'

It was even better than the first time. So he's a macho pig with no sense of humour, she thought. Nobody's perfect.

Anna, who had watched them from her towel,

couldn't believe her eyes. What happened to Betsy? she wondered. Has she been too long in the sun?

'Don't burn that delicious complexion.' Juan was squatting in front of her. He was wet from a recent swim and his hair was slicked back. Anna looked at his tanned chest and muscular arms and shoulders. His teeth gleamed in his dark face. 'Let me put some suntan lotion on your back.'

Betsy had helped her with that only ten minutes ago, but what the hell. Anna closed her eyes as she felt Juan's hands on her back.

'It's time for lunch, darling,' Juan whispered into her ear. 'Try to cool off first.'

Anna shook herself. What was she doing? She rose and walked quickly to the water's edge. She ran through the waves and threw herself into the crystal-clear water. The cold suddenly woke her from her lethargy. She felt at once wide awake, alert and ravenously hungry.

Three long tables had been set out under the awning on the terrace of the taverna. The guests slowly drifted around the tables and sat down. Anna found herself beside the man from the European Commission. He had a friendly face with warm brown eyes behind steel-rimmed glasses.

'Oh, hello,' Anna said in French. 'You're the man from the Commission.'

'Please, call me Jean-Claude. You make me sound so boring.'

'OK. Jean-Claude.' He turned out to be much more amusing than he looked, with an easy charm, a wonderful sense of humour, and a mischievous smile which lit up his face. He is really very attractive, she thought, half an hour later, but by that time she had drunk several glasses of the deceptively light white wine, and everyone around her seemed beautiful and witty. Anna devoured the lunch, which consisted of a variety of Greek appetisers – olives, taramasalata, cucumber in garlic-flavoured yoghurt, and vegetables marinated in olive oil – followed by grilled fish.

'Your husband is a hard-working man,' Jean-Claude remarked as they ate.

'He is very ambitious.' Anna smiled ruefully. 'I don't see much of him these days.'

'That's a pity. For him, I mean,' Jean-Claude said, as he admired her auburn hair drying in ringlets, her incredibly blue eyes fringed by black lashes, and her sun-kissed face.

'But he wants to make a good career. And he's so interested in the European Union. It's very important for Ireland.'

'Yes, but all the issues are not that important. We spend a lot of time in Brussels discussing trivia. If you only concern yourself with what really matters, you don't have to work that hard.'

'Really?' Anna found that very difficult to believe. What about all the dossiers Conor brought home? And the mountains of papers, the reports and long phone calls? It couldn't all be a waste of time.

'Just to give you an example: last week we spent two days trying to decide the standard size of the cages for battery hens. Important to the hens, but does anybody else really care?'

'But what about the big issues? The foreign policy,

the monetary union, the Common Agricultural Policy? Surely they take a lot of time and work.' Anna had heard these things mentioned by Conor and Sarah. They had sounded very serious.

'Of course. The important work has to be done. And it does demand a lot of time. I'm simply saying that if you leave the battery hens and the rest of the trivia to other people, you wouldn't have so much work. Your husband is a good diplomat and a very clever man. But he should be a bit more focused and learn to relax. He should follow the example of one of his colleagues here, who manages to do some amazing work without appearing to be really trying.'

'Who do you mean?'

'Juan Valverde. A brilliant man with very good contacts.'

'Juan?' Anna asked, confused. She decided not to drink any more wine.

'Yes, that's right. He gives the impression of being lazy and careless. Everything seems to be a joke to him. By acting this way, he manages to pick up a lot of information. Other diplomats feel safe with him because he always looks as if he isn't really listening. Brilliant. Quite brilliant.'

Anna looked down the table at Juan, who was sipping wine and looking at her through half-closed eyes. He looked like a sleepy lion. Lazy and content, without a serious thought in his head. Was Jean-Claude pulling her leg?

Further down the table, Patrick and Betsy were looking into each other's eyes, giggling and sharing olives. They seemed oblivious to the rest of the world.

Anna wondered how Betsy was going to manage her work for the rest of the trip.

'Those two look happy.' Nick, who was sitting on Anna's other side, smiled as he followed the direction of her eyes.

'Yes. Amazing, isn't it? What about you, Nick? Are you married?' Anna realised that she didn't know anything about him.

'Not at the moment. I have been married four times. My first wife was Italian, my second wife Greek, the third German. I have just broken up with my fourth wife, a fierce woman from Iceland.'

'But that's terrible. How sad to go through so many divorces.'

'Not really. You get used to it. When it doesn't work out, it's better to cut your losses. And there were no children.' Nick shrugged.

'So you are between countries at the moment?'

'You could say that.' His eyes glittered as he looked at her. 'I've never tried a Swedish girl.'

'Stop.' Anna laughed. 'I don't want to be next.'

'Don't worry. I wouldn't dream of trying. Your heart is already lost.' He glanced at Juan. 'I want to be your friend. Anyway, fantasies are often a lot more exciting than reality.'

'I don't know what you mean,' Anna replied. 'I'm very happily married.'

'Really?' Nick raised his eyebrows. 'Very. Happily. Married.' He pronounced each word separately. 'Does your husband know?' He turned his head to look at Conor on the far side of the terrace. He was listening to his small radio and taking notes.

Anna was feeling sleepy. The sun, the wine and food were beginning to have their effect. She wanted to lie down in the shade and sleep for the rest of the afternoon. The sun was high in the blue sky and still blisteringly hot, and Anna was not looking forward to the walk back to the harbour. She closed her eyes and would have fallen off her chair if Nick hadn't caught her.

'Feeling a little drowsy?'

'Totally zonked.'

'Here, try this.' Nick helped her up and brought her to a deckchair in the deep shade of the terrace. 'Try to rest for a while. I'll call you when it's time to go back.' Gratefully, Anna closed her eyes and dropped off.

'Anna. Wake up.' She half opened her eyes. Conor was standing in front of her holding his radio. He looked upset.

'Can't you let me sleep?'

'I just picked up something on the news. It's incredible.'

'Can't it wait?' she pleaded.

'You won't believe what I've just heard.'

'Don't tell me,' she murmured sleepily. 'Kinsale has sunk into the ocean without a trace.'

'Please, Anna! Wake up and listen,' Conor appealed.

'OK.' She straightened up in the deckchair and tried to concentrate. 'I'm listening.'

'Well,' he began, squatting beside her on the sand. 'It appears that Sanchez Construction paid a huge amount of money to a politician in return for the permission to build the hotel in Kinsale.'

'I don't believe you!'

'It's true.'

'How come they admitted to doing that?'

'They said that they were told that a contribution to the party fund would be most welcome. They thought it was normal procedure, as they had done the same thing in Morocco last year, when they built a big hotel in Tangiers.'

'Why has this come out now?'

'Well, there is talk of reversing the planning permission because of the huge public outcry. You wouldn't believe the riots there have been in Kinsale. It's been like a minor civil war. And another thing: my father is missing.'

'Isn't he on holiday in Kerry?'

'I rang the hotel he usually stays in, and they said my parents had not arrived. They cancelled their booking.'

'Maybe they're staying somewhere else?'

'I rang Mrs Murphy, their cleaning lady. She told me my parents left for the airport in a taxi a week ago. They didn't say where they were going.' Conor was looking worried. 'It's not like them to just take off like that without telling anyone where they're going.'

'They probably just wanted to go somewhere different this year. I know your dad was a bit tired of looking at the rain in Kerry every summer.'

'It's very strange all the same,' Conor muttered. 'I hope nothing's wrong.'

'Don't make a big drama out of everything,' Anna

exclaimed. 'They left for the airport in a taxi. It's not as if they were taken away at gunpoint. They're probably sitting on a beach in Spain or Portugal right now, sipping wine and having a lovely time.'

'I suppose you're right,' Conor replied, looking far from reassured. 'But it's a bit annoying not being able to talk to Dad when all this is going on.'

'I know, I know. But go on with your story,' Anna continued. 'I suppose Sanchez and Co. are looking for their cash back?'

'That's right. But no one in Fianna Fáil knows anything about this money.'

'How much are we talking about?'

'Well, a cheque for £100,000 is missing.'

'That's incredible!'

'It's a lot of money to lose.'

'But they have to be able to track it down. It must be in someone's pocket. Let's see,' Anna mused. 'Which one of the government ministers is living it up? Who has recently been on a fancy holiday, or bought a big house?'

'I can't think of anyone,' Conor said, frowning, 'except maybe . . .'

'Who?' Anna demanded. 'You mean . . . I can't believe it.'

'No,' Conor agreed. 'He wouldn't. He's a shit, but he *is* the . . .'

'. . . Taoiseach,' Anna filled in.

Mykonos is a wonderful island, Anna thought, as she and Conor walked through the narrow streets of the little town. Night was falling and lights were being lit in the little houses. It was cooler now, with a soft breeze that smelled of flowers. Conor and Anna were admiring the window displays of the many small jewellery shops that were still open. They had an hour to kill before they were to meet the rest of the group at a taverna in the harbour. They had been promised a typical Greek evening.

They had spent the early evening in their cabin listening to Conor's small radio. RTÉ was barely coming through, but it was just possible to hear the main points of the evening news. Anna and Conor stared at each other in disbelief as they listened to reports of the missing cheque and denials from the government's official spokesman.

There had been a heated discussion in the Dáil, with demands from both Labour and Fine Gael for an explanation from the Taoiseach, who denied any knowledge of the affair. He said that he had never heard of Carlos Sanchez, let alone met him. Carlos Sanchez was reported to be furious and had promised to reveal the name of the recipient of the cheque the following day. He would also mention how the cheque had been conveyed to the politician in question.

'It'll probably mean another . . .' Conor remarked.

'What?' Anna asked.

'Another tribunal.' Conor laughed. 'God, I wish I had done law at university. I could have been a millionaire.'

The radio signal had become weaker after that, and it had not been possible to hear the rest of the programme. 'I can't wait to listen to it tomorrow,' Anna had said. 'It's better than a novel.'

'I'd like to buy you something,' Conor now suddenly announced, looking at a display of gold bracelets in the shop window. 'Something small,' he continued as he saw the light in her eyes.

'Really? Why?'

'To make up for having left you on your own so much.'

'That's sweet of you. You haven't been exactly entertaining lately.'

'But you have to understand how important my work is. I'm not here to have a holiday.' Conor was beginning to sound annoyed. He hated it when Anna made him feel guilty. She looked lovely tonight, dressed in a simple black and white polka-dot silk top with thin straps, a black fitted linen skirt, a red belt, and high-heeled sandals on her tanned feet. But she had no earrings. That was what he would buy her. Then maybe she would leave him alone. Gold was much cheaper in Greece than in Paris, and the jewellery on Mykonos was known to be beautiful.

After a lot of searching, discussing and trying on of different types of earrings, they finally settled on a pair of dolphins with lapis lazuli backs, bent into a loop. The blue brought out Anna's eyes and the gold gleamed against her light tan.

'Thank you, darling.' Anna gave Conor a kiss. She knew he was feeling guilty and the gift was meant to humour her, but she loved the earrings and decided not to worry about his motives. Maybe he was going to improve. Maybe not. At the moment she just wanted to enjoy herself. Conor was trying to be nice.

Both Juan and Nick were being charming. Who wouldn't like to bask in that kind of attention?

It was completely dark by the time they reached the restaurant. The stars glowed in the dark sky like a million diamonds set into a canopy of black velvet. The lights from the harbour glinted close by, and the *Agamemnon*, all lit up in the distance, looked like a fairytale ship. The guests were finding their seats at the round tables on the terrace. Anna found herself between Juan and Patrick. Nick was sitting opposite with Betsy and Susanna.

'Careful with the ouzo,' Patrick told her. 'It has a kick like a mule.'

The evening became more and more lively as the dinner progressed. The food and wine were delicious, and everyone was feeling wonderful after the day on the beach and the siesta most of them had indulged in when they got back to their cabins.

At the next table, Conor was for once paying attention to his table companion, the attractive wife of the French ambassador to the European Union. She seemed to be explaining something to Conor, and he was listening with rapt attention.

Juan interrupted Anna's thoughts. 'I saw you talking at length with Jean-Claude Bonhomme today. I didn't think you were interested in politics.'

'We weren't talking about politics. We were talking about you.'

'Much more interesting. What did he say?'

'I'm not going to tell you.'

'You don't have to. I know what he said.'

'What?'

'He said that I'm the big bad wolf and that Little Red Riding Hood should beware.' Juan grinned at her, showing his even white teeth, and at that moment he looked remarkably like the wolf in the book of fairy tales Anna remembered from her childhood.

'You're not a wolf, you're a big pussycat,' she joked.

'I think Little Red Riding Hood is whistling in the dark.' Juan's eyes narrowed as he took a swig of ouzo.

A group of musicians had arrived as they were talking, and now they began to play a Greek tune. For a moment Anna forgot about Juan and just listened to the music. She sipped the ouzo, and started to feel very relaxed and happy.

When the musicians ended their performance, Juan clapped his hands in slow applause. 'Wonderful, absolutely divine,' he drawled. He leaned toward Anna. 'What a performance, eh, darling?'

Anna looked at him with a frown. 'You're drunk.'

'Just a little tipsy. Nothing to worry about.' He squinted at Anna. 'You should have some too. It will make you feel wonderful. Here.' He held his glass to Anna's lips. 'Just a little sip.'

'Stop it.' She brushed away his hand.

'How sad. A lovely woman so hard and cold.' Juan took a swig of his drink and smiled at Anna.

As the evening came to an end, the guests began to walk down the steps at the end of the terrace and on to the path which led to the harbour. Juan rose and brushed off Nick and Patrick, who were trying to help him. 'I don't need any help. I'm not drunk!' He walked slowly toward the steps, but somehow lost his bearings and ended up against a huge six-foot urn which was part of the decoration. He put his arms around the urn and rested his head against it. 'Sorry, darling,' he muttered, 'I'm just not in the mood.'

Patrick and Nick were on either side of Juan and gently dislodged him from the urn. In the harbour, the launch had already started its engines. They boarded carefully because of the darkness, Patrick and Nick holding tightly on to Juan. Anna thought it was a miracle that Juan managed to get back on the yacht without falling into the black water or slipping on the deck. Patrick and Nick didn't let go of him until they were safely in the lobby. Juan excused himself and went to his cabin.

'How do you drink that ouzo? It's lethal,' Anna asked Nick. She was feeling a little unsteady herself.

'Filthy stuff. Never touch it.' Nick laughed.

Conor and a few of the men wanted to continue the evening in the bar of the yacht, and Anna decided to join them. She wasn't really tired and she didn't want yet again to go to bed on her own.

The bar was furnished exactly like a bar in a luxury hotel in New York. The walls were of black marble and the carpets and chairs were a rich red. There was a bar counter with high stools, and more comfortable chairs around the walls. A small disco adjoined the bar. Anna sank down in a soft chair with a glass of water. Conor, Jean-Pierre, Jean-Claude and a few of the other diplomats settled into a corner and proceeded to continue a discussion that had started earlier that evening. Jean-Claude flashed a smile at Anna before turning to the other men, who were already deep in conversation.

'Charming.' Monique, who had joined Anna in her corner, was glaring at the men with distaste. 'Wouldn't you think they could take just one evening off for a change?' She kicked off her high-heeled shoes and tucked her feet under her in the chair.

'Hello! Two lovely women on their own.' Patrick stood in front of them with a glass of beer in his hand.

'Please, Nick,' Monique pleaded, 'we need to be entertained. I want to dance.'

A few minutes later, music was playing in the disco. Monique and Nick started to dance, followed by Patrick and Betsy. A few minutes later they were joined by Anna and Jean-Claude, who had grown bored with the discussion in the far corner.

It was two in the morning before Anna left the disco. Conor had already retired to bed. Anna had shared a bottle of champagne with Betsy and Patrick, and that combined with the ouzo was making her a little dizzy. She tiptoed unsteadily into the dark cabin and undressed. She didn't bother to try and find her nightgown. Conor didn't stir, as she crawled into bed. The cool sheets felt silken on her bare skin. She fell asleep as soon as her head touched the pillow and didn't wake until the next morning, when the maid knocked on the door to bring in their breakfast.

'Come in,' Anna called. Conor was hidden under the bedclothes. She shook him gently.

'Breakfast.' She sat up tucking the sheet around her

as the maid came in. Why was the maid staring like that? Anna turned to Conor. But it wasn't Conor!

'Anna. Darling,' Juan exclaimed. 'What a lovely surprise.'

CHAPTER II

Anna stared at Juan in horror. Was it a dream? No, she had a terrible headache and that never happened in dreams. She must have lost her way in the dark last night. And she had no clothes on! How was she going to get out of this situation? And how was she going to get out of Juan's cabin and into her own without Conor noticing?

As these thoughts flashed through her head Juan was sitting up in bed grinning as if he had just won the Lotto. The maid put the tray with Juan's breakfast on a table and, smiling, disappeared through the door.

'You look lovely, my darling. I don't seem to remember everything. Was it wonderful? Did the earth move? Did bells ring?' He moved as if to embrace her.

'No. Don't touch me. It's all a terrible mistake.' She crawled backwards out of the bed with the sheet wrapped tightly around her.

'No woman has ever been to bed with me and told me it was a mistake. Should we try again?' Laughing, he started to get out of bed. She saw that he was wearing as little as she was. She grabbed her clothes from the floor and rushed into the bathroom, locking the door.

She quickly pulled on her clothes and washed the makeup off her face. She used Juan's hairbrush to tidy her hair. It was very quiet on the other side of the door. She slowly opened the door a crack and peered out. Juan was sitting at the small table near the porthole tucking into his breakfast, humming to himself. He had put on a pair of jeans but no shirt. Anna opened the door wider and started toward the door that led out of the cabin, her shoes in her hand.

Juan turned around. 'There you are! Have some breakfast. I always find it very romantic to have breakfast after a night together.' He put a piece of croissant into his smiling mouth.

'We didn't spend the night together!' Anna exclaimed. 'I mean, we did, but it was an accident. Nothing happened. I just slept with you . . . I mean . . .' She was becoming muddled. 'You *do* know what happened. Please try to help me instead of laughing. It's not funny! And if you tell anyone I'll kill you. For God's sake, stop giggling.'

'OK. I'm sorry.' Juan had calmed down a little. 'Nothing happened. And I won't tell. I promise.'

'I'm going to my cabin to see if Conor is awake. If he is still asleep, I'll just get into bed.'

'Make sure it's Conor this time, darling. We wouldn't want this to happen again.'

'Shut up! If Conor is awake, I'll just say that I've been for a walk.'

'In your party clothes? Won't he think it's a bit odd?'

'Well, I'll think of something. Don't be so negative!' She opened the door.

'Anna,' Juan said softly.

'Yes, what is it now?' she snapped impatiently.

'I just wanted to tell you, that if we had made love, neither of us would have forgotten.' He blew her a kiss as she gently closed the door.

Anna tiptoed through the silent corridor to her own cabin. Everyone must still be sleeping off the ouzo. Well, that was lucky.

As she came into their dark cabin she found Conor still in bed, barely awake. 'Are you already up?' he asked sleepily.

'Just going to have a bath.' Anna went into the bathroom, locked the door and started to fill the tub. She took off her party clothes and stuffed them under some towels. She would sort them out later. Phew.

She sank thankfully into the warm water and made an effort to relax. She sighed deeply and tried to sort out her feelings. She smiled as she remembered the scene in Juan's cabin. It was funny, now that she was safely in her own room. But the thought of being naked in Juan's bed gave her goose bumps all over.

Anna was coming out of the bathroom, tying the belt of her robe, when there was a knock on the door.

'Get that, darling. It's probably the maid with our breakfast,' Conor murmured sleepily.

Without thinking, Anna opened the door to the same maid who had brought breakfast to Juan earlier. The poor woman looked at Anna in total confusion.

'I'm sorry, but I only brought breakfast for one,' she stammered.

'Why on earth did you do that?' Conor asked, puzzled.

'I thought *madame* was not here. I thought she was . . .'

'Never mind,' Anna said quickly. 'Just put the tray on the table. I'm not very hungry anyway.' Behind the maid's back, she looked at Conor and pointed to her head, as if to indicate that the woman was not all there.

'Oh,' Conor said. 'Right.' He looked kindly at the woman as she left their cabin. 'It's all right,' he said to her reassuringly.

'It must be hard to get good staff on a ship,' Anna mumbled.

That day had started strangely and it became worse with every passing hour. Anna checked her calendar twice to see if maybe it was Friday the thirteenth. There must be some explanation for all the bad luck. First, Conor's radio broke, making it impossible to listen to the lunchtime news and the continuing drama in Dublin. His mobile phone was out of range, causing a total news blackout. Then there was a problem with the ship's engines, leaving them stuck for hours in very choppy waters just off the mainland. A number of guests, including Anna, were violently seasick. This, on top of a major hangover from drinking too much ouzo, made her feel terrible. The memory of her embarrassment that morning did not help to cheer her up.

Ill and tired, she lay on the bed in their cabin while Conor, neither seasick nor hung-over, wandered up and down complaining about the loss of his radio link with Ireland. 'I know something awful is happening and I have no way of finding out. This is bloody terrible,' he stormed. 'It's so frustrating, can't you see that?'

'Please, Conor,' she pleaded, 'go and be frustrated somewhere else. I can't take any more.' At that moment there was a knock on the door. Conor opened it to admit the ship's radio officer.

'There is a phone call for you, Mr O'Connor,' he announced. 'It's urgent, they said.'

'It'll be my father,' Conor suggested. 'He probably wants to tell me what's going on.'

'No, it's from your department,' the officer replied. 'You can take the call in the radio room.' He turned and left.

'I'll be back in a minute, sweetheart. Can you manage without me for a while?' Conor asked.

'Yes, yes, go on,' she replied, waving her hand limply and hoping that she might be able to sleep off her nausea.

'Will I bring you something to eat?' he asked with the insensitivity of someone who had never been seasick. 'Maybe a ham sandwich? Or some cold chicken? They'll be serving dinner soon.'

'Please. Just go.' Anna groaned, nausea rising in her throat.

As he closed the door, Anna fell back on the pillows. She closed her eyes and drifted into a light sleep.

She woke up an hour later feeling weak but no longer sick. The ship's engines were humming steadily again and she assumed that they had been repaired. The sea had calmed somewhat and the rolling motion was not as strong as before. She rose slowly from the bed and tried to stand up. Yes, that was all right. She glanced at her watch. It was ten o'clock. Where was Conor? He must have finished his phone call by now. At that moment, he walked in the door, looking agitated.

'Were you on the phone all this time? What's going on?'

'I'm not sure. I have been called to Dublin by the minister.'

'Robert Sullivan? Why?'

'I don't know. They wouldn't tell me. All I know is that they want me there as soon as possible. I'm leaving tomorrow. In the afternoon.'

'What about me? Am I going with you?' Anna asked.

'No, it's better if you stay here. What are you going to do in Paris all alone?'

'But can't I come to Dublin with you?'

'You'll just be in the way. And you'll be bored. The cruise is nearly over, anyway. You might as well stay and enjoy yourself.'

'But, but . . .' She wanted that they should celebrate his promotion together. It was all her doing!

'Please, Anna,' he snapped. 'Do as you're told for once!'

'All right,' she exclaimed. 'I will. I don't care about you. I'm going to have great fun!' She swished out of the cabin, slammed the door shut, stomped down the corridor and ended up on deck, where she bumped into Juan who was having a brandy and a cigar by the railing.

'Careful, darling. You'll topple into the sea,' he exclaimed, grabbing her arm. 'What's wrong? You don't look well.'

'Gee, thanks.'

'You're not the only one who's been ill. Susanna looks even worse than you do.'

'That's supposed to make me feel better?' But it did.

Juan looked at Anna and thought she was beautiful. Her eyes were enormous in her pale face, giving her beauty a romantic quality. She looked like a woman in a Pre-Raphaelite painting, all auburn ringlets, translucent skin and limpid eyes. He was beginning to feel more than a passing attraction for her. She was stubborn, irritating and strong-willed. But ill and tired like this, she was adorable. He wanted to take her in his arms and carry her to bed. He knew he should ask her for another favour but he didn't want to use her any more. He wanted to make love to her.

'Would you mind throwing away that stinking cigar?' she demanded. 'It's making me feel queasy.'

'Of course,' he replied, tossing the offending object into the sea. 'I'll get you a cup of tea. That will make you feel a lot better. Sit down on that deckchair over there. I'll be back in a little while.'

Anna sat down on the lounge chair and put up her feet. The air was lovely and warm, and the soft breeze felt like a caress on her face. Juan arrived a few minutes later with a cup of tea and some crackers. She gratefully drank the tea and nibbled on the crackers, feeling instantly more human.

'Thank you. That was heaven. How did you know it was exactly what I needed?'

'I know what it's like to be seasick.' He smiled tenderly at her. 'Was Conor sick as well?' he asked.

'He was in great form. He drove me crazy. And now he's leaving to go to Dublin. He's been called to an urgent meeting with the Minister for Foreign Affairs.'

'Oh no!' Juan exclaimed.

'What's the matter?'

'Nothing. I just remembered something. Nothing to do with Conor,' he assured her. 'Are you going with him?'

'No. I'm staying to the end of the cruise.'

'Really? That's wonderful,' Juan said. 'Don't worry. I'll take care of you.'

'I'm quite capable of taking care of myself, thank you,' she replied stiffly. Why did men always assume she had to be taken care of?

'Now, you have the number of my mobile and the office number? Don't call me except in an emergency.' Conor was preparing his departure.

Jean-Pierre and Jean-Claude were also leaving for the airport. They were flying to Brussels for a meeting. The ship was riding at anchor outside Piraeus. The launch would take the men to the quay, where a car was waiting.

'Do try to concentrate on something other than your suntan for a change,' Conor continued. 'I need you to be charming to the French officials who are staying. It's very important to keep them happy. When you come back, we have to discuss the question of you working. I don't want you to continue with that nonsense much longer. So think about it while I'm gone.'

'I will.' Anna was feeling very annoyed. But she didn't want to start a row just then. Things had been decidedly chilly between them since the previous evening. Anna was disappointed Conor did not want her with him. He just thought she was being difficult.

'Try to be a bit more friendly to Juan. You have been positively frosty to him. We have to keep in with the Spaniards. They could be powerful allies in Brussels.'

'Yeah, OK,' Anna muttered.

'Anna! Did you hear me? Be nice to Juan, there's a good girl.' Conor sounded like a cross parent.

'Yes, I heard. I will be nice to him.' Very, very nice, she thought. And I won't be a good girl.

'Conor! We have to get going.' Jean-Claude had already boarded the launch. Jean-Pierre kissed Monique warmly and jumped aboard. Conor followed without a second glance at Anna. As the launch roared off, Anna saw him checking the papers in his briefcase.

'What a touching scene. Your husband was so romantic. It nearly made me cry.' Juan was leaning against the railing on the upper deck. He pretended to wipe a tear from his eye.

'Don't be stupid.' Anna wasn't in the mood for playing games.

'How about going to Athens for dinner, girls?' Juan asked. 'There are some lovely restaurants in the Plaka. That's the old part of town,' he explained. 'It's really lovely. Especially in the evening.'

'Why not?' Monique replied. 'It sounds like fun.'

They made arrangements to meet in the lobby an hour later. Juan would organise the launch and a car to bring them to Athens.

Anna went to her cabin to change from the shorts and T-shirt she had been wearing all day. She put on a black sleeveless cotton dress with a full, ankle-length skirt. She decided to bring an embroidered shawl, bought in Italy the summer before, in case she felt cold on the way back. She didn't need much makeup on her tanned face, only a little mascara. The dolphin earrings were her only jewellery.

'You look like a lovely young peasant girl,' Juan told her when they met in the lobby. The launch was ready with the engines idling. There was no sign of Monique.

'Where is Monique?'

'She has a headache. She is resting in her cabin.'

'Oh, no. I don't believe you. I'm not falling for that!' Anna turned to go back up the stairs.

'Go and ask her if you don't believe me. It's one of her migraines, she said.' Anna realised with horror that Juan must be telling the truth. He couldn't possibly have known about Monique's migraines.

'I don't want to go out with you alone. God knows what you'll get up to. I'm going to have dinner here on the ship.'

'Dinner was served over an hour ago. You missed it. It's me, or you go hungry.'

'OK, I'll go hungry.'

'Please, Anna. I won't lay a finger on you, I promise. And I'll take you back as soon as we've had dinner, I swear.'

Anna decided to enjoy herself for a while. Nobody cared what she did. Why not have some fun?

'All right. But no touching!'

'Not as much as a handshake.' Juan held up his hands. 'I won't even help you on to the launch.' His brown eyes were pleading, and he looked incredibly handsome dressed in a light blue shirt, navy slacks and a red sweater slung across his shoulders. Conor told me to be nice to him, Anna thought.

'What's this?' she asked suspiciously as she looked at the red open sports car that was waiting for them on the quay when they arrived.

'It looks very much like a car to me. But maybe it isn't? I'll ask someone what this curious object could be.'

'Don't be silly. You know very well what I mean.'

'You mean why isn't there a big black limousine complete with middle-aged driver to act as chaperone? I thought this would be more fun. It's not meant to be a sexual object or a way to lure an unsuspecting young girl into my bed. I just thought you might want to have fun. Just that. Nothing else. What do you say, Anna? Relax.'

Anna decided to try to relax. Juan was in the mood to enjoy himself. What would be the harm in that? He was, after all, wonderful company and the best guide you could have in Athens, as he had spent a few years there as a child when his father was attached to the Spanish embassy. He even spoke a little Greek.

Athens by night was a different place from the noisy, polluted city Anna had driven through the evening they arrived. The Plaka, situated just below the Parthenon, is where the inhabitants of Athens go for an evening out to have a drink, a meal and meet friends.

Anna and Juan wandered through the narrow streets looking into shop windows and quaint restaurants. They found an old inn where they could have dinner in the garden under trellises covered with vine leaves. Two cats wandered around, winding their tails around the legs of the guests. Soft Greek music was being played on an old gramophone.

They enjoyed a Greek meal with what seemed like a hundred different courses. Dish after dish of wonderful vegetables, fish and meat were brought to their table. Everything was deliciously flavoured with herbs and spices Anna had never tasted before.

'I'm stuffed,' Anna at last announced, pushing away a half-eaten dish of chicken in wine sauce. She sighed contentedly and stroked one of the cats which had jumped into her lap. She felt relaxed and happy.

Suddenly, Juan's mobile phone rang, breaking the spell.

'Sorry, darling,' he said. 'I've been waiting for this call. It won't take a moment.' He picked up the phone, rose from the table and walked a few yards away. A rapid discussion in Spanish followed, which lasted longer than the promised few minutes. Anna could see that Juan was looking increasingly annoyed. The conversation finally ended and Juan came back to the table, his handsome face in a frown.

'Is there something wrong?' she asked.

'A bit of a problem, yes,' he replied, looking at her thoughtfully. After a moment's silence he asked, 'Anna, you did deliver the letter to Nolan, didn't you?'

'Of course.'

'You're sure? The very same letter I gave you?'

'The very same. I put it in my handbag and then I transferred it to my evening bag and gave it to the Taoiseach. He was very grateful.

'I see,' Juan said. 'Hmm . . .' he continued, looking thoughtful.

'What's the matter? Is there a problem?'

'No, it's all right. I'll work it out,' he replied and rose from the table. 'Time to go,' he announced.

They walked slowly back to the car. A lot of people were still sitting around drinking ouzo at the small tables outside the bars and restaurants. Greek music could be heard here and there. The air was warm and fragrant with the smell of flowers and Greek food. Juan drove slowly through the winding streets, speeding up as they reached the open road to Piraeus. They did not speak until they were back on board the ship.

'Look, no hands,' Juan whispered as they arrived into the deserted lobby. He leaned forward holding up his hands, and placed a kiss on Anna's mouth.

'Good night, my beauty,' he murmured. 'I will never again be as well behaved.'

'I hope not,' she whispered. 'I couldn't bear it.' She ran up the stairs to her cabin without looking back. The ship moved in the calm water. They would be in Santorini just before lunch the next day.

Santorini. What a beautiful place, Anna thought, as she sat on the terrace in Franco's Bar sipping a drink which consisted of orange and pineapple juice and something very alcoholic. Far below, she could see the *Agamemnon* anchored in the bay.

The group had spent the day exploring the island, sunbathing and swimming at one of the beaches, which were curiously black from volcanic sand. They would go back to the yacht later to change and then return to the island for a party in a villa perched on the highest point of Santorini. The owner of the villa was a friend and associate of Pavlos Patmos.

Santorini is unlike any other island in the Greek archipelago. The whole island is one huge pile of volcanic lava. It rises from the sea in colours of red, black and brown against the dark sapphire of the sea and the brilliant blue of the sky. The white houses climb up the hills in a jumble of terraces and balconies, creating wonderful shapes with breathtaking views.

Anna was enchanted with this island, with the black sand and the cold, clear water, the dazzling white houses and the churches with their light-blue domed roofs. She was fascinated by its history and the ruins of many different periods. They had visited the archaeological site of Akrotiri, where remains of a town dating from 2000 BC had been found under the volcanic ash. Unlike Pompeii, the inhabitants had had plenty of time to leave the area. Only the houses and all they contained were left, perfectly preserved by the ash.

Lunch had been served at a little inn on a beach, and afterwards the guests had been taken by bus to the small town of Oia with its steep, winding streets.

Juan and Anna had spent the day avoiding each other. Now that Conor had left, there was a curious shyness between them. Anna was irresistibly drawn to Juan but did not want anyone to notice how she felt. Conor's behaviour the day before had hurt her and she did not want to think about him. Instead she concentrated her thoughts on this island, the beauty of the day, the sea and the delicious food they had eaten. Juan kept his distance, watching her from afar the whole day. Now he was standing by the bar, some distance from where Anna was sitting looking across the bay.

The sun had finally disappeared into the sea. The guests from the yacht made their way down the hill to the launch. There would be time for a short nap before it was necessary to dress for dinner. Anna was feeling sleepy. Juan joined her as she walked down the hill.

'I'm looking forward to dancing with you tonight,' he said, taking her hand.

'I have never seen you dance.'

'You will tonight. Believe me, you will.'

Anna felt a certain trepidation as she dressed for the party. Conor and his career seemed to belong to another world. She felt a sense of danger which excited her. She wore a black sleeveless dress with a very deep neckline. She felt reckless and dangerous.

The villa of Alexis Kollaros was perched on a cliff top high above the sea. Far below, the lights of the nearby villages could be seen like a row of pearls around the bay. It was a hot, windless night with a black sky. The guests climbed up the many steps to the terrace where their host was waiting for them. He was a good-looking man in his early sixties with a thatch of pure white hair, lively brown eyes, and a wonderful smile. He kissed the hands of the ladies and expressed his pleasure at meeting them.

As this was a very special evening, the guests had taken trouble to dress up. Most of the men wore black tie. Juan wore a white tuxedo jacket with his. Of course he would have a white jacket for a hot evening, Anna thought.

An elaborate buffet had been laid out in the big dining room. The windows were open to let in the cooling breeze that was beginning to blow. Alexis had invited some of his Greek friends to meet the guests from the yacht. Anna chatted with a couple from Athens, and asked many questions about Greece and this wonderful island.

When the guests had finished eating, coffee was served on the vast terrace where it was intended they would dance later. Anna was sipping her coffee, looking at the view, when Juan came up beside her. He put his arm around her and held her against him. 'What a lovely evening,' he mumbled into her hair.

'Mmm,' she replied dreamily and sighed.

'Why the sigh? Are you sad?'

'We have to leave this magical island tomorrow.'

'Don't think about it. There is only tonight. And only you and me.'

Music could be heard from the stereo. Frank Sinatra was singing 'I've Got You Under My Skin'. Some couples were already dancing.

'Come, Anna, let's dance.'

Anna turned and went to the improvised dance floor further out on the terrace. She put a hand on Juan's shoulder. His arm went around her waist and, looking into each other's eyes, they began to dance.

Anna had never had a partner who danced with such perfect rhythm. Even Pierre and other professional dancers did not move with such utter perfection and soul. It was as if Juan could feel her every thought. She forgot the other people and where she was. There was only Juan and the music. They danced as if they were one. They were a stunning sight, and many of the guests stopped to watch them. Their dancing became more and more intense.

'That's the best sex I've seen in a long time,' Nick whispered to Betsy.

'I wonder how it will end,' Betsy sighed, sounding worried.

'It seems fairly obvious to me.'

'I wish there was something we could do,' Betsy murmured.

'Maybe there is . . .' Nick replied slowly.

When the music stopped, Anna and Juan stood still as if rooted to the floor, eye to eye, their faces expressionless, breathing hard. Neither spoke, neither moved. For a split second, the world had stopped.

The music changed again, to a fast number, and

suddenly, everybody was dancing. Juan and Anna moved, without touching, to the fast beat for a few minutes, then Juan pulled Anna down the steps into the dark garden.

'Anna.' His arms went around her and his lips were on hers. Her head was dizzy from wine and dancing. She put her arms around Juan's neck and kissed him back with a fervour she didn't know she possessed. The feel of his body against her, his hands around her waist and his warm lips made her forget time and place. She gave herself up to the sensations and slipped her hands inside his jacket to feel his muscular body.

There was a sudden explosion and the sky lit up with a thousand lights. The earth shook. Millions of stars of white, red, green and blue erupted across the black sky.

'Fireworks!' someone shouted and there was another blast of lights. The garden filled with people running and shouting, looking up. Anna and Juan sprang apart.

'But Nick. It's too soon!' Alexis shouted angrily. 'I had planned the fireworks for much later.'

'So had I,' Juan muttered between his teeth.

Alexis could be heard still arguing with Nick on the terrace. 'I thought I told you to start the fireworks at midnight. It is only half past ten. What were you thinking of?'

'Alexis, don't be angry. It was my fault. I asked Nick to do it,' Betsy soothed. 'In any case, the display was beautiful.' Alexis seemed to accept Betsy's words of comfort. He had a soft spot for her.

The fireworks display signalled the end of the

party. Sadly, the guests took their leave of their host, thanking him for a wonderful evening. When they returned to the ship, they gathered in the bar for a last drink. No one wanted the evening to end.

'Meet me on the sun deck in five minutes,' Juan whispered to Anna, and left the bar. A few minutes later she finished her drink and, pretending to yawn, said goodnight to Betsy and Patrick.

'Have another drink,' Betsy pleaded. 'It's not that late.'

'No, I want to go to bed early.' Anna slipped out and ran up the stairs to the sun deck, where she could see Juan's white shirt gleaming in the dark. He had taken off his jacket and somehow procured a bottle of champagne and two glasses.

'To us,' he said and held out a glass.

She drank the champagne in one gulp, which made her cough.

'Take it easy! It's not medicine.' He poured her another glass. 'Sip it slowly, darling.'

She laughed and sipped the champagne more slowly, looking at Juan over the rim of her glass. She could see him clearly in the light of the full moon that had just emerged from the clouds. She felt as if she was in a film or a dream. Nothing seemed real.

Juan took the glass from her and put it with his own on a nearby table. 'I think that's enough for tonight.' He put his arms around her and looked into her eyes. 'We want to be conscious and clear-headed so we can enjoy the sensations.'

'What kind of sensations?'

'Like this,' he whispered, and started to kiss her.

'And like this,' he continued, kissing her neck. 'Anna, I love you,' he breathed.

Her arms went around his neck and she pressed her body against his. His hands were everywhere, touching her all over. How many hands has he got, she thought crazily, running her fingers through his hair.

Juan slipped down the straps of her dress to kiss her shoulders. His hands were inside the front of her dress. She opened his shirt and ran her hands over his chest. His skin was warm and smooth.

'We can't continue this here, darling,' Juan muttered into her cleavage.'

Anna was about to answer when the ship's public address system crackled.

'Urgent telephone call for Mrs Anna O'Connor,' a loud voice announced. 'Please come to the purser's office at once.'

All the lights came on, illuminating the deck in a ghostly glare. Juan swore loudly in Spanish. Anna pulled up the straps of her dress and Juan buttoned his shirt and put on his jacket. The lights went out.

'Telephone call for Mrs O'Connor,' the loud-speaker boomed again.

'*Mierda*,' Juan exclaimed. 'I'll wait for you here.' He took her hands and stared intently into her face in the dark. 'You will come back? Promise.' Wordlessly, she nodded, feeling suddenly cold. He pressed a kiss on her mouth and she left.

'Anna? Is that you?' Conor's voice came through after a lot of interference. 'Were you in bed?'

'No,' she replied. Not yet, she thought.

'I'm having awful problems. In fact, I have some bad news.'

'What?' She suddenly woke up from the dream. She felt as if a bucket of ice-cold water had been thrown in her face. 'Bad news? But what about your promotion?'

'Promotion? You must be joking! I'm in danger of being fired and possibly arrested.'

'What are you talking about?'

'They think I have something to do with the missing cheque.'

'What?' Anna demanded. 'Who are *they*? What's going on, Conor?'

'OK. I'll explain. Carlos Sanchez announced this morning that he had conveyed the famous cheque to the Taoiseach through diplomatic channels. It was the Irish embassy in Paris that is supposed to have acted as go-between. He said that a Spanish diplomat had looked after it. This man had sent Mr Nolan the cheque by way of the counsellor of the Irish embassy. But Anna' – Conor's voice was rising hysterically – 'I never saw the cheque or anything like it. I didn't give Nolan as much as a postcard. But no one believes me. They think I'm lying and that I have pocketed the money. They've been grilling me for hours. I'm being suspended from my duties. It's in all the papers.' Conor was nearly sobbing now. 'It's the end of my career.'

'Calm down, darling,' Anna soothed. 'I'm sure there's an explanation for all this.' Slowly, she realised that the explanation was very simple, and her blood ran cold. Of course, she thought. I know who delivered the cheque. And it wasn't Conor.

'I hope you're right,' he replied, but without conviction. 'Anyway,' he continued. 'I rang to tell you to look out for Juan. You see, he must be the diplomat in question.'

'Yes. He must be,' she replied, her voice shaking.

'He's a crook. Do you understand? And he's dangerous, so be careful.'

'I will.' Anna was in a state of shock. She replied automatically to everything Conor said.

'That's not all,' he continued, 'there's more trouble; my parents have been found. It's terrible.'

'Dead?' she whispered.

'Don't be silly,' Conor snapped. 'They're very much alive. They had a lovely holiday!'

'But how can that be bad news?' Anna was totally confused.

'It's not the holiday that's the problem. It's where they spent it. They were in Carlos Sanchez's villa in Marbella! How do you think that looks?' Conor growled. 'A member of the county council in Kinsale being wined and dined by the very man who is proposing the destruction of the town!'

'Oh,' Anna stammered.

'And *we* have been living it up on a cruise ship in the Greek islands. The journalists are having a great time with this.'

'Have you talked to your father?'

'Yes, I have. He doesn't understand what all the fuss is about, he says. What a mess,' Conor moaned. 'You have to leave as soon as possible, Anna.'

'But the cruise is nearly over. We are going back to

Paris the day after tomorrow,' she stammered.

'That's right. OK. I'll see you when you come back. I'm in Paris now to collect a few things and arrange for someone to replace me. Then I'm supposed to go back to Dublin and wait for the outcome of this affair. They are expecting me to cough up the money. But how can I?'

'I don't believe this is happening,' Anna whispered. 'You can't manage this on your own. You need a lawyer.'

'I have one. Dad's solicitor.'

'Mr O'Dea? But he's at least a hundred years old.'

'What does it matter? I'm doomed,' Conor declared. 'And my family is in disgrace.'

'Don't give up,' Anna soothed.

'I would love to get my hands on the bastard who has that cheque,' Conor raged. 'But I have to go now. I'll see you in a few days. Bye.' He hung up.

Anna stood with the receiver in her hand, as if paralysed. She realised now what she had felt but had not wanted to admit to herself. Juan had used her. He was a liar and a cheat. He had pretended to be attracted to her in order to make her do what he wanted. He had managed to get her and Conor to go on the cruise and to get Conor's father invited to Marbella while the application for planning permission was decided on. He had also tried to get her into bed (and, let's face it, she thought, nearly succeeded). She had been such a fool. And she had got Conor into trouble as well.

God, I'm stupid, she thought. Vain and selfish too, a little voice added. Tears of self-loathing, anger and hurt started to course down her cheeks. She hung up the receiver and slowly walked out of the purser's office and down the corridor to her cabin. Once inside, she locked the door.

Anna was now sobbing hysterically and frantically looking for a handkerchief. She grabbed her large handbag, which she hadn't used since the flight, and rummaged around in it to find a tissue to dry her streaming eyes and nose. She found a crumpled packet of Kleenex, and, tucked beside it, a white envelope. Oh, yes, Declan's report card. She had forgotten to open it because of all the hassle of the past week. Darling little Declan! The thought of him made her cry even harder. She realised how much she missed the children. They wouldn't be very proud of their mammy right now, she thought, and blew her nose. She decided to look at Declan's report card.

I hope he didn't fail maths again, she thought, opening the envelope. But it did not contain anything that resembled a report card, just a folded piece of paper. She unfolded it and stared at the letters and numbers.

'What the hell . . .' she muttered. Then she realised what she was holding in her hand. It was a bank draft for one hundred thousand pounds made out to Seamus Nolan.

CHAPTER 12

The next morning, when Anna looked at her face in the big mirror in the bathroom, she looked terrible. Her eyes were red and swollen from crying, her cheeks were pale, and her hair looked limp. She had a splitting headache. She hadn't slept a wink, but had laid awake all night trying to think of a way out. There was no one she could ask for help. She couldn't bear the thought of telling anyone what she had done. I'll have to sort it out myself, she decided.

After an agonising few hours, she finally found a solution. The only solution. But it didn't make her stop crying. It wasn't the thought of the damage she had done to Conor that upset her the most, but the fact that Juan had betrayed her.

She felt a little better after a long, hot shower. There was a knock on the door as she was brushing her tangled hair. Probably the maid, she thought, carelessly wrapping the huge bath towel around her as she went to open it. Juan, dressed in a suit, with a face as terrible as her own, stared back at her.

'You look awful,' he said. 'Don't worry,' he

continued, as she backed away from him. 'I won't touch you. I wouldn't force myself on an unwilling woman. I looked for you last night but you were gone. Your Swedish cool took over, I suppose. Control is more important than love to you, isn't it? Thank God I didn't fall for your pretended warmth.' He stepped into the cabin and closed the door.

'You bastard!' Anna yelled. 'How dare you come near me. How dare you talk of love!' She threw her hairbrush at him. He ducked, and the brush hit the closed door.

'I beg your pardon?' Juan stammered, no longer in control.

'I know everything! That was Conor on the phone last night. He is in awful trouble, thanks to you! And me,' she added.

'What's happened?'

'The cheque is missing. That cheque I gave to the Taoiseach. Yeah, that's right, you can wipe that surprised look off your face! I know all about it. They think Conor nicked the money. Nolan denies receiving as much as a penny.'

'What a shit,' Juan groaned.

'It takes one to know one. I know all about you now. Thanks to you, Conor is being suspected of theft.'

'That is truly awful. I never wanted him to get into trouble. You must believe me. Nolan was supposed to fix the planning permission. But he must have either just taken the money and done nothing, or the cheque was lost somehow. Carlos is left with no hotel and a loss of £100,000. What a mess. The problem is, I can't come clean and explain the truth. That would put you into a terrible position.'

'And you. That's your main worry, isn't it, you coward.'

'No, Anna, please. I don't want anything to happen to you.'

'How touching,' she sneered. 'What a gentleman. But don't worry. I have just thought of a way out. Everyone will come out smelling of roses. Even you. Not that you deserve it. Just one question. Try to tell the truth for once, if you know what that means.'

'What's your question?'

'Who else knows about my part in this charade?'

'No one. Just you and me. And of course Nolan.'

'Is that the truth? Sanchez doesn't know? If you're lying . . .'

'No, he doesn't. He thinks it was Conor. It's the truth. I swear.'

'I'll have to believe you. OK. Then it will work.'

'What will work? How can you do anything? Do you know what happened to the money?'

'Yes I do,' she replied. 'But I'm not going to tell you where it is.'

'You know where it is?' Juan stammered. 'How is this possible? You said . . .'

'I made a mistake. I gave Nolan the wrong envelope.'

'What was in it?' Juan demanded.

'Declan's report card.' Anna started to sob. 'Poor little Declan's report card. If he failed maths, the Taoiseach will know about it. You see,' she explained, 'the envelopes were identical. That's why I mixed them up.'

'Oh my God,' Juan whispered. 'No wonder Nolan's so angry. He's being blamed for receiving money he doesn't even have. And Carlos is as mad as hell. He'll blame me, of course.'

'I hope he tears you limb from limb,' Anna snapped. 'But never mind that. There is only one way to get Conor out of this mess. And I'm going to do it.'

'What can you do?' Juan demanded.

'I'm not going to tell you a thing.'

'But sweetheart,' he pleaded, 'please . . .'

'Don't sweetheart me,' she snarled. 'Just get out. I don't ever want to see you again.'

'I suppose this is goodbye,' Juan said.

'You bet it is. I'm so glad I realised what you were like before it was too late. Thank God nothing happened between us.'

'I wouldn't call it nothing,' Juan replied. 'It wasn't nothing to me.'

'Please. I don't want to hear any more. Just leave.' She tightened the grip on the towel. She was feeling a little exposed.

'Anna,' Juan pleaded, grabbing her shoulders. 'Please listen.'

'I don't want to hear any more from you. There is only so much bullshit a woman can stand,' Anna replied, trying to wrench free of his grip.

'No. You are going to listen.' Juan's fingers were digging in to her flesh and his eyes looked deeply into hers. 'It's true that I flirted with you in the beginning to make you pass on the cheque. But then my feelings became stronger. I fell in love with you. Last night I told you the truth. I do love you. I have never wanted a woman more. Not for a long time,' he added.

'I don't believe you. I may be foolish but I'm not a complete moron. Leave me alone!' she shouted and burst into tears.

Juan's arms went around her and, feeling totally helpless, she leaned her head against his shoulder.

'I hate you,' she sobbed into his suit. 'I wish I had never met you, you big shit.'

'I know,' he soothed. 'I agree. I suppose you couldn't forgive me?'

'No. Never. I hope you'll rot in hell forever.' Anna pulled herself free from his embrace, and, with tears dripping on to her towel, stared at him for a moment. 'Please, just go,' she whispered.

'I'll go,' he said softly. 'The ship's helicopter is taking me to the nearest airport. Then I'm going to Madrid. We won't see each other again.' Juan gently placed a finger under her chin. 'I'll never forget you,' he mumbled. 'I'll try, but I won't succeed. And for God's sake don't drop that towel. You won't have a chance in hell if you do.' He leaned forward, kissed her mouth and suddenly let her go. The door slammed as he left.

Anna sank down on the bed, her feelings in turmoil. She knew she should hate him after what he had done to her. She felt deeply guilty about her part in the whole mess with the cheque, and realised she had nearly wrecked her marriage and Conor's career.

If only Conor hadn't been so annoying, she

thought, if only he hadn't ignored me like that. Flirting with Juan had been a kind of escape, like watching a soap opera on television where she was the star. Any woman would have been carried away, she thought. Juan is like a big box of chocolate to someone who has been on a diet for months, a glass of water in the desert. He was probably sent here by the devil to tempt bored housewives. Well, I was strong enough to resist him, she thought with pride, conveniently forgetting that if it hadn't been for Conor's phone call . . .

Anna arrived back in Paris on a rainy evening. There was the usual pushing and arguing at the airport to find a taxi but she finally managed to elbow herself and her luggage through the crowd and into one. The past week of luxury living had left her ill prepared for real life. She felt physically and mentally exhausted by the events of the past days. The trip back to Piraeus had seemed endless. Alone in a deckchair, unable to enjoy the perfect weather and beautiful scenery of the last day, she could hear the other passengers have their lunch on the sun deck below, chatting about the wonderful time they had had. The last evening Anna did not share the farewell dinner with the other guests. She asked for a sandwich and a pot of tea to be sent to her cabin. The following morning, after the ship docked, the breakfast with Pavlos Patmos, which under different circumstances would have amused her, was rather a strain.

Pavlos was a tiny, chubby man in his late seventies. He had appeared in the ship's dining room to greet his guests. He was accompanied by two of his daughters, who greeted Betsy with squeals of delight and warm kisses.

One by one, the guests shook their host's hand and expressed their thanks for a wonderful week. Pavlos accepted their thanks and proceeded to make a short speech in French. He told them he had been delighted to organise a cruise for diplomats from the European Union and that he hoped it would bring good fortune to his country. He said he was putting his private jet to their disposition for the trip back to Paris.

Everybody then lined up to say goodbye to Nick who had taken such good care of them during the trip.

'Goodbye, my sweet,' he said to Anna when it was her turn. 'Don't look so sad. A pretty girl like you should look happy.'

Tears welled up in her eyes. Nick put his arms around her and whispered, 'He isn't worth it, believe me. Chin up.' Anna stuck her chin in the air and tried to smile. 'That's my girl,' Nick said. 'And don't worry, I took care of your letter. It was sent by express mail early yesterday morning. It will probably arrive today.'

'Thank you so much, Nick,' Anna said. 'You've been a true friend.'

'You're welcome,' he replied. 'Have a good trip.' He turned to speak to the next person in line.

A fleet of cars brought them to the airport where the Patmos jet was waiting. The plane was tastefully decorated and furnished with cosy sofas and chairs. It was certainly a lot more comfortable than a commercial aircraft.

Anna settled into a seat by one of the windows and closed her eyes while the plane took off.

'Tired?' Betsy asked gently beside her.

'I'm exhausted. I didn't sleep a wink last night.' They were interrupted by Patrick, who touched Betsy's shoulder.

'Please, honey, let me explain.'

'No,' Betsy snapped. 'Go away.' Patrick straightened up and walked to the rear of the plane.

'What's the matter?' Anna asked. 'I thought you were . . .'

'We broke up,' Betsy replied with a grim expression on her face.

'What happened?'

'I don't really want to talk about it. But OK, I'll tell you, if you promise never to mention his name to me again.'

'I promise,' Anna said, momentarily forgetting her own misery.

'Last night was so wonderful. Really magic,' Betsy started. 'We were in bed drinking champagne, and I thought all my dreams had come true. Then he started being superior. He criticised the decor of the ship. I told him I had designed it, but that didn't make any impression on him. He actually laughed at my design and said it was kitsch and naff. I told him anyone who wore those awful ties had no right to talk about taste.'

'Oh God,' Anna exclaimed. 'Then what happened?'

'Well, the row got worse and he threw me out of his cabin, wearing only a sheet. I had to sneak through the corridors to my room, hoping no one would spot me. Oh, Anna, I made such a fool of myself. I should have known what he was like.' Betsy's eyes filled with tears. 'I thought I had met Mr Right. Boy, was I mistaken.'

'He threw you out of his cabin?' Anna gasped. 'Half naked? What a shit.'

'Weeeell,' Betsy muttered. 'Maybe I went a little too far. I said a few things that no man would be able to take.'

'Like what?'

'Oh, I just criticised his performance in bed. Unjustly. He's actually unbelievable. But I wanted to really stick the knife in.'

'And now he's trying to make up,' Anna remarked.

'I know. But I don't want to. We would just make each other miserable.' Betsy sighed and turned to Anna. 'What about you? You look awful. Is it Juan?'

'Well, partly.'

'Oh God. I told you not to get involved with him. You didn't sleep with him?'

'No. Of course not.'

'Thank goodness for that. But what's the problem then? Are you sorry you didn't?'

'No.'

'You need therapy. You seem to be totally confused.'

'Look who's talking,' Anna retorted. Then she started telling Betsy some of what had happened the night before, leaving out the part about the cheque and the whole mess with Seamus Nolan.

'So, you got into a clinch with Juan on the deck,'

Betsy said, 'when the phone rang. Talking to Conor made you realise what you were doing. You just left Juan waiting with a big . . .' She started to laugh.

'. . . bottle of champagne.' Anna smirked.

'How terribly disappointing for poor Juan. You really got him where it hurts a man the most. Good for you. He'll probably never recover.'

'I hope not. It serves him right,' Anna declared, feeling quite cheerful again.

'That's right.' Betsy smiled. 'Cheer up, darling. You will soon have forgotten Juan. Conor will be waiting for you when you come home and he will be so happy to see you.'

Anna thought about Betsy's words as she sat in the taxi. Betsy was right. She would try to make her marriage come to life again, as soon as the mess Conor was in had been sorted out. She was sure it would be, very soon, now that with Nick's help she had taken care of the cheque. I got him into it, she thought, but I also got him out. And I hope he'll never find out I had anything to do with it.

It was a horrible night. Anna was looking forward to the bright apartment and dinner with Conor. Maybe he would take her to a restaurant? There was a lovely little bistro around the corner. They could have a light meal and a few glasses of wine. The thought cheered her up. I'll make him feel better, she thought, as she went up in the lift.

But the apartment was dark and empty. Where was Conor at this hour? Did he not know she would arrive home? He had said that he would see her tonight. Anna put her suitcase down in the hall, picked up the post and went into the living room. The place was dusty and stuffy.

There was a dead plant, a dirty tea cup and a scribbled note from Conor on the coffee table. *Gone to Normandy with Sarah*, it said. To Normandy? With Sarah? Had he left her? Was this the end? Oh God, he has found out, she thought. He must despise me. And now he has another woman. Sarah has finally got her claws in him. Anna's knees went from under her and she sat quickly down on the sofa. What am I going to do now? she thought.

She glanced at the post. There was a card from the children asking if they could stay longer, they were having such a good time. *Grandad is taking us camping and Gertrude (the dog) has had puppies. Please can we stay a bit longer, we don't want to come home yet*. It was signed Lena and Declan. There was a PS: *Have you seen Declan's report card?* The children didn't want her either. She felt totally alone and abandoned.

Anna picked up the extension on the little side table to ring Betsy. She needed a friend to talk to on this bleak evening. The phone rang many times before there was an answer.

'Hello?' answered Patrick's voice. He sounded breathless.

'Patrick? What are you doing there? I thought ...' She stopped. 'It's Anna. Is Betsy there?'

'Just a moment.' Anna could hear giggling and rustling. Betsy's voice came on the line. She sounded a little strange.

'What are you doing with Patrick?' Anna demanded.

'What do you think?' Betsy giggled. 'Oh stop that, darling,' she gasped. 'I'm on the phone.'

'But you said . . .'

'I know, but . . . Well . . . you know . . . I changed my mind.' More giggling.

'I see,' Anna muttered and hung up.

She put down the receiver as if it had burned her. Nobody wanted her. Conor had run away with Sarah, the children didn't want to come home, and Betsy was making wild, passionate love with Patrick. Monique had left for the south of France with her children for a last holiday before their departure to Australia. And Teresa, her friend from Portugal, was away for the summer. Anna felt as if she was stranded on a deserted island, adrift on the ocean without a life raft.

She put her head in her hands and gave herself up to her feelings. Tears started to course down her face and she began to sob. She cried for a full hour without stopping, until there were no tears left. She felt drained, and terribly hungry. She rose and went out to the kitchen. Maybe Conor had done some shopping.

There was hardly any food in the fridge, just a dried-up piece of cheese and half a carton of milk well past its sell-by date. Anna found two pork chops, a bag of French fries and half a chocolate cake in the freezer. That would do for a start. She could cook the chops in the microwave and do the chips in the oven. The cake would thaw while she was cooking. If she was still hungry after that, she would ring for pizza. She needed to fill the void inside her.

Anna was eating the last crumbs of the chocolate cake when she heard the front door open. Maybe Conor was back? She rushed out to the hall, where Mícheal was closing the door. He turned around and looked at her, surprised. He was carrying a big white box.

'Jesus! You scared me. You look like shit. Did you have a bad trip?'

'What the hell are you doing here? And with a key. Did I forget to make you give it back?'

'I didn't know there would be anybody here. Sarah's television is on the blink, and I thought I could watch the news here.'

'So you broke in? Charming.'

'I have a key,' he replied, waving it in front of her face. 'I had a copy made. By the way, darling,' he continued, 'your husband is in it up to his neck. He stole that money and now he'll be in jail forever.' Mícheal broke into a cackling laugh.

'He's innocent,' Anna protested.

'My eye! He did it all right. He looked as guilty as hell in that picture on the front page of the *Telegraph*. Prison is too good for him. He should get the chair.'

'I know he didn't do it,' Anna declared. 'The whole thing is about to be sorted out. Wait till you see.'

'Sorted out?' he snorted. 'I bet. It'll be some diplomatic fiddle again. I know you're very thick with the Taoiseach. They have let your husband out, I heard. Temporarily. But the news will start in a minute. I have to watch it.' He walked into the living room.

'No you don't. Get out at once,' Anna shrieked, running after him.

'Just let me watch the news,' Mícheal pleaded.

'The news? Why do you want to watch the news?'

'Don't you know? Sarah is gone to Normandy.'

'Yes. With Conor. They have run away together. Why would that be on the news?'

'You bloody fool. Don't you ever listen to the news or read the papers? Haven't you heard about the crisis?'

'Crisis? In Normandy? Have the cows gone on strike?'

'You really are the most stupid woman I have met in my entire life.' Mícheal raised his eyes to the ceiling in despair. 'The French fishermen have blocked the ports. Thousands of English and Irish tourists are stranded because the ferries can't leave. Conor had the bright idea to go and see if he can help them in any way. He asked Sarah to come with him.'

'But Conor has been suspended from his duties,' Anna stammered. 'He was only supposed to come here to pick up some papers and organise someone to replace him while he is away.'

'Yeah, I know,' Mícheal replied. 'But he asked for permission to go to Normandy and the Department was more than happy to let him go. That's what Sarah told me. No one else would be mad enough to face those bastards.'

'Tourists. Of course. Saint Conor to the bloody rescue. I should have known.' Anna suddenly felt relieved, but very angry.

'You have no idea what it's been like here for the past few days,' Mícheal remarked. 'Sarah said the phones haven't stopped ringing at the office. Everyone is looking for help. They are somehow blaming the embassy for the whole mess. You know how people are when they're in trouble. They look for a scapegoat.'

'So Conor thought the embassy would be criticised if he didn't go up there?'

'Criticised? They'd be fucking crucified. We're talking angry Irish tourists with no money or food,' Mícheal exclaimed. 'I'm sure your Department thought it was proper punishment for what he's done. A bit like throwing him to the lions. They are probably hoping he won't come back alive.'

'Conor hasn't done anything!' Anna protested. 'Can't you get that into your thick head?'

'Yeah, right,' Mícheal muttered.

'So what is he doing?' Anna sighed. 'Handing out the loaves and the fishes?'

'He filled the car with bread, ham and beer. I think he even brought whiskey. But we can find out what's going on if you'll just switch on the TV. I'll leave when the news is over.' He put the box on the coffee table.

'Is that pizza I smell?' Anna asked, feeling hungry again. Finding out that after all Conor might not have left her had calmed her down.

'Yeah. I was going to eat it here. But I'm not sharing.'

'Ah, please,' Anna begged. 'I'll open a bottle of wine.'

'Wine? OK.' Mícheal sat down on the sofa and opened the box. 'There's extra cheese,' he announced.

'Lovely. Let's check the wine rack.' Anna didn't want to be alone any more. She was even prepared to put up with Mícheal tonight. I must be really desperate, she thought. Well, it's less dangerous than dancing with Juan. There will be no temptation.

'So, Mícheal,' Anna said an hour, a huge pizza and two bottles of wine later, 'how come you're here? I mean, if there is a crisis in Normandy, why aren't you there, interviewing the victims of this humungus disaster? As I asked you once before, a long time ago, aren't you supposed to be a journalist?' She hiccuped. ''Scuse me. It must be the pepperoni.'

They had had their meal in front of the television watching the news, which had only devoted three minutes to the situation in Normandy. They had caught a fleeting glimpse of Conor walking down the long line of cars, looking stressed, handing out sandwiches to Irish people in distress.

'Well, my dear. Since you ask, I don't give a shit, actually. I find people in trouble a shagging bore. I prefer a good political scandal. Especially a sexual one. Talking of which,' he continued, 'what did you really get up to with that bloody Mexican?'

'Spaniard,' she corrected.

'Whatever. They're all the same to me.'

'Nothing,' Anna replied.

'What?'

'Nothing happened.'

'Really? Was he a fucking queer?'

'No, no. It was me.' Anna was losing track of the

conversation. She didn't really know what they were talking about or why.

'You? You're queer?'

'No, no. I messed it all up.' She burst into tears. 'I hate myself,' she wailed, 'I hate my life.'

'Come on! It can't be that bad.'

'Yes it is. You don't understand. I've done something terrible.'

'What have you done? Shagged a bloody Mexican?'

'No. Will you listen for once?' Anna grabbed him by the front of his pullover. 'Pay attention.'

'Right, right,' Mícheal slurred. 'I'm lishtnin. Tell me all about it.'

'I can't,' she sobbed, 'it's too horrible. I can't tell anyone.'

'Why not? Come on. Spit it out. It won't go any further, I swear.'

'No,' Anna sniffed. 'I've changed my mind. I don't trust you. You're one of *them*.'

'Them?'

'Journalists. It would be in the papers tomorrow if I told you.'

'Would it?' he asked, looking confused. 'Who'd put it in the papers? Anyway,' he continued, 'so this Argentinian wanted to shag you, and you didn't? Wash dat the problem?'

'It's none of your business,' Anna replied, looking suddenly prim. 'I'm not going to tell you a thing.'

'About wha'? I forgot what we were dishcussin. How about shum more vino?' He poured them both another glass.

Anna drank the wine in one gulp. The alcohol dulled the pain a little. She had been relieved to learn that Sarah and Conor were not eloping, but maybe the tourists were worse rivals than another woman? Conor loved helping people. He was always handing money to beggars and would be the first person to assist anybody in distress. He is kinder to strangers than to me, she thought. He would give a poor woman he didn't know everything he had in his wallet. But if I want to buy a new dress, it's like blood out of a stone.

She was tired and more than a little bit drunk. She wanted to get rid of Mícheal and go to bed. He was leering at her over his glass. I hope he is not thinking what I think he is thinking, she thought.

'How about a cuddle?' Mícheal slurred. 'All this talk of sex has made me feel affectionate.'

'How can you? What about Sarah?'

'She's not here, is she? A man has needs, you know.' He leaned forward. 'So how about it? It will cheer us both up. And I won't speak a word of Spanish.'

'Are you out of your mind? Do you really think I would sink so low? Why does everybody want to have sex with me?' she shouted. 'I'm sick of sex! And you can shove your needs. Now, get out! I want to go to sleep.'

'Don't get excited. Just let me smoke a cigar before I go. I always smoke after sex but since we skipped the main course, I have to go straight on to dessert.' He took a big cigar from his pocket.

'No, you don't. You won't smoke that filthy thing in here.' She snatched the cigar from him, walked a little unsteadily to the open window and threw it out.

'You really are a party-pooper.'

'Go home.'

'I know you want me. You're just too tired tonight. How about getting together some other time? How about tomorrow night?'

'How about when hell freezes over?'

'Tell me, your highness,' he enquired, slowly getting up from the sofa. 'Why did you ask me to stay for dinner if you despise me so much?'

'Because you were there.'

'Well, thank you so much for a delightful evening! I especially enjoyed the revelations of your nonexistent sex life. But don't worry. I won't tell anybody. Your reputation as a tease is intact. When your husband is rotting in jail, you'll be very lonely. You'll be singing a different tune then.'

'Goodbye,' Anna snarled as she held the front door open. 'Please don't bother to come back. And you can hand over that key while you're at it.'

'Why should I?' Mícheal glared at her drunkenly, leaning against the wall.

'Because if you don't, I'll tell Sarah that you tried to get into bed with me.'

'And I'll tell your husband that you nearly shagged that Portuguese.' They stared at each other in silence.

'If you don't hand over the key this instant,' Anna snarled, 'I'll tell everybody about your true identity.'

'Jesus Christ, woman, you drive a hard bargain.' He groped in his pocket and produced the key. 'OK. I won't bother you again, even if you beg me.'

'That'll be the day.'

Mícheal shuffled through the door and into the lift. Anna could hear him mutter to himself as the lift slowly brought him down.

She closed the door and went into the living room to tidy up. What an evening. She felt queasy and she had a splitting headache. Her stomach churned from all the food she had eaten. Never again, she thought, I'll never drink wine again. And as for pizza. She wanted to meet the man who had invented it and force him to eat a very big one and watch him writhe in agony. She couldn't believe that she had revealed details of her sex life to Mícheal. It was the wine and the loneliness that had done it. She had needed to confide in someone, and Mícheal had been the only person available.

As Anna lay in bed, she looked at the framed photo of Conor she kept on her bedside table. She looked at his handsome face, his reddish-blond shaggy hair that curled behind his ears, his lovely brown eyes that crinkled when he smiled, and his generous mouth. She remembered his muscular body and how it felt to be held in his strong arms. Safe, she thought, I feel safe in his arms. But maybe it's too late? I have really been stupid, she said to herself. It is partly my fault that he has been ignoring me. I should have tried to make him notice me. She fell asleep with the photograph pressed against her bosom.

The phone rang early the next morning. Anna's head was aching, her mouth felt dry and furry, and her stomach was in a knot. She groped for the receiver.

'Hello, this is the telephone,' she said irrationally

into the receiver. 'I mean, this is me on the telephone.' She realised she was at home in her own bed.

'Anna? Is that you?' Conor's voice asked. 'Are you all right? You sound a bit strange.'

'Yes, darling. I'm fine,' she croaked. 'Just a bit tired.' She tried to clear her throat. 'Could you try not to speak so loudly?' This is one hell of a hangover, she thought.

'OK. But Anna!' he was shouting again, sounding happy.

Anna winced and held the receiver further away from her ear. 'Yes?'

'There's some wonderful news.' Conor laughed.

'What, sweetheart?' she whispered.

'I'm in the clear,' he exclaimed. 'The cheque has been found. They just called me from the Department.'

'Really? That's fantastic,' Anna replied. 'What a relief. Did Nolan have it?'

'No. Mr Sanchez has explained that the cheque was never given to the Taoiseach in the first place. It had accidentally been sent to Greece. Isn't that strange? Anyway, whoever had it, sent it back to Sanchez. There are still some honest people in the world.'

'So everyone's happy?'

'Not everyone,' Conor said. 'The Secretary General of the Department told me that the Taoiseach seems annoyed with me. I don't know why. He is supposed to have said something about someone in my family not being very clever and that they would get theirs in the end. I haven't a clue what he means.'

'Don't worry about it,' Anna soothed. She hoped

she wouldn't meet the Taoiseach for a long, long time. 'Just be happy everything is all right. How are things in Normandy?'

'It's bloody murder up here. You have no idea what it's been like. The Irish are giving me hell, blaming the government, the embassy and the European Union for this. They don't seem to understand that it's the bloody frogs who are the source of the problem. Someone screamed he was going to sue when he came home but he didn't seem to be sure who he would sue. Bloody fishermen. Jesus, I'll never eat fish again.'

'But weren't they happy to see you?'

'Only because it gave them someone to shout at. I have even fed the bastards. If I hadn't had the bright idea to bring beer, they would have attacked me.'

'Irishmen can be really vicious sometimes!'

'It's the women. And the language. I'm telling you, I was bloody terrified they were going to lay into me.'

'Why don't you just come home? There can't be much more you can do.'

'I will. I'm coming home soon. By the way, you'll never guess who is here stuck in one of the queues.'

'Who?'

'My cousin, Kieran. You know, the dentist in Dublin?'

'Was he happy to see you?'

'No, he just shouted abuse at me. What's the embassy doing to help? he called. Nothing as usual! What do we pay taxes for? To let the likes of you live it up in Paris? Bloody typical! I didn't give him any beer.'

'Good for you. Let him stew.'

'I will. Anna,' he continued, 'it looks as if the blockade will be over soon. I'll be able to go back to Paris.'

'How are you getting back? With Sarah?' Anna didn't much like the prospect. She still wasn't sure Sarah wouldn't try to seduce Conor.

'I hope not!' Conor exclaimed. 'The thought of two hours in a car with that woman gives me the creeps.'

'Why? What has she done?' Anna asked, with relief in her voice.

'She hasn't done anything. She's just so annoying. She keeps lecturing me on how to do my job. She has these theories on how to make the office more efficient. In fact, she seems to think she can reorganise the entire Department! I can't stand much more of it.'

'Wasn't she any help during the blockade?'

'She was bloody useless. She annoyed people by telling them to cheer up. She also told them that it was their own fault for coming to France by car: It would have been better if you had travelled by air, a much more efficient way to go on holiday.' Conor mimicked Sarah's prissy voice. 'She gave out to a group for throwing litter out of their car as well. What impression of Ireland do you think you are giving the French? she asked.'

'I'm sure they didn't care.' Anna laughed.

'They couldn't give a damn. They were ready to murder any Frenchman they saw.' Conor grunted. 'I would have managed much better here without that bloody woman. The Irish were in a mood to kill us by the time she was finished. She's a menace. I'm going to catch a lift with one of the journalists. I'll probably be home early this evening. Around seven or eight.'

'That's great!'

'I can't wait to come home and have a bath and a meal,' Conor said. 'I have lived on sandwiches and beer for the past two days and I haven't had a chance to shave or wash. You won't like the look of me.'

'Yes I will,' Anna replied. 'I love the caveman look. Conor,' she continued, 'I'm so looking forward to seeing you again. I've missed you. Do you love me?'

'Of course. What's this all about? Are you feeling all right?'

'I'm feeling great. I didn't before, but now I do. See you tonight, darling.' Anna hung up feeling a lot better. Conor seemed his usual self. All she needed to do was to make him realise that they should spend more time together and that there were things more important than Irish politics and his career. It would be tough and take a lot of effort, but she loved a challenge. Sexy underwear, she thought, I'll buy some sexy underwear today. That should make him sit up and take notice.

The phone rang again. Anna picked up the receiver thinking Conor was calling her once more. 'Darling.'

'What? Is this the O'Connors'?' asked an annoyed voice.

'Yes, yes it is. Indeed it is,' Anna answered happily.

'Oh. Hello, Anna. It's Susanna Fuchs. You sound happy.' Susanna sounded as if it was rude to be happy.

'I am. What can I do for you?'

'I just wanted to know if you are coming to my coffee morning today. Remember, I gave you the invitation weeks ago but you didn't reply. I tried to remind you during the cruise, but you weren't listening. So what about it?'

'A coffee morning?' Anna stammered. Why is she having a coffee morning in the middle of summer and the day after coming back from the cruise? she thought. 'But it's July,' she protested. 'Hasn't everybody gone on holiday?'

'There are lots of people still around. Nobody goes on holiday until August. I thought you knew that,' Susanna corrected, as if it was a huge *faux pas* to leave town before the end of July.

'But we only just came back from Greece.'

'So? That doesn't seem to have worried anyone else. Everybody is coming.'

By 'everybody', Anna knew Susanna meant those ladies of the diplomatic corps who wouldn't dare not to appear at one of Susanna's functions. Anna was one of them.

'I'm terribly sorry I didn't reply to your invitation, Susanna, but ... I ...' she was trying to think of an excuse, but couldn't.

'That was very rude. Are you coming?'

'Well, I ...'

'Good. See you later. Eleven o'clock.' Susanna rang off.

Shit, Anna thought, that's the last thing I want to do. But she knew she had to go.

She had a long hot shower and washed her hair. She dressed in clothes suitable for a ladies' coffee morning, a white straight skirt and jacket, the navy Versace T-shirt and sandals. She felt nearly normal again, even though she was still a bit tired. Her face reflected in the dusty mirror of the lift showed no signs of the despair she had felt the day before. She looked fit and happy. She had an hour to spare before it was time to go to Susanna's. She would spend it in the boutique further down the street that specialised in expensive lingerie.

Anna emerged from the boutique an hour later, having parted with what seemed to her a small fortune for just a few pieces of silk and lace. But if it worked, it was worth it, she thought. She had been amazed at how she looked in the beautifully designed underwear. Her very feminine body was displayed to its utmost advantage, even though her thighs were a bit wobbly and her stomach not quite flat. Wait till Conor sees this, she thought: he will forget about the poor and starving.

The sun was shining again and Anna enjoyed the feel of the warm air. Susanna's apartment was only ten minutes' walk away. Anna arrived at the building at ten past eleven. She knew that most of the guests would already have arrived. Nobody dared be late for one of Susanna's dos! She didn't hear any of the expected din of conversation as she came to the front door. That's funny, she thought.

Anna rang the doorbell. Its sound echoed inside. Nobody came to open the door. She rang again. When she had waited another few minutes and still nobody had come, she decided to leave. There must be some mistake, she thought. Suddenly, the door opened and Susanna appeared, looking upset.

'Sorry I'm late. Am I the last?' Anna asked.

'You're the first. And probably the only one. Nobody came.' Susanna stared at Anna and tears started running down her face.

'Maybe they're just late? The traffic . . .'

'Traffic my eye. They all live nearby. Don't just stand there. Come in. I could do with some company.'

Anna wanted to turn around and leave but remembering how lonely she herself had felt the night before, she decided to stay. In any case, she wouldn't mind a cup of coffee and she was curious to see what would happen next. She couldn't believe that nobody would turn up, but maybe the other women had finally had enough of Susanna?

Anna entered the big, modern apartment. It was sparsely furnished. The colour scheme was almost exclusively white and the chairs and sofas looked hard and uncomfortable. The only splashes of colour were some abstract and, to Anna, completely incomprehensible paintings hanging on the wall of the living room. There was a big tray with coffee cups and a strawberry cheesecake on the sideboard.

'Sit down. Make yourself comfortable.'

How? Anna thought as she perched upright on one of the hard chairs. Susanna sat down on an identical chair opposite. Tears were still running down her cheeks. Anna suddenly felt desperately sorry for this strange woman.

'Susanna, I'm sure there must be some explanation for this.'

'There could only be one. Nobody likes me.' Susanna sniffed, wiping her face with the back of her hand. 'Except you. You like me, don't you?'

'Yes, of course,' Anna lied. 'I really, really like you.'

'That's the problem with living abroad,' Susanna sighed. 'You have very few friends. Nobody really cares.'

'That's true,' Anna had to agree, thinking back on the evening before. 'It can be very lonely.'

'Oh yes.' Susanna blew her nose. 'Sometimes I think that we could be lying dead here in our apartment for weeks and nobody would know. Nobody would miss us and we would only be found when the smell was too unbearable. But even that could take a while. My French neighbours might just think that I was trying a new type of cheese.' She smiled. Making fun of the French seemed to cheer her up.

'That's going a bit far,' Anna remarked with a smile, 'but I know what you mean.'

'Let's have some coffee.' Susanna rose, went to the sideboard and lifted the coffee pot. 'Do you like our apartment?' she asked as she poured.

'Interesting art,' Anna began feebly, looking up at the paintings.

'Do you think so? I painted them myself. That one,' Susanna said, pointing to a large painting which consisted of two cubes, one blue and one green, 'is my husband and me. It really expresses how we feel about each other and how we fit into society, don't you think?'

'Absolutely.' Anna's eyes drifted to the collection of framed photographs on the chest of drawers. She felt it would be safer to comment on those. One particular picture caught her eye.

'Why do you have a photo of Chancellor Kohl in your living room?'

'It's my mother.'

'Oh,' Anna stammered. 'She's a very striking woman.'

'No, she isn't. She is fat and ugly.' Susanna snapped. 'I was fat like her when I was a little girl. Everyone teased me about it but my mother did nothing to help me. She just gave me more cheese, cream and sausages. She thought it would make me feel better to eat but it only made me *fat*.'

'Maybe she meant well?'

'She was so stupid. She should have realised that what I needed was not food but help. She should have known how terrible it was when the girls in my class teased me for my *dikke kont*!'

'I beg your pardon?'

'It means fat bottom in Dutch.'

'I see,' Anna said, relieved.

'My bottom was enormous. I was so fat that I couldn't fit into a seat at the cinema or on a bus. *And I couldn't ride a bike*. Do you realise how serious that is if you live in Holland?'

'Yes, I can imagine. But how did you become so thin? How did you manage to make your body so perfect?'

'I met a girl at university who had been fat like me. She taught me how to lose weight. It took me about two years to make my body what it is today. I decided that I would teach others to do the same. That's why I became a keep-fit instructor.'

'So that's why.'

'Yes, of course. What did you think?'

'I thought it was so that you could tell people what to do. You seem to enjoy shouting orders so much.'

'What do you mean? I just think people should learn how to stay thin. I can't understand why they don't want to be like me.'

'Maybe everybody doesn't think that being thin is the ticket to happiness. But if you're happy, that's the right thing for you. It may not be the same for everybody.'

'But I'm not happy!' Susanna burst into noisy tears. 'Before, I was fat and sad, now I'm thin and miserable. I have no friends and everybody hates me.'

'What about your husband? At least you have him,' Anna said reassuringly.

'I never see him. He is too busy with work and his stamp collection. He is a very boring man, actually. I wish someone really exciting would fall in love with me.'

'Really? Like who?'

'Someone like your husband or Juan Valverde. I saw how you were always cuddling him. I thought that since you had such a dishy husband already, you wouldn't need to flirt with anybody else. But you want everything, don't you? You weren't content to have just one man, you had to have two.'

'It wasn't really like that,' Anna tried to explain.

'Don't try to fool me. I know what kind of woman you are. I can't understand why men seem to find you so sexy. You don't have a perfect figure.'

'Listen, Susanna,' Anna interrupted. 'You wouldn't be so miserable if you didn't try to push people around all the time. You're so ready to criticise others and point out how perfect you are. If you once, only once, did something crazy and irresponsible, it would be a great relief.'

'Irresponsible? Like what?'

'Like, like . . .' Anna tried to think of something. She caught sight of the cake. 'Like eating a large slice of that cheesecake.'

'Cake? No, I couldn't.'

'Yes, yes, you can.' Anna went over to the tray and proceeded to cut two enormous slices of cake. She brought them over to Susanna.

'One for you and one for me! Let's try. I know you can do it. Look, I'm eating.' Anna took a big spoonful and put it in her mouth. 'Mmmm, delicious. Better than sex,' she lied.

'Is it?' Susanna slowly put a piece of cake in her mouth. 'You're right,' she mumbled, her mouth full of cake. 'It's heaven.' She had soon polished off the large piece of cheesecake on her plate.

'How do you feel?' Anna asked.

'Good. Really good. And calm. Let's have some more.'

'No, that's enough for today. You mustn't overdo it the first time. I have to go now,' she added. 'Conor is coming home from Le Havre tonight. He's been there to help during the fishermen's blockade.'

'Will you come back another time?'

'Of course.' Anna gathered her parcels and prepared to leave. 'I'm going to the Tuesday market in Neuilly on my way home to pick up some of Conor's favourites. They have free-range chickens and lovely cheese.'

'But today is Wednesday,' Susanna exclaimed.

'No, it's only Tuesday,' Anna replied. 'Look, I have today's *France Matin*.' She showed Susanna the newspaper and the date at the top of the front page.

'Bloody hell!' Susanna exclaimed and started to laugh. 'My invitation is for Wednesday. That means that all those women will arrive tomorrow.'

'There you are,' Anna said. 'I knew there was an explanation. They'll all come tomorrow.'

'Do you really think so?' Susanna looked doubtfully at Anna.

'I'm absolutely certain. But I must go. Bye, Susanna. And thanks for the coffee.'

'Goodbye.' Susanna leaned forward and kissed Anna on the cheek. 'And thank you.' Anna was a little shaken.

The lift brought her smoothly down. Susanna called a last farewell.

'Anna?'

'Yes?'

'The cheesecake was low-fat.'

It was half past seven. Anna was in the kitchen cooking up a storm. She had spent over an hour at the market, choosing the best meat, vegetables and cheese for Conor's welcome-home dinner. She was cooking all his favourites: scallops *St Jacques,* fillet of beef with Madeira sauce, mushrooms, haricot beans and new potatoes, grilled goat's cheese, mixed salad and hot chocolate pudding with whipped cream. It was the kind of dinner he would have had after playing rugby, but tonight there would be something better than rugby. We'll score more than one try, she thought to herself with a little smile. And what a scrum there would be.

She had laid the table with the best china and crystal and put a vase with red roses in the middle of the table.

At eight o'clock the scallops were ready to go into the oven, the steaks were waiting to be cooked quickly in the frying pan, and the sauce, vegetables and potatoes were keeping warm on the heating tray. The grilled goat's cheese would only take a few minutes to prepare while they were having the main course, and the chocolate pudding would have completed its cooking time when they were ready for dessert.

Anna went in to the bedroom to change. The news on the radio had announced the end of the blockade in Normandy. Most of the tourists had been taken on board the ferries. That's a relief, she thought, no more bloody tourists in distress. She put on her new underwear, admiring herself in the mirror. She decided to wear a blue summer dress with a low neckline. It showed off her wonderful tan and bright blue eyes, which sparkled with excitement. She was looking forward to their romantic evening.

At nine o'clock there was still no sign of Conor. She had rung his mobile evey ten minutes, but he must have switched it off. Where the hell was he? The dinner would be a disaster if he didn't come home soon. She was tired and annoyed and the new underwear was beginning to feel uncomfortable.

At ten o'clock she started to worry. Maybe he had

been in an accident? She went into the living room, sat down on the sofa and switched on the evening news. The very first headline made her stare at the screen in horror.

CHAPTER 13

'*Bonsoir.*' The woman newsreader smiled. 'Here are the main points of the news. Hijack drama in Normandy. Irish plane forced down at Le Touquet airport. Mad monk armed with explosives threatens to kill all on board. Irish diplomat boards plane in attempt to save passengers. Police on full alert.'

'Oh, my God,' Anna whispered, 'what is Conor doing?'

She listened intently for the next few minutes, her eyes glued to the screen. The story that unfolded was unbelievable. A man dressed as a monk with a hot-water bottle hung from his neck, which he claimed was full of nitro-glycerine, had forced an Aer Lingus plane bound for Paris to land at the tiny airport of Le Touquet. He threatened to blow the plane up if his demands were not met. Nobody seemed to know what they were and 'Irish diplomat Conrad O'Connard' had boarded the plane in an attempt to talk sense to the monk. Nothing had been heard from them for over an hour. French gendarmes, armed with machine guns, were surrounding the plane.

'Wouldn't you think they could at least get his name right,' Anna sobbed. She was squeezing one of the sofa cushions with both hands and biting her lip. I have to go there, she thought, I have to go to Normandy. She stared at the TV screen, willing something to happen. The scene at the airport was quiet. The plane, surrounded by armed men, was bathed in light. A group of journalists and television cameramen were assembled near the aircraft.

There was a sudden movement at the door of the plane. More lights were trained on the man who appeared. It was Conor. He looked tired, dirty and unshaven. He waved his arms and said something.

'Speak up,' a journalist called. 'We can't hear you.'

'He has revealed what he wants,' Conor shouted.

'What is it then?' asked another journalist.

'He wants to know the third secret of Fatima.'

There was total silence while the journalists digested this. The secrets of Fatima, Anna thought, what was that again? Oh yes, now she vaguely remembered the story of the three children to whom the Virgin Mary was said to have appeared. She had told them three secrets, the third of which the Catholic Church had not divulged at the time. It had happened in the village of Fatima in Portugal, at the beginning of the twentieth century.

'The secret of what?' a French journalist asked.

'I have tried to make Fatima reveal her secret for years,' another journalist joked. There was a burst of laughter.

'But the third secret of Fatima was announced by the Pope earlier this year,' shouted an Irish journalist.

'It was the prediction of the attempt to assassinate the Pope.'

The other journalists nodded and muttered among themselves.

'I know,' Conor replied. 'But he says he doesn't believe it. It can't be the real secret, he said, it isn't important enough. He says it has to be something more earth-shattering.'

'What are you going to do?' someone shouted. 'Call the Pope on your mobile?' There was more laughter. Anna was appalled that they could joke about such a serious matter.

'I'm going to pray,' Conor announced, looking stressed. 'I suggest you do the same.' He disappeared back into the plane. The scene fell silent again.

The news programme switched to a different story with a promise to return to the hijack drama as soon as there were any new developments.

Anna sat as if paralysed. Conor is in terrible danger, she thought. She was both terrified and angry. If he dies, I'll kill him. I'll never speak to him again. Oh my God, what am I thinking? I have to go there. I have to speak to him. What if I never see him alive again?

She quickly went into the bedroom and changed into a shirt and jeans. She threw a change of clothing and toiletries for Conor into a small bag and looked around for the car keys. After some frantic searching, she found them in an empty jar in the kitchen. She tidied away the food, hoping that Conor would get a chance to eat it soon. She took her bag, grabbed her suede jacket from the hook behind the hall door and left.

The two-hour car journey was terrible. Anna found it hard to concentrate on driving because of her terrible fear. She twice nearly crashed the car. Once she just managed to avoid a huge lorry coming the other way. A little while later, a dog ran into the road, forcing her to swerve dangerously. She was relieved to see the lights of the small airport as she approached the scene of the hijack. She screeched to a halt outside the terminal building and jumped out of the car without bothering to close the door.

She raced around the building, her heart in her throat. The plane was still standing, all lit up, at the end of the tarmac. There seemed to be some sort of commotion around it. People were shouting and flashbulbs from what seemed like a thousand cameras were exploding in the black night. Anna ran faster toward the plane.

'Ouch!' She had run straight into someone.

'Anna! What are you doing here?' Sarah stared at Anna with big eyes.

'What do you think?' Anna babbled. 'What's going on? Where's Conor? Is he all right?'

'It's all over,' Sarah announced importantly. 'He didn't have a chance. He's finished.'

'Conor!' Anna screamed, grabbing Sarah by the arms. 'Conor's dead. Oh my God.'

'No. He's alive. I meant the monk. Conor attacked him and got him to surrender. He's been taken away by the police. Conor's . . .' her words were drowned by the sound of a jet plane landing.

'What's that?' Anna shouted.

'It's the Taoiseach. He's flying in to help his fellow

Irishmen in danger,' Sarah replied when the noise had died down.

'He's coming to cash in on the publicity, you mean,' Anna snorted, having calmed down a little.

'He's not like that. He's a wonderful man,' Sarah protested. 'I think he's a bit of a saint, really.'

'Yes, yes he's so special,' Anna replied without interest. 'But where's Conor?'

'He's over there by the plane being photographed and interviewed. The air hostesses can't stop kissing him.' Sarah smirked. 'Awful tarts.'

'OK, thanks.' Anna began to walk toward the aircraft and the group of people.

When she came a little closer, she spotted Conor, flanked by two air hostesses, at the bottom of the steps being questioned by a huge group of journalists. She tried to get to him, but couldn't push through the crowd. She stayed behind the reporters and cameramen, listening intently.

'What happened?' a journalist asked. 'How did you make him surrender?'

'It was the sandwiches,' Conor said.

'The sandwiches?'

'Yes, and the warm beer,' he added.

'What do you mean?'

'Well,' Conor started, 'the mad monk had just announced his demands and I had divulged them to the police and the press. We all sat down in the plane to wait for a response. I was keeping an eye on him, to make sure he wouldn't do anything crazy. The atmosphere was very tense. Some of the passengers were in tears and the others were going in and out of the toilets. I had the feeling the situation would soon become very serious indeed. I told the crew to serve drinks, but they ran out of booze very quickly. About half an hour ago, one of the air hostesses asked if it mightn't be a good idea to serve the sandwiches and beer that were left over from lunch. Without thinking, I said yes. I asked the monk if he would agree to that, and he said OK.' Conor paused.

'What happened next?' the journalists shouted.

'Well, I took one look at the sandwiches, and that was it,' Conor explained. 'Something inside me just snapped.'

'And?' the press shouted, waving their microphones in front of Conor. 'Keep going!'

'I realised that if all of this hadn't happened, I would be sitting down to a lovely meal with my wife. I have been living on sandwiches and warm beer for the last few days. I felt I would rather be blown to kingdom come than eat another bloody sandwich.'

'So what did you do?' the journalists shouted. They were finding that getting the story out of Conor was like pulling teeth.

'I realised whose fault it was I was there. It dawned on me what this lunatic was doing to my life. I looked at him and just saw red.' He paused again, wiping his brow.

'*Allez!*' a French television reporter shouted, 'we haven't got all night! Could we hear the rest of your story, *please*.'

'All right!' Conor snapped. 'Give me a chance. OK,' he continued, 'this is what I did: the monk was sitting there playing with his hot-water bottle and looking at me with his beady little eyes. I walked over to him and grabbed him by the throat: If you don't hand over that thing, I said, I'll tell you a secret you won't forget. When I'm finished with you, you little creep, you'll be sorry you ever started all of this. And the Pope won't be too impressed either. He'll strip you of your robes and send you to a monastery for the rest of your miserable life.' Conor took a deep breath. 'That's exactly what I told him.' He cleared his throat and pushed the ends of his shirt into his trousers.

'We'll never hear the end of the story at this rate,' a man muttered at the back of the crowd.

'For God's sake, give him a chance,' Anna snapped. 'Can't you see he has been through hell?'

'Who are you?' The man sneered. 'Mother Teresa?'

'I'm his wife,' Anna announced proudly.

'Maybe you could make him speed it up a bit, then.'

'Don't be so impatient,' Anna replied. 'What's your hurry?'

'We want to make the morning edition,' came the reply, 'but at this rate, we'll be lucky to get it in by Christmas.'

'So, anyway ...' Conor was saying. The reporters snapped to attention. 'The madman seemed terrified by my outburst. He begged me not to hurt him and promised to do anything I said. Please don't tell the Pope! he pleaded. The rest was easy. The pilot contacted the police and that was the end of it.'

'What about the hot-water bottle?' a reporter shouted. 'What was in it?'

'It sure as hell wasn't nitro-glycerine,' Conor

replied. 'I wouldn't be standing here if it were. The police took it. Probably full of chicken soup.'

There were more questions and demands for photographs. But Conor had spotted Anna. He pushed through the crowd.

'Darling,' he exclaimed and threw his arms around her. 'How wonderful of you to come.' He squeezed her until she could hardly breathe. Some of the reporters stared at them, but a moment later they turned their attention back to the plane. Seamus Nolan had arrived.

'You're a hero,' Anna said to Conor when she could draw breath. 'But I'm really so angry with you! I thought you were dead.' She started to cry. 'You idiot,' she raged. 'You could have been killed. What made you risk your life like that?' She beat her fists against his chest.

'I just didn't think,' Conor replied. 'I'm sorry I scared you. But I'm OK.'

'I'm so happy,' she sobbed. 'I've never been so happy in all my life. You stink,' she added, 'and I love you.'

'And I love you,' he replied still hugging her.

'Can we go home now?' Anna demanded. 'I want to show you how happy I am.'

'I just have to sort out a few things with the Chief of Police,' Conor replied, 'and I must speak to the Taoiseach.'

'The Taoiseach?' Anna asked nervously. 'You have to talk to him? What's he doing anyway?'

'What do you think?' Conor grunted and jerked his head towards the plane.

Anna glanced over in that direction. Seamus Nolan, dressed in a tweed jacket, had taken Conor's place between the two air hostesses. He had his arms around them and he was smiling to the cameras.

'We got the situation under control very quickly,' Anna could hear him say. 'Mr O'Connor is one of my best officers.'

The passengers were beginning to file out of the aircraft. The Taoiseach let go of the two women and started to greet the people coming down the stairs. He shook hands with the men and gave each woman a little hug. They all looked dazed and slightly surprised to see him there. The cameras blazed. Nolan beamed.

'Let's go into the terminal building,' Conor said, grabbing Anna's arm. 'I might get something to eat while I wait for that ham to finish his performance.'

Together they walked to the terminal, where Conor had a short discussion with the Chief of Police, who managed to get Conor some chicken salad and a glass of wine.

'That's better,' Conor announced, devouring the last piece of chicken. They were sitting in the small cafeteria. Anna had a cup of coffee. The last few hours had made her too nervous to eat.

'Conor.' Sarah stuck her head through the door. 'The Taoiseach wants a word. He's in the VIP lounge.'

'Does he know I'm here?' Anna asked.

'No, why should he?' Sarah demanded.

'Don't tell him.'

'I won't,' Sarah replied. 'Why would he be interested in you, anyway?' She closed the door.

'I'd better go in.' Conor rose from his chair. 'I

won't be long.'

'I'll wait in the car,' Anna told him.

Conor came out of the terminal building a while later and got into the passenger seat.

'Please take me away from here,' he muttered and put his head on Anna's shoulder. He was nearly asleep.

Half an hour later, they drove up in front of the Hotel du Casino in Deauville. 'Where are we?' Conor asked drowsily. 'Home already?'

'No, this is a hotel.'

'Why are we here?' Conor muttered.

'I didn't want to drive all that way. I'm so tired and my underwear's killing me.'

'What? OK.'

Anna walked into the luxurious lobby of the hotel. Conor shuffled after her like a big, tired dog.

The night porter looked at them with ill-disguised contempt. He took in Conor's unshaven face and dishevelled clothes, Anna's jacket and jeans, and their small piece of luggage.

'*Madame?*' he asked in a snooty voice.

'Do you have a double room?' Anna asked. 'With a bathroom?'

'We have no rooms free,' he sneered.

'Oh,' she replied, disappointed.

'What did he say?' Conor mumbled.

'They have no rooms.'

'No rooms? In the middle of the week?'

'No, *monsieur*,' the porter replied.

Conor suddenly snapped to attention. He straightened up, leaned across the desk, and stared at the porter. 'Listen,' he snarled, 'I've had a terrible few days. I've had to deal with the mess that your stupid fishermen created. Then I had to spend hours on a plane with a mad monk. I haven't slept for nearly a week. Now I just want to go to bed. If you don't give us a room this instant, I'll ... I'll complain to your foreign minister ...' He paused for breath. '... who I know personally.'

There was a curious silence broken only by the heavy breathing of the two men.

'Very well, *monsieur*,' the porter muttered. 'You can have number fifty-six. It's the bridal suite, all I have left.'

'Perfect,' Conor replied. 'The bridal suite. Will that be all right, darling?' he asked, turning to Anna.

'Lovely!' she gushed.

The suite was enormous, decorated in tones of pink, white and blue, with mirrors everywhere. Conor undressed and had a long shower in the huge bathroom.

'I feel human again,' he announced as he stepped into the bedroom wearing only a towel around his waist.

Anna was turning the knobs on the radio. She was in her underwear and feeling a little shy. 'You can probably get RTÉ on this thing,' she suggested.

'Who cares? Come here,' Conor growled.

'Don't you want to tune in to the news?'

'No!' he commanded. 'Forget the news.' He walked over to Anna and took her in his arms. 'It's the middle of the night,' he whispered. 'We have to go to bed.' He picked her up and walked over to the enormous four-poster bed and laid her on the silk bedspread. 'What's that you're wearing?' Conor asked looking down at her. He leaned over and touched the lacy front of her new bra.

Anna shivered with delight as she felt his touch. 'I bought it to turn you on,' she murmured.

'It worked,' he muttered and joined her on the bed. 'Take it off,' he ordered and tried to undo the bra.

'Careful!' she exclaimed. 'Don't rip it. It cost a fortune.' But it was too late. The little scraps of silk and lace were lying on the floor. Conor ran his hands over her naked body. She sighed happily and snuggled up to his strong hairy chest. She had come home.

Anna woke up late the next morning not quite knowing where she was. She looked around the huge luxurious room and it all came back. She stretched and smiled. It was all right. Conor was all right. Last night had been wonderful. Conor stirred beside her.

'Good morning,' he muttered and put his arms around her. 'Where am I?'

'Don't you remember? You're in the bridal suite. Isn't it just heaven? And there are mirrors everywhere.'

'All the better to see you,' Conor growled. He started to kiss her. 'Hello, stranger,' he whispered. 'I'm sorry if I have been ignoring you. I wanted to make it up to you, but then I got kind of busy.'

'It was my fault too,' Anna mumbled.

'Never mind. We'll forget about it. Let's get to know each other again.'

'I thought you might still be tired,' she muttered into his neck.

'I can feel my energy coming back. How about some massage?'

Anna slipped her hands around his back. 'How about a little yoga?'

Anna and Conor were having breakfast dressed in identical white hotel robes on the balcony outside the bridal suite. It was a beautiful day and they were admiring the view of the beach and the sea. Seagulls squawked overhead and the flags on the beach snapped in the fresh breeze.

'I can't believe yesterday really happened,' Anna remarked. 'It seems like a dream.' She smiled. 'The porter must have thought you were dangerous, the way you looked last night. I was a little frightened myself.'

'You should have seen the tourists! Some of them looked worse than I did yesterday, and that was only when they arrived. After a few days not even their mothers would have wanted to come near them.'

'What about cousin Kieran?'

'He was prepared, as usual. He had a complete set of toiletries and a change of clothes. He also had a camping stove and a mini-shower that he had invented himself and a supply of tinned food and bottled water. There are no flies on cousin Kieran. He looked as fresh as a daisy all through this ordeal. I'm surprised he wasn't murdered by some of the other passengers.'

'That must have impressed Sarah.' Anna licked some jam off her thumb.

'It did. She kept telling him what a wonderful example he was to his countrymen and how proud his mother would be if she could see him. Cousin Kieran is the best example of Irish manhood, in Sarah's eyes.'

Anna laughed so much she nearly choked on her coffee. 'But he is such a nerd,' she finally spluttered. 'He wears sandals and socks.'

'So does Sarah,' Conor said.

CHAPTER 14

The drawing room of the Canadian embassy in Paris was packed with people and was very hot. It was the end of September and Patrick and Betsy were celebrating their engagement with a reception. They had invited the entire population of Paris, or so it seemed to Anna as she pushed through the crowd.

'I didn't think they knew that many people,' she said to Monique as they waited in line to congratulate the happy couple.

'They are very popular,' Monique replied. 'I never thought they would get their act together, though. They seem to fight most of the time. I saw them screaming at each other in the street last week. She threw her ring at him and he had to search through the gutter to find it. Then I saw them cuddling in a restaurant a moment later. That woman is crazy.'

'I know. Imagine throwing away such a huge diamond,' Anna exclaimed.

'They'll be very happy.'

'I wonder. It seems to be either love or war most of the time.'

'That's what I mean,' Monique said. 'It will be like most French marriages. And they will never be bored.'

'Just like Conor and me,' Anna smiled. Things were very good between them at the moment. The summer had been wonderful. They had stayed nearly a week in Normandy, not telling anyone where they were. Conor had not switched on the radio once. Then the children came back from Sweden, and the whole family had gone to Ireland for a month.

All the Irish Sunday newspapers had still been full of reports of the hijack and its happy ending. There were pictures of Seamus Nolan on every front page. *Taoiseach saves Irish passengers*, one newspaper reported. *Seamus Nolan risks his life for his countrymen,* said another. He had never been more popular. Lizzie Dobbins was even rumoured to have taken him back, and the people of Kinsale had presented him with a big silver dish to thank him for saving the town from developers. 'That man's a saint,' a grateful citizen was reported to have said with tears in his eyes, after having had the honour of shaking Nolan's hand.

The cruise and Juan seemed very far away in Anna's mind. The memory of her infatuation with him had faded with her suntan. He had sent her one red rose with a card signed with the letter *J*. That was all. Anna had thrown them away with just the slightest twinge of regret. I think I'm cured, she thought. She hoped he was really suffering.

Anna and Monique finally reached the happy pair, who were standing in the doorway greeting their guests. Betsy was looking beautiful in a shapeless white knitted dress that hung down to her ankles.

'Wow,' Monique whispered in Anna's ear. 'Sonia Rykiel.'

'Where?' Anna asked looking around the room.

'No.' Monique sighed. 'The dress. It's a Sonia Rykiel.'

'Oh,' Anna mumbled. 'You mean that dress that looks like a dishrag knitted by a five-year-old? It's a designer thing?'

'Yes,' Monique replied. 'It must have cost a bomb. It's from her latest collection.'

'I must get into knitting,' Anna said. 'I'd make a fortune.'

'But you can't knit.'

'Exactly.' Anna smiled. Monique shook her head.

A huge diamond glinted on the third finger of Betsy's left hand. Patrick smiled broadly as he accepted the congratulations of his many friends and colleagues. Anna hadn't seen Betsy for a while, because the hotel job was finished, and Betsy and Patrick were busy preparing for their departure to Canada, where they would be married.

'Love your twin set,' Anna joked when she greeted Betsy.

'And the gardener is cute,' Betsy replied and winked.

'Are you sure you know what you're doing?' Anna muttered in Betsy's ear.

'No, but whoever does? I like to live dangerously.'

'You're very brave. Don't say I didn't warn you, though.'

'Who's being gloomy now?' Betsy laughed.

'Where's Conor?'

'I'm sorry, he couldn't make it. He had to work late. But he sent you his best wishes.'

'Work again?' Betsy demanded.

'He couldn't help it,' Anna explained. 'The Taoiseach is in town for the French summit meeting tomorrow. There is a working dinner at the embassy. I'll be picking him up there later.'

Betsy had to turn her attention to the next guest, and could not continue their conversation.

Anna made her way through the crowd towards the dining room, where drinks and food had been laid out on the big table. She was very hungry. On the table there was a mouthwatering array of various canapés and salads. Anna took a plate and piled it high with smoked salmon, cold chicken, crab sandwiches and tiny meatballs.

'Stuffing yourself again?' a familiar voice asked. Anna nearly dropped her plate. She turned around. It was Mícheal, wearing a bright orange pullover with a green shamrock on the front.

'Mícheal! What a nasty surprise!'

'I was invited, you know. You might be amazed to know that some people actually *like* me.'

'That *is* hard to believe,' Anna agreed.

'Great to see a woman eat. But you look a bit heavy around the middle. Expecting a happy event? Won't your husband be surprised when the baby comes out speaking Spanish.'

'You're disgusting,' Anna declared. 'Where's Sarah?'

'We broke up.'

'Oh? Was it another woman?'

'Nah. Sarah's not interested in women.'

'God, you're thick. I meant . . . Never mind. So, why did you leave her?'

'I didn't. She threw me out. She caught me kicking the cat. Then we had a row. It's that animal or me, I said. Next thing I knew, I was standing on the street with all my stuff. Vicious bitch.'

'Where are you living now?'

'I have my own pad. I found a little place on the Left Bank. No one can make me leave. I'm staying in Paris until I've finished my book.'

'That'll be a long stay.'

'You know, I tried to tell your husband what you were up to with the Taoiseach, but he wouldn't listen. I'm not responsible for my wife, he said. What she does has nothing to do with me. She's her own woman. Bloody fool. Well, as I always say: there's none so blind as those who will not listen.'

'What a charming man you are,' Anna mocked. 'And a true friend.'

'You know,' he said, putting an arm around her, 'it would be better if you were a little more friendly.'

'Why?'

'Because we Irish should stick together.'

'You're nuts!' Anna exclaimed, shaking his arm off. 'You need a doctor.'

'I see someone I know,' he announced, ignoring her remark. 'Got to go. See ya.' He disappeared in the crowd.

'Who's the tramp?' Monique asked. She was

nibbling on a stick of celery.

'It's Mícheal. You know, the journalist who stayed with us last spring,' Anna replied.

'Yes, I remember him now,' Monique replied, looking across to where Mícheal was cuddling a blonde woman at the other end of the room. 'Just look at him! Where does he get them?'

'The women?'

'No, the pullovers!' Monique shuddered. 'What a horrible man. How can you stand even talking to him. He's so crude.'

'I know,' Anna replied. 'Puts you off your food. Maybe we could market him as a slimming aid?'

'I'm sure I will meet plenty of men like that when I'm in Australia.'

'Except for the pullovers. It will be string vests and hairy armpits instead,' Anna teased.

'I can't wait.'

'God, I'll miss you,' Anna exclaimed. 'Both you and Betsy are leaving at the same time. I'll be all alone.'

'There's always Susanna.' Monique helped herself to a glass of champagne. 'You know, she's nearly human these days. I think she's on drugs.'

'What are you talking about?'

'You weren't at her coffee morning. Just after the cruise. I heard she was most peculiar. The apartment was a mess and she nearly forced her guests to eat a monster of a cheesecake. Then she told them to relax and do what they felt like. It was scary. But we all know how relaxed the Dutch are about drugs. So that must be it.'

'Don't be silly. She is just trying to be normal.'

'Susanna? Normal? Impossible.'

'Oh, give her a chance.' Anna took a bite of a crab sandwich.

'What are you going to do now that the hotel job is finished?'

'I'll think of something. If I don't have anything to do, I'll just get fat again.'

'You have already put on a few pounds, *chérie*. You have to be more careful.' Monique looked at Anna's plate with a frown.

'Don't nag. I was thinking of doing some kind of course. Maybe a degree. Do you think you can do medicine on the Internet?'

'Maybe. There are so many medical web sites. You could probably get enough information for a medical degree.' Monique finished her champagne. 'Got to go. I have to finish my packing. Call in to see me tomorrow. We have to get together before I move.' She kissed Anna on the cheek and turned to leave.

Later that evening, Anna parked the car near the embassy. She was hoping the dinner would be over and the Taoiseach gone. But the lights were still on in the upstairs windows and two black limousines were waiting with their engines idling outside the huge entrance doors. Anna decided to slip into the building and wait in the downstairs cloakroom. She nodded at the drivers, who were chatting softly to each other, as she passed. She was tiptoeing across the vast marble hall toward the door of the cloakroom when she heard voices at the top of the stairs. One voice in particular was horribly familiar. Anna raced towards the cloakroom, trying not to make a sound, and just managed to get inside and close the heavy mahogany door as the party reached the hall.

She waited, her heart thudding, for the group outside to go, but to her dismay she heard the Taoiseach's voice terrifyingly clearly.

'I'll just get my coat. Won't be a tick.'

'I'll get it for you, Taoiseach,' said the voice of the ambassador's wife.

'No, it's all right. No trouble.'

The handle moved and the door started to open. Anna looked around for somewhere to hide. A big potted plant was the only thing big enough to conceal her. She pushed herself behind it, but it was too late. Nolan had spotted her.

'Well, well,' he purred, 'who have we got here?'

'Eh . . .' Anna stammered. 'Hello . . .'

'Helping out with the houseplants? I didn't know you had green fingers.'

'No, I . . .' Anna came out from behind the plant.

'So, my dear,' Nolan said with a smile that made Anna shiver, 'we meet again.' He put his hand on hers.

'Yes,' she whispered.

'Interesting letter you gave me.'

'I didn't mean . . .' Anna had never felt so stuck for words in her life.

'Not quite what I was expecting,' he smirked.

'I'm . . . I'm really sorry,' Anna mumbled.

'Caused all sorts of problems.'

'I can imagine . . .' She tried to pull her hand away.

'But I forgive you. Plenty of fish in the sea.'

'Thanks . . . I mean, yes there are. Fish, I mean.' She had no idea what to say.

'Pity about your son, though,' he added.

'What?'

'Not so clever, is he?'

'What do you mean?' Anna asked, mystified.

'The little bastard failed maths.' Laughing, the Taoiseach took his coat and left.

Also available from
beeline

LEO CULLEN

Clocking 90 on the Road
to Cloughjordan
and other stories

'The setting is rural Ireland in the 1950s, and the
subject is the adventures of the Connaughton family,
headed by Lally senior . . . a marvellous creation.
The final effect is atmospheric and poignant.'

Anthony Gardner, *Daily Telegraph*

'Both subtle and funny . . . Leo Cullen memorably
paints the picture of Connaughton's worlds . . . and
the realities that drive him, in the emotional sense, at
90 miles per hour along the back roads of Tipperary.'

Owen Kelly, *Irish News*

'I tried to remember when I had read a book as
funny. I couldn't find one . . . With this effort alone
the author has assured himself a lasting place in
comic Irish literature.'

John B. Keane, *Sunday Independent*

ISBN 0-85640-722-4

£5.99 €8.99

Available now at all good bookshops

BEELINE
COMPETITION

Win the chance to become a Beeline author!

Beeline is an exciting new popular fiction imprint from
Blackstaff Press presenting entertaining and original books of
broad general appeal.

We are looking for new authors for future Beeline books – why not
enter our Beeline competition? The winning script will be published
by Beeline, and will be edited, designed, printed and marketed by our
award-winning team. The winner will also be offered a professional
author's contract with Blackstaff Press.

Submitted novels can be in any genre – romantic, historical,
detective, thriller etc – but must be original (i.e. previously
unpublished), well-plotted, with strong characterisation and
above all a lively, readable style.

Your complete typescript should be submitted on A4 paper, double-
spaced, and should be available on disk if required. Please enclose a
short covering letter (make sure you include your address etc!), a
one-page synopsis of your novel and a brief CV including details
of any previously published work. Send everything to:

BEELINE COMPETITION
BLACKSTAFF PRESS
WILDFLOWER WAY, APOLLO ROAD
BELFAST BT12 6TA

If you wish your material to be returned, please enclose sufficient postage.

The closing date for submissions for the Beeline competition is
31 December 2002. Details of the winning entry will be announced
by 30 April 2003.

The judges' decision will be final. No correspondence will be entered into. In the event of
none of the entries being of a publishable standard, the most promising writer will be
offered advice on script development by an experienced Blackstaff editor.

Good luck!